I0655378

Unwitting Witnesses

A Paul Marzeky Mystery

Stefan J. Malecek, Ph. D.

Copyright ©2019 Stefan J. Malecek, Ph. D.

All rights reserved.

ISBN-13: 978-1-7335382-0-6

DEDICATION

This book is dedicated to all those through the years who have supported and encouraged me on my voyage to greater mental and spiritual health. I am grateful to have been able to survive my long journey to wisdom, acquired only through many decades of trial and error, discovering and distilling the raw "stuff" of Life. As Ram Das once said, "All is grist for the mill." I am grateful for everything I have experienced that has informed, supported, and inspired me and fed my writing habit.

ACKNOWLEDGEMENTS

As Henry Miller once famously said "Even a bad novel needs a bit of privacy and a place to sit." I am ever grateful to acknowledge the beneficence of the Creator and the ever-present inspiration and illumination I have been provided.

To Topher Allan and Harold Dick Jr., my two oldest friends and brothers, I want to acknowledge the ongoing love and support. They have shared innumerable unique life experiences with me, and decades of some of the best experiences of my life that will never be repeated. I love you and thank you deeply.

To Sharon Curtis, one of the most trustworthy and genuine of all of the women I have ever known. Thank you for saving my life, and helping me become the man that I am.

To the "Dawgs of Manzanita"—Darel Grothaus and Michael Hithe—with whom I have shared many adventures (and tragedies). Wow! I could not have asked for better brothers. I love you and thank you deeply.

To Andrea Scholz, my all-round administrative and personal assistant who has never failed to be supportive of my work in many ways, especially when I grumble irritably about technology that doesn't work for me. She is steady and reliable, and always does sterling work assisting my works that would never otherwise have escaped my laptop. I send love and great thanks to her.

PRELUDE

September 16th, 1988   1311

He'd managed to survive his "banging" years without an adult bust, and had created a new identity for himself. Though he had had his gang-tattoos laser-beamed off, he retained the aura of his "gansta" days, he still called himself "Fast Eddie." He also tended to identify strongly with people from the streets, drug users, and the downtrodden.

He and Teresa had a little boy one year old. He thought he had moved away from the barrio "forever"—naively believing he had left his past behind as well.

He had even landed a job as a Pre-Licensed Psychiatric Technician at the County Psych facility. Teresa was working part-time, but the cost of good childcare was heavy. Children always seemed to require extra money.

So, when the mysterious voice (Latino-sounding and rough) called him, and threatened to reveal the past he had kept so very carefully hidden. He would inevitably lose his job. All The Voice asked of him was to provide a "few small favors." He intimated that he knew everything about his past, and Eddie was scared. But all he (or she) seemed to want wasn't anything too important: information about unit census and staffing patterns; a report on the busiest times on the Acute Unit; admission procedures from the Crisis Clinic.

When The Voice called the next day, it told him to come to the Taqueria at 25th and Mission, one of Eddie's favorite spots. They used flank steak in their burritos and made dynamite fresh salsa. When he was told to bring his work keys, he knew he was seriously in over his head. He refused, and then heard a tape recording of his own voice giving up information. He didn't even have his license yet. He told Teresa that he was going to go get them some dinner and would return shortly.

"How will I know who you are?" he asked The Voice when he finally capitulated.

"It doesn't matter. I will know you."

CHAPTER ONE
Chaos Rules!
San Francisco   September 21st, 1988 1215

What had started out as a routine Day shift, for the Acute Adult Unit at any rate—where yelling, screaming, occasional fist-fights, arguments, threats, outright violence, take downs and seclusion were commonplace, even expected—changed the instant the Psych Police brought Zack Hawkins in.

In spite of his otherwise repulsive appearance, Zack called himself "The Mack," because he delusionally considered himself to be a pimp and procurer of young women, all of whom (actually almost all women *in toto)* universally rejected him because of, take your pick: greasy, stringy hair; malodorous body odor; acne-scar pitted face, pocked, oleaginous, body covered crown to toes with a thick mat of dense black hair; broken, twisted, yellowed teeth; and/or a rare brand of halitosis officially banned by the UN Health Organization in seventy three countries.

Zack's presentations ordinarily followed a relatively enormous overdose, or alternatively, at the end of a week-long binge when he ran out of his favorite substance. He was usually shipped in after being seen at one of The City's ERs, after he was medically cleared of not being in immediate danger of dying, either from medical conditions or his impending detox.

Zack was grunting, cursing, and shouting, wildly flailing, vainly trying to unencumber himself of the steel handcuffs that encased his wrists and linked them solidly to his waist chain, and thence to his ankle chains. His eyes were wide and as crazed as a terrified horse foaming at the mouth. His clothes were completely stained in layers of the deep unknown, and torn in a variety of places. He was missing his left shoe, and on the right was a graying white sock and an untied orange tennis shoe, both feet encircled by ankle cuffs.

He was the center of a whirling, swirling montage of grunting, sweating men and women who were attempting to contain him as he threw himself against their living wall of arms and legs, hands and fingers, breasts and chests, feet and toes, heads and minds—a united staff and police presence marshaled against his force.

Rivulets of foul-smelling perspiration poured off him like the Johnstown flood, and his exertions became more agitated as the gathered forces attempted to contain him. He swung his triangularly shaped head from side, spitting and snapping at his captors like a berserk turtle, as if possessed by aliens fighting to be freed of his imprisoning human body; his voice was a strident shriek that sliced like glass slivers through ears, neurons and nerve endings.

"Leave me alone, motherfuckers!"

As he violently twisted his head, he hacked a large, green phlegm ball in the face of a deputy sheriff, who loosened his grip and violently wiped it from his face with his shirt sleeve. One of the female techs had partially secured a towel around his mouth. When one the deputies reached to help, Zack chomped firmly down on the edge of her hand, and she screamed and slapped him, yelling "Goddamn you!" as she withdrew from the fracas. The other deputy smashed his hand sideways into the face of the recalcitrant man who grunted and snarled.

One of the male RNs detached himself to escort the injured woman to the Treatment Room. She had blood running off her palm that splattered her clothing from her waist to her thighs.

Daniel, a senior Psych Tech, stepped in and took charge of the errant towel on one side, and another Tech named "Beef"—young, burly, and buff—risked fully exposing his meaty forearms to the potential trap of the salivating patient to pull the towel tightly around the raging client's mouth on the other side. They both held the towel securely as strident conversation whirled around them, while a young pre-licensed Tech named Eddie Chacon kept a firm grip on his right leg.

"Fuck this! Just take him down!"

"Get him on the floor!"

"Somebody get his legs!"

Zack was the wild neutrino at the core of the writhing human centipede that suddenly shifted forward and down. No one was especially careful to cushion the struggling man. Beef went to a knee, and then rolled to his side, still holding his end of the towel. Joe Torrance, the Psych Police supervisor, landed full-force on the right side of the condign man's back who grunted, then spewed yellow chunky vile-smelling vomit that splattered onto the feet, hands, and clothing of various staff members.

"Yeech!"

"Fuck!"

"Bastard!"

A female deputy stepped up with the leather restraints, then hesitated for a moment as if to aim a blow at the psychotic man's head, but Tom caught her eye and shot her a look, so she simply continued to hand them out.

"Call housekeeping STAT!"

"Is the seclusion room door unlocked?"

"John's down there, standing by and waiting!"

Having fallen face down and dislodged the towel, the malodorous man began campaigning agitatedly to be released, but with considerably less gusto. Someone pulled his pants down, exposing the pale, pimpled white moons of his buttocks just as the Med Nurse arrived carrying a loaded and capped syringe.

"Make way! Make way! The Haldol Express is coming!"

"What'd ya got?"

"Haldol 5 IM STAT as per Doctor Stephens!"

"Does he know this guy probably has drugs on board?"

"I told him! He said 'Get some STAT labs, give him the meds, and maybe we can give him some benzos later.'"

Benzodiazepines were anti-anxiety agents that were routinely withheld pending laboratory results, because they could confuse the clinical picture; but Haldol, an anti-psychotic, would hopefully and rapidly decelerate the agitation.

One of the Techs, Joann Novisk, grimaced as she grasped Ted's left butt cheek, and puckered a packet of skin up in her gloved hands, readying it for injection.

"Whew! This son of a bitch needs a bath!"

"Just shoot him quick!"

She swiped his buttock with an alcohol sponge, stabbed the syringe in and aspirated with the same thumb, then smoothly injected the drugs.

"Prepare to transport!"

The team positioned themselves to lift the patient face down by the restraints. The towel had been replaced and was taped firmly in place, all of his appendages were firmly entrapped in top quality cowhide leather cuffs, tightened down with the belts pulled all the way through. Someone had each arm and leg, and another firmly grasped his belt. Paul exchanged a glance with each in turn.

"Prepare to lift! On three! One, two, three."

With practiced ease, Zack was rapidly lifted into the air, and moved to the waiting seclusion room, placed face down (to prevent aspiration), and the restraints fitted securely to the rigid metal handles on the sides of each of the four legs of the bed, which themselves had been sunk in two feet of concrete. In another twenty minutes, if his vitals were within normal limits (WNL), he would get another 5 milligrams of Haldol intramuscularly to further reduce his agitation (via its strong anti-dopaminergic action).

Though still cursing, he was left to his own machinations, mumbling and spitting, as the Haldol invaded his brain, and subverted his neurons. The staff dispersed as if dandelion spores in the wind, with the shift yet young—and more paperwork than ever to which they had to devote themselves. Some would rehash the incident while others went to get a fresh cup of coffee, and still others to retell old "war stories" to the newer staff. And the shift was yet young.

CHAPTER TWO

The Beat Goes On

September 18th, 1988   1645

Eduardo sat in a booth, fidgeting, and sipping a Pepsi. The Voice was already ten minutes late, and he was vacillating between anger, fear, and worry. He had even entertained a fleeting fantasy about punching the guy out, but he wasn't sure who he was up against.

Just then, a small Latino woman approached his table and asked, in sultry tones, if she could sit down.

"Vamanos, puta!"

She leaned closer to him, and Eduardo's eyes widened in total terror as The Voice spoke to him, commanding him to get up immediately and come outside. They walked south down 25th and turned onto Lilac Alley as Eddie's systolic blood pressure rose twenty points. The Voice (still didn't know his/her name) had told him tersely just to walk. When they got to the middle of short lane, the man pulled out a small metal box, and asked for his work keys.

"Why, Man? What you want with my keys?"

"Do what I tell you and you will walk away from this. Otherwise I will kill you. Your choice, *cabron*."

The Voice quickly pressed Eddie's #1 key into the clay inside the metal container, then handed back his keys, and told him to turn around.

"Why, man? What are you going to do?"

Eddie listened to the ominous silence, punctuated only by the night sounds of the Mission District—salsa music, laughter, sirens, buses and cars.

Eddie asked again, and then ventured to turn around. He saw he was standing completely alone. He wondered if he'd been hallucinating. He jogged back to La Taqueria, ordered dinner and was home shortly thereafter. The more he thought about it, the more confused he became. Who in the hell was The Voice? What was so compelling about The Voice's voice, what made him want to obey? And those eyes! Like a snake, or a Gila monster. He decided to bury this latest dark and bizarre encounter of his.

CHAPTER THREE
Intervention?
September 21st, 1988   1715

Zack Hawkins' first psych admission had been at age eight. He had attacked his mother when she found him huffing airplane glue and masturbating to porn magazines. Since then he had been institutionalized in every facility in San Francisco, and most of the outlying counties, as well as numerous trials in both Napa and Atascadero State Hospitals. Not even ECT had ever seemed to alter his path of destruction through life.

He had lain in the furthest seclusion room, gleefully absorbing all of the noise and confusion happening outside his door, greedily sucking it in as if it were a prime-time banquet for his warped senses. With all the uproar on the floor, he had been relatively forgotten—though he had earlier had his own moment in the spotlight, and created his own spectacle that resulted in his being secluded and restrained since just after lunch. He lay pinned face down on his bed like a raging praying mantis on a cork board. His arms and legs were restrained to the legs of the metal-framed bed, which were, in turn, sunk into the concrete floor. The bed shook as he rattled his restraints and turned his head to get a better view when he felt the presence of an intruder, someone peeking at him through the chicken wire-reinforced Plexiglas window in the center of the solid wood door, just before a key was inserted into the lock, and turned.

The polluted odors of the seclusion room assaulted the senses of the intruder, who took small, shallow breaths and approached the pinned patient. As if in defense of his squalid demesne, Zack turned his head to spit on the intruder.

"What the fuck do you want? You motherfuckers already shot me full of fucking drugs!"

His belligerent incantation echoed off the pale, faded walls that were permeated with decades of amalgamated fear, urine, and the cloying cupric odor of unleashed and unintegrated emotions.

"What're you gonna do? Suck my dick?" said Zack, attempting to rotate his hips in a failed lascivious gesture, held firmly in place as he was by sturdy cowhide straps. He grunted his frustration, and then laughed coarsely.

Zack felt suddenly very vulnerable. His most provocative taunt had not elicited hostility, or a response of any kind. He tasted the air with his tongue like a reptile, and his eyes bugged out exothalmically as he worm-wriggled in his restraints, feeling very much as if he were on a hook watching the approach of a huge hungry fish.

"Who the fuck <u>are</u> you, dude?" he whispered, sweat coating his furrowed brow, and dampening his fetid pajama pants. He whimpered as his terror-filled pleas fell on uncaring ears.

He thrashed vigorously as his fear mounted, shredding the skin at his wrists and ankles, bleeding into his restraints as he grew exponentially more agitated. He coughed up a yellowish blob of phlegm and attempted to launch it at the intruder. It fell short of its mark like a failed missile, and yet more desperation perspiration poured out of his acne-pitted pores like toxic waste at a superfund site.

The interloper swiftly slipped his right arm under and around the ensnared man's head, simultaneously clamping off both carotid arteries with such speed and force that Zack almost immediately slipped into unconsciousness, lungs shuddering, disbelieving brain shutting down, as his retinas registered a brief last image of the intruder's radiant smile as the only words ever spoken danced in the air as if frozen in gelatin.

"I am The Avenging Angel!"

CHAPTER FOUR

A New Day

September 21st, 1988   1400

The day crackled with promise as Paul surveyed the day from the front window of the house he was renting on Kensington Way in the West Portal, most previously occupied by Jack Cassidy and Jorma Kaukounen of the Jefferson Airplane.

He took a last check of himself in the full-length mirror in the foyer. Although he was critical of the extra twenty pounds he carried, he was pleased with the image that looked back at him. Six feet tall, face healthily weathered from daily walks in the ever-changing Bay Area weather, he was currently weighing in at 235 pounds, and his dark brown hair had grown beyond his shoulders. All in all, he was pretty proud of his presentation.

Paul always ran a high body temp, but he always prepared for the weather. Today he wearing a long-sleeved emerald green t-shirt under a snap-button chambray shirt with jeans and his denim jacket with desert boots on his feet. Living in The City inevitably required a jacket at some point in the afternoons. He packed a dinner of leftover meatloaf and a salad he had prepared the night before, his journal, an extra set of underwear and a pair of socks (he usually changed mid-shift) into his backpack.

It was exactly 1400 as he walked down Kensington Way in the West Portal toward the Dewey traffic circle. He still kept the much more efficient military/hospital time. He breathed deeply as he stepped out and looked up toward the cross on the top of Mount Davidson that dominated the Miraloma Park District. He stepped into what San Franciscans called "Indian Summer," September and October being the warmest and best weather that The City ever got to experience—sun bright, skies clear, wind crisp and fresh, more spring than autumnal, April often being cold, windy and miserable. He felt stimulated as he strode off on his way to work, luxuriating in the scintillating day and celebrating another day of being a San Francisco resident.

He greeted "Baghdad-by-the-Bay," as Herb Caen had called The City, his city, in an earlier, gentler time. Despite the magnificence and ever-changing beauty all around him, and a chilly tang that wanted to ease his angst, his brain turned him inward, to chew on yet another of the knotty issues with which, it seemed, he was always concerned, that always seemed to want to capture his attention.

Even though he was theoretically entitled to sign "BA" behind his name along with the required "LPT" (Licensed Psychiatric Technician), he was always a little hesitant to do so, especially as he was usually surrounded by so many Ph.Ds. and MDs, even MD/Ph.Ds.

Going back to college eight years after getting clean had admittedly been thrilling, having the opportunity to unleash the hidden capacities of his brain in pursuit of a desired goal that required concentrated effort, slogging through research, and the occasionally tedious writing assignments. It had been fun to be in the classroom one weekend a month with the members of his cohort who demographically ran the gamut from full on underground characters with tattoos and piercings and resumes to match, to straight-looking housewife types with their own incredible stories to tell. What united them all despite the many differences (they were straight and gay and in-between, every race and creed, professionals of every sort and tradespeople, youngest 24 oldest 68) was the desire to get an education and prove to themselves and others that they had the fortitude and energy to "get the paperwork" to validate their intelligence and life experience.

It seemed now, in retrospect, that all of the work and anticipation he had engendered driving toward the goal of being college educated, had disappeared in an instant, as if it had been written on flash paper. It had been so fleeting. It disproved his cherished belief that educational parity with his father would bring him the soul satisfaction he had always sought; disabused him of his cherished belief that having a BA would really bring him love and blessings; would validate him by having achieved this goal after having survived what he considered to be the waste ground of his earliest life, and even more especially all of the years he had spent drinking and using.

The anniversary of his "End of the Cocaine Era" still glowed brightly, probably always would. It was the initiation of his "clean years" that was still paying dividends in large and small ways every day. It was something of which he was inordinately proud, an accomplishment that had taken tremendous courage and dedication initially, and required ongoing fortitude and reinforcement since. He considered it to be a personal gateway, a sort of mental and emotional monument to his inner strength and willingness to persevere in the face of the most horrendous, almost incalculable, odds.

He had met so many people who had gotten clean and relapsed; who had had multiple treatment programs; interventions and "second chances" ad nauseam; and still failed to achieve a life consistently free of obsessive-compulsive substance use. To stop using was just the bare beginning, the ante, as it were. The far more difficult part was remaining firm in the decision to never use again. Never. Such a huge word. So final. So permanent. So encompassing. It demanded a depth of purpose, of soul strength, of genuine burning desire to remain free, not only of the consciousness-clouding substances, but of the mental and emotional traps and quagmires that lay behind them; being willing to work on them, unravel them, free oneself of their pernicious influence, and integrate the previously lost energies into one's larger beingness. Such recovery was an ongoing process that required daily refreshment, devotion and care. Even more, it involved the deep and true forgiveness of the self, and the willingness and ability to allow the gilded strands of love to permeate the essence of one's self—allow, not create, because they have been there all along hidden, obfuscated, buried under the detritus of the traumas and tragedies of life in a perpetrative, tyrannical society whose warped lived principles were learned at the mother's breast (perhaps in the womb itself), and were inculcated into each and every newborn's nerve endings along with the myelin sheathes that covered them, rendering them seemingly irrefutable and untouchable, irredeemable.

The net result, of course, was generation after generation of individuals who mirror-copied the bad habits and behaviors of all those who came before them, seemingly unable to comprehend the great manipulative program in which they were trapped and therefore unable to cooperate in their own liberation from prisons more formidable than any of iron or steel, often with jailers far more cruel than any institution and punishment far more severe than bethought by the Inquisition's practitioners or Gestapo sadists. The key and most salient point being, of course, that each of us knows the most exquisitely excruciating castigations and reprimands, the most extraordinary knots and screws and clamps that can be applied to our own minds.

It was part of what had made the long journey so exhausting, enduring the slow passage of time's crucial ache, developing the kind of patience that he himself had never had (or never wanted to have), yet knowing it was something he needed to develop were he to ever get to the golden shore of his dreams.

Purity of motive was involved too. It was not enough for him to attain a baccalaureate in order to proclaim that he had equaled the level of his father's educational standard, feeling as if that at last would garner the love and support he had never had while the man was alive. That seemed a tainted motivation, driven not by love and appreciation and gratitude, but by fear and hatred and anger. It furthered neither him nor the Universe, especially as it seemed that when he made a positive shift, the entire Universe changed too.

By the time he reached the corner where Kensington met Clarendon at the Dewey Traffic Circle, he felt lighter, as if yet another piece of the cosmic puzzle had been carefully slotted into place in his mind and he was ready to take on the next mini-challenge of his complex life. He took different routes every day, and stopped for a moment to consider which way to go today. Even though the total distance was only seven miles, with all of the twists and turns of the contours of the geography, it took quite a bit longer than if it were a straight course.

It only took him forty five minutes to walk the seven miles to work—sometimes he walked over to Portola, and across the spine of The City with its spectacular views of downtown with the Bay Bridge and the East Bay in the distance; and then trip down steep Clipper Street, lovely Clipper Street with its vast panoply of different styles and shapes and colors of houses like a picture postcard, to where it dead-ended at Dolores; or north on Sanchez to 30th Street. Other times he might take Portola to Diamond, and then negotiate all of the dead-end streets to his destination where Church dead-ended. If he was late or tired, he could take the "J Church" car to the end of the line; or he could take the K, L, or M car to Forest Hill Station, and walk. Only very rarely he could take a cab, usually after a double shift.

No matter what route he chose, he liked to arrive fifteen minutes early to do his usual reconnaissance of the unit and suss out which of the patients he felt might potentially be building to "blowing up." Though at first disbelieved, now the staff listened to his prognostications since he had been proven correct numerous times. His intuition had developed considerably since he got home from Vietnam, and apart from a few years off as a full-time professional drug dealer, he'd been working on psych units ever since.

He used his Master key (called a "Number One") that opened all of the doors on either of the units, except for the med rooms and narcotics cabinets, to unlock the secure steel front door. Then he entered the sally port, off of which were the locked doors to the two units—the Adult Acute Unit and the Alcohol Detox Unit. There were ten beds on each side, each with three seclusion rooms that could be used by patients from either unit, depending on the flow and intensity of the population. They were often asked to take overflow when either Mount Zion Crisis or San Francisco General Emergency Psych Services were on diversion because of acuity, even once when they were both on diversion simultaneously, something that was never supposed to happen.

The staff routinely managed rude, inebriated, bellicose, malodorous, depressed, stoned, dysphoric, rowdy, combative, disturbed, angry, delusional, raging, belligerent, morose, hallucinating, obtunded, bizarre, belligerent, manic, florid, violent, mute, rapid-cycling, unresponsive, demented, paranoid—and/or all of the above in some form or fashion. It was all part of the job description.

All seemed relatively well and quiet tonight (so far) as he made his way through the dayroom. Even patients who had formerly been difficult or intransigent tonight seemed to be, at least superficially, with the program. He even got a few smiles and greetings.

Then he went to the staff room (he was working Acute tonight), he went to the staff room for a cup of his own home-brewed coffee. He was the only one there who really gave a shit about good coffee, so he set up his single cup Melita coffee holder, and put the water on to boil. He pondered, not for the first time, how different his life might have been, had he either not joined the Army, or not repeatedly volunteered for Vietnam. Both decisions seemed relatively foolish in retrospect, though he was massively better off than if he had not fled St. Louis or just stayed gritting his teeth at Fort bloody Riley, Kansas!

He certainly would never have managed to make his way to The City by the Bay; would never have experienced the amazing, loving women he had; would never have rocked out at a thousand concerts at The Fillmore, Family Dog, Matrix, Lion's Share; would never have lived the life he had had, certainly never become a Licensed Psychiatric Technician and so much further unfolded his journey within.

His voyage had led him ever deeper into unravelling his own psyche, revealing the intensity of his emotions, unveiling the magnitude of his shame and pain and bringing him repeatedly to the gates of redemption and integration. He would be living in an entirely different Universe. All he had become would not now exist, would never have been born! He sometimes pondered where and who, even when, would he be, or have been if he had not made the critical decisions he had made, often in moments of panic and confusion, frequently in deep states of anger and depression?

He shook his head as he poured the boiling water over the coffee, and smiled ruefully. *Quel domage!*

The shift slipped quickly by, with many of the patients sleeping or involved in the watching the Giants game on TV, on the verge of sweeping a three-game series with the San Diego Padres. He was almost feeling secure that it would be a quiet night for a change. All he had left was nine o'clock meds and case notes—then he would be out of there!

Of course, it was just at that moment that the Psych Police brought them a little "gift."

CHAPTER FIVE
Dismay
September 21st, 1988   1845

The Psych Police was a unique sub-unit organized by the City and County of San Francisco to specialize in the application of the tenets of the Welfare and Institutions Code 5150, mandating a 72-hour involuntary evaluation for those who, as a result of mental disorder, posed a danger to themselves or others; or who appeared so grossly unable to care for themselves as to be designated gravely disabled. There was a Sergeant Supervisor and five other officers who rotated through the twenty-four clock of each and every day. They were trained and ready to evaluate anyone who might possibly meet the legal qualifications "as a result of mental disease or disorder," generally called by other officers.

When Paul responded to the door buzzer, he immediately groaned at the sight of the handcuffed disheveled man being held upright and slumped between two uniformed officers. The man might once have been described as foppish, but now he simply looked tattered and bedraggled—stained gold silk shirt, mauve bell-bottoms with multiple holes and tears, and purple velvet jacket that had seen far better days. They were extremely old, as if he had been wearing them continually since the 1970s.

On the streets, Jack Denton was called "The Dark Disciple." He always referred to his guidance by the Dark Master, Satan, whose gravelly-honey toned voice gave purpose and direction to all of his actions. He indulged daily in his sacramental marijuana to induce what he, in his more lucid moments, called "ecstatic union with the King of the Dark Forces." Psychiatric authorities simply called it psychotic decompensation.

He was a frequent flyer, with an old case file folder a foot and a half thick, and a swiftly growing volume two. Somewhere between the 3rd and 5th of every month, having smoked up the bulk of his Social Security Disability check in the form of the finest weed available, he would arrive on the unit, having become either delirious or delusional or both. Invariably he would begin to preach the "word of his one true God," even when no one was inclined to listen. Often this lack of attention led Jack to become "a little physical" in order that someone might better "receive the word of the Dark Lord." Generally, he would rant and scream when ignored, and then apply an iron grip on another person's body part, even more forcefully insisting that they turn their lives over to the specious care of Satan.

The police, of course, considered it to be assault and battery, especially when, on more than one occasion, this particular maneuver resulted in injuries, once a broken bone. Several times he had managed to avoid being charged with the far more serious charge of aggravated assault by being admitted to Atascadero State Hospital for a court-committed 180-day stay. Tonight, he'd been medically cleared at the SF General's ER, but they were on psych diversion, and Mount Zion Crisis close behind, so Sergeant Green made some kind of casual arrangement with hospital administration, and they hustled him right over, promising toxicology results within the hour.

There were rumors and suspicions that he might have been involved in kidnappings, even murders, as a result of his delusional system, and had been taken advantage of by a perpetrator far more organized, and devious to achieve nefarious ends. It was widely acknowledged that Jack was far too disorganized to accomplish such deeds on his own, but the police had never had any solid proof of any such an association.

Jack's demeanor shifted to what might otherwise pass for "normal," once he entered the unit. He started loquaciously conversing with two uniformed officers as if they were all old friends. The officers greeted Paul, and rolled their eyes as

Jack attempted to enlist their cooperation in his campaign to win souls and influence people.

"You could be of tremendous assistance! You could just not arrest people anymore! It would be a wonderful gift!"

His smile was magnetic, though slightly cockeyed, as he reached up with his manacled hands, and pushed a bushy wave of thick, blonde hair away from his weathered, leathery face, one that all-too-clearly reflected how he had saturated himself with drugs. The records stated that he was only twenty-eight, though he appeared to be at least fifty. There were a pair of holes in each ear where silver hoop earrings had been removed for security reasons as well as a number of plastic and metal bracelets he habitually wore.

"Hello, Paul! Jenny! How's the kids? Stevie! It's like old home week here!" he chortled. His enduring roller-coaster spirits were a permanent aftereffect of the methamphetamine he'd injected into his arms, legs, neck, and any other site he could find. (He'd even been known to take the gauze out of nasal inhalers to cook down the wyamine to inject). A massive overdose two years earlier had left him in a coma for two weeks, and led him to swearing off all other substances but the magical weed.

Through the years he had had numerous diagnoses: Manic-Depressive Disorder, Mixed; Manic Depressive Disorder, Manic; Substance Induced Mood Disorder; Substance

Induced Psychosis; Schizophrenia, Undifferentiated—even Schizophrenia Paranoid Type once, when he'd completely over-amped on a potent mixture of marijuana, alcohol, methamphetamine, LSD, and Valium. After many "trials" of neuroleptic meds (billed to the taxpayers of the great State of California), Outpatient Services had finally decided that he was, in fact, Manic-Depressive Mixed; and he was officially prescribed Lithium, and Klonopin to smooth his edges (the latter which he sold on the street). He absolutely refused to take Haldol or Stelazine for his delusions.

Nonetheless he still carried diagnoses of Manic-Depressive Disorder Mixed, and Drug Induced Mood Disorder (in Remission) as well as rule-outs for Schizoaffective Disorder and Drug Induced Delusional Disorder.

His demented cackle echoed through the unit, as the officers walked on either side of him, and Paul walked drag, trailing behind to block that as a possible escape route.

One of the new Techs attempted to take his vital signs, but he was resistant until Stevie managed to cajole the old burnout into allowing her to take them while Paul and the Nursing Supervisor waited. As soon as she took the blood pressure cuff off his arm, he broke free, and went skipping into the dayroom, twitching and cackling. Several patients looked askance while others seemed magnetically drawn to him, his aberrant charisma radiating as he danced around the dayroom with a Mephistophelean glee, his thin sallow face and pointed waxed goatee punctuating the air erratically.

"We should throw him in the seclusion room," Paul murmured.

"But he's still in cuffs!" said Eddie, just out of training and on his first assignment.

Tom Sutton, the Nursing Supervisor, sniggered, then snorted through his nose.

"Last time he was here he complained to the Patients' Rights Advocate, and they said it was 'abusive' of us to seclude him just to shut him up."

"But he'll get everybody else jacked up!"

"And we'll have to deal with the aftermath!"

While the policemen pursued Jack, George Squires appeared as if by magic. He was still smoldering after an almost-lethal dose of phencyclidine (PCP) he had smoked earlier in the day. When he caught sight of the whirling manic figure of Jack Denton, he screamed at the top of his lungs and he ran directly at Jack, who simultaneously threw off the two officers attempting to restrain him. It was as if a plutonium meatball had been fired into a mass of uranium, creating a fissionable event.

Since George was committed to spreading the word of the Lord Jesus, and "smiting the unrighteous," he yelled at Jack, "I cast thee down, Beelzebub!"

Reaching for the manic figure, the younger officer fell directly into the knees of the Med Nurse who'd been crossing the floor holding a plastic tray filled with small paper med cups. She panicked, threw up her arms and screamed. She'd been preoccupied and not paying attention. She had initially believed she was being attacked by hordes of sexually preoccupied male patients (one of her greatest fears, and an occasional masturbatory fantasy). As she collapsed to the floor, the med cart turned a cartwheel in the air before discharging its contents, spilling a veritable cornucopia of substances—Valium, Thorazine, Haldol, Synthroid, Cogentin, Ativan, Percodan, Lithium, Metamucil, Navane, Lasix, Benadryl, Cardiazem. The pills and potions rolled and tumbled across the highly polished linoleum floor,

Almost all of the patients converged at the scene of the debacle like a human avalanche crashing. Men and women; young and old; in wheelchairs and with walkers; on crutches and canes; drooling and dribbling; with tongues wagging, and pajamas sagging; continent and incontinent, they came, on and on, like a Biblical surge that kept gaining momentum, strength and speed; on and on with ravaged courage and deluded determination, they came, intent as any pilgrim on a quest as staff from both units responded to the Panic Button alarm, pouring through the doors like a horde of Vandals sacking Rome—bright, educated mental health professionals whose faces all reflected excitement at the opportunity to join in the mayhem.

Like a human tsunami wave, a rush of patients flowed after the spilled treasurers, stuffing them into mouths, pockets, purses, and body cavities. A shoving match broke out on the floor as the more aware inmates wrestled with the less compensated over territorial rights.

"Give me that Valium!"

"I want them Percodans!"

"I'll trade you!"

"Ecchhh! Fucking Thorazine!!"said one patient said spitting.

As the older officer crawled away from the human stew boiling and bubbling on the floor, he climbed cautiously to his feet and scurried away from the pandemonium. Since everyone was wearing street clothes, it was virtually impossible to distinguish the patients from the staff. The two officers struggled to each other's sides, shifting from foot to foot for a moment, momentarily overwhelmed. They looked into each other's eyes and waded into the teeming storm of humanity, two dark blue monoliths immediately surrounded by the roar of voices, akin to nothing less than the world immediately after the fall of the Tower of Babel. They focused on the one person they knew of a certainty was crazy as he flailed around in handcuffs, leg and belly chains.

"Grab his wrist!"

"Motherfucker's trying to bite me!"

"That's my leg! Take the goddamn restraint off my leg!"

"Pull them apart and seclude them. Separately!"

"Oh, Great Lord Satan, deliver me..."

"Help! Help me!"

Johnny J had secured George around the chest, and was attempting to prevent him from biting a nurse on the neck, like a berserk vampire. He had been speaking softly, attempting to soothe him when George turned around to try to strangle him with his cuffed wrists. The very air swam with cries and chaos, redolent with aberrance and confusion, punctuated by calls for help and screams for assistance.

"I NEED SOME HELP HERE! RIGHT NOW!"

Responding to the intensity of the plea, both officers let go of Jack momentarily, as the Panic Button continued bleating and adding to the collective dissonance.

"Just take it easy, George. You're safe here!"

"Ain't none of you motherfuckers gonna be safe, I get my hands on you!"

As George shouted, spittle flying from his lips. As his liver became more re-stimulated, more and more PCP from his saturated fatty tissue leached out into his whole body. While

PCP works exceedingly well as a large animal tranquilizer on horses, bears and hippopotami, the effect on George was immensely different. Highly stimulating rushes shook him like repeated tsunami waves flashed through him illuminating him with tremendous urgency as a dynamic power pulsed through him, accompanied by a growing numbness of his peripheral nervous system—the anesthetic effect of the tranquilizer simultaneously struggling for dominance of his nervous system. His pain receptor response was all but nullified and his florid exertion burned incredible energy, pulling toxic-drug saturated fat stores into the oven of his metabolism dissociated from the executive control of his prefrontal cortex, leaving him completely at the mercy of his raging limbic system that was absolutely hammering at him with imperative fight-or-flight messages.

Johnny J had secured George around the chest, and was attempting to prevent him from biting a nurse on the neck, like a berserk vampire. He had been speaking softly, attempting to soothe him when George turned around to try to strangle him with his cuffed wrists. The very air swam with cries and chaos, redolent with aberrance and confusion, punctuated by calls for help and screams for assistance.

"I NEED SOME HELP HERE! RIGHT NOW!"

Responding to the intensity of the plea, both officers let go of Jack momentarily, as the Panic Button continued bleating and adding to the collective dissonance.

"Just take it easy, George. You're safe here!"

"Ain't none of you motherfuckers gonna be safe, I get my hands on you!"

As George shouted, spittle flying from his lips. As his liver became more re-stimulated, more and more PCP from his saturated fatty tissue leached out into his whole body. While PCP works exceedingly well as a large animal tranquilizer on horses, bears and hippopotami, the effect on George was immensely different. Highly stimulating rushes shook him like repeated tsunami waves flashed through him illuminating him with tremendous urgency as a dynamic power pulsed through him, accompanied by a growing numbness of his peripheral nervous system—the anesthetic effect of the tranquilizer simultaneously struggling for dominance of his nervous system. His pain receptor response was all but nullified and his florid exertion burned incredible energy, pulling toxic-drug saturated fat stores into the oven of his metabolism dissociated from the executive control of his prefrontal cortex, leaving him completely at the mercy of his raging limbic system that was absolutely hammering at him with imperative fight-or-flight messages.

CHAPTER SIX

The Beat Goes On

September 21st, 1988   1700

When the Panic Button was pushed, the Charge Nurse from Detox sent three of her four male staff, and all of the female staff who chose to respond. The male staff had been instantly galvanized and raring to go. The unwritten rule for female staff was that they were not "required" to respond—though more often than not the women Techs were often high testosterone types who enjoyed the adrenaline rush as much as any man. Since everyone was paid the same, the "party line" had it that everyone was equal as concerned duty and danger. In actuality, it usually worked out that the male staff spearheaded the bulk of potentially violent situations. The extra staff who arrived to help stanch the situation instead actually fed it, as they were mostly younger and less experienced. As such, they tended to cluster together on the periphery like baby chicks looking for a hen, and were not able to actually contribute to helping restore order as they tended to get in the way of the long-standing practices associated with takedowns and well known to the more experienced staff.

The net result of this was a kind of concordance amongst the patients. Each of the gathered groups' energies was amplified by the cybernetic feedback. Manics used the lack of individual attention and boundary-setting to begin frenetically patrolling the unit, becoming increasingly grandiose and aggressive. Their speech and intrusiveness intensified too, and they started making lewd remarks about, and sexual comments to, both male and female patients. A few started exposing themselves—to the fright of some, and to the delight of others. The schizophrenics' voices warned them of impending doom, or castigated them for not attempting to flee. The paranoiacs broadcast, sometimes quite loudly, that they'd been right all along—the staff <u>was</u> out to get them! And there was <u>nowhere</u> to run to! The obsessives had a field day with all of the additional chaos that had been created. They went into overdrive attempting to order and categorize their ever more detailed and fanciful schemes, preoccupations, and rituals. The depressives murmured and sighed deeply, then retreated further into their internal landscapes, ruminating and perseverating about ancient lost opportunities. The religiously preoccupied evangelized all who would listen (or not) that the Apocalypse had finally arrived, exhorting everyone to beg forgiveness before the arrival of the Rapture ships. Through it all, the tangled mass of patients gyrated, whirled, and swirled in a wild dervish-like dance. Most of the any patients were singing and swinging while gleefully knocking over older and less-oriented geriatric patients who had wandered in disoriented through the unit door that had been left open.

Into the midst of this teeming confusion stepped Tom Sutton, a Senior Nurse Supervisor, a veteran of many crisis interventions. As the old saw had it, a diamond is only a chunk of coal that makes good under pressure. Tom absolutely sparkled as he waded in like the Rock of Gibraltar, standing steady and directing traffic, untangling Gordian knots of patients and staff, issuing orders and galvanizing staff members into positive action. Paul had gravitated toward him, and he stood shoulder-to-shoulder with him, sorting out the chaos like tangles from a knotted skein.

"Goddamn it! Get those patients sorted out! Who is that on top of Marilee?"

"Some patient!"

"I don't care! Get him off her, and get him secluded!"

"They're all full!"

"Then four-point him on a gurney in the hallway!"

In the midst of the mêlée, George's internal thermometer had skyrocketed as more and more of the PCP stored in his liver metabolized, and he falsely believed that his body was filled with superhuman strength. As the policemen attempted again to secure him, a massive drug surge smashed into him. He pulled away with all of his might—and ripped his left hand free of the handcuff, along with the epidermis, dermis, and a chunk of flesh, flaying the skin from most of his hand. Gouts of blood spurted from severed arteries, mangled nerves and shredded muscles exposed in a kind of macabre anatomy lesson. He flailed his damaged appendage, spurting arterial blood on the walls and floor as well as numerous people as he and started backing toward the locked unit doors. Though he was still running on high-grade internal fuel, his eyes glazed as he went deeper into shock.

The massive blood spray had immediately caught Tom's attention. He made a quick eye contact with Paul and they encircling the drug-emboldened man from opposite sides.

George was within a yard of the first locked door when he suddenly noticed his damaged paw. Holding it up in front of his face, he gripped it with his right hand as if it were an alien artifact, shifting his attention back and forth, left to right, as Tom and Paul closed the pincers on him. Paul grabbed him around the chest, pinning his right hand to his side with the handcuffs still attached. Tom then secured his damaged hand, and wrapped a length of rubber tube as a tourniquet around it just above the wrist as other staff closed on them, and they took George to the floor. Tom dispensed hands full of 4"x4" pads from his pockets for a pressure dressing, followed by yards of tape.

Soon the entire area from above the wrist to fingertips was encased in a kind of gauze cocoon. Blood from both major arteries slowed, but continued to seep through the mass of packing in spite of the hastily applied tourniquet. George's skin was clammy; he was sweating profusely; his face was chalk white; and his breathing was rapid and shallow. Then, as if he had just come back into his body, George's eyes lit up like electrified saucers. Then he exhibited what was the least serious symptom medically, but the most painful to every other human close by: he loosed an enormous scream as his tortured nerves and neurons finally communicated with his benumbed brain.

"AAAHHHHH! EEEEAAAGGGHHH! EEEAAAGGGHHHH!"

"BP is 80/48 and dropping! Pulse 120, rapid, and thready!"

"Start a line with normal saline! Use his ankle! Get a gurney! Get him to the ER!"

"How about some Ativan?" asked a younger Tech.

"Hell no! He's probably loaded on fucking PCP!"

"Jane! Take this hand! Go with him!"

Another of the Techs and both police officers immediately volunteered to help make the precipitous transport with two other staff.

"Make sure they know he's got PCP on board!"

They got the patient carted, strapped securely, and on his way to the ER, all the while Jane recited a constant flow of worsening vital sign information like an ominous mantra.

Jason Albritton Junior was the Ward Chief, and the psychiatrist ultimately responsible for the running of both units. He had stopped by to retrieve some case study materials he needed for an article he was writing. He spoke directly to the Charge Nurses of both units, and to a third year Medical Student doing his "tour of duty" in psych.

"Fuck a bunch of Doctor's Orders! Just start giving all these people PRNs! We'll write the orders later!"

Paul immediately went to the Med Room, and began furiously filling med cups with standard dosages of each patient's PRN. Then he gestured to the bulk of the staff who had gathered in a cluster by the Med Room looking like nothing other than a bunch of human grapes to get the pipeline to the patients moving.

Tom started issuing orders.

"Make sure the rest of the patients are still here and safe. Do a head count! NOW!"

Then, almost as an afterthought, he called out, "Better check vitals on everybody! Who knows who took what! Check pupil responses too!"

Techs and nurses made a steady shuttle to the half-open door of the Med Room, and then out onto the floor to dispense their wares to patients who had had their vitals taken and recorded. Most of the spilled meds had been recovered and were in a large plastic container in the Med Room waiting to be wasted by being dissolved in the sink in front of two witnesses who would both be required to sign the med sheet. All the patients had been properly accounted for and identified before they got meds—the more disturbed of whom were asked to lie down and take injectable meds. For any who did not evince immediate cooperation, a "show of force" of two or three tensed and ready staff members materialized to reinforce the implicate order.

Tom had just returned from making a quick round of the unit when a young pre-licensed Tech wobbled toward him. Tom noted his pale complexion and profuse perspiration, then told him to sit. He checked his wrist, and saw that his pulse was racing.

"Are you hurt? You look shockey! I need some help here! NOW!"

"Tom," he said, voice cracking, dragged out of his throat as if held captive, each syllable seemingly purchased at the highest of prices. "I think Hawkins is dead!"

CHAPTER SEVEN
A Day in the Life
Same Evening   1735

Samuel X. Smith sat mute. He silently witnessed the exodus of the intruder, his besotted brain recording all of the vivid pictures and intimate information, but unable to attach any emotional significance to it. His blood alcohol was two and a half times the legal limit. His amygdala and limbic system were temporally occupied with keeping the memories of his past from flooding his hippocampus, and from swamping his forebrain with the urgent awareness of his having no future at all.

CHAPTER EIGHT
A Time to Break Down
September 21st, 1988   2210

Tom Sutton felt a distinct aversion to the always weird energy, foul odors and the claustrophobic confines of seclusion rooms, even as many times as he had entered them. A veritable phalanx of staff had heard the rumor about the dead patient. A casual observer might have thought they were at a Hollywood grand opening though to Paul they appeared more to be a gaggle of ghouls. Some were anxious, others cracked inappropriate jokes, still others were superficially stoic—but all were intent on the supine figure lying on the bed. They leaned on the walls and door, craning their necks to see around one another, touching everything, leaving thousands of fingerprints the police would later have to eliminate. They were typical "looky-loos" who gathered at any disaster, fascinated by the damage and relieved that it had not happened to them.

The patient's skin was cooling quickly, but still warm. Tom did not find a carotid pulse. He immediately started shouting orders.

"Get those restraints off! Initiate CPR! Call 911! NOW!"

Staff scattered to implement his commands. Paul went to stand by the front door to direct traffic.

"Take some of these fucking 'spectators' here and put them to work! If anybody gives you any shit, tell 'em it's orders from the Nursing Supervisor!"

Paul turned to follow his orders, directing staff to immediately implement group therapy sessions to ally patients' fears, while re-directing the patients to follow staff directives at the far end of the unit.

Eddie Chacon monitored the door, directing the in-coming Code Team to the seclusion rooms. Like a juggernaut, two paramedic teams, a fire crew, and four more uniformed police officers arrived in very short order. Alfredo Tomasetti, one of the docs from the Code Blue Team, took immediate charge of resuscitation efforts.

The Crash Cart was standing by, and another Nursing Supervisor was stationed in Medical Supply to immediately dispatch anything not readily at hand. Tom quickly apprised Alfredo and the paramedic team in a rapid burst like a coded satellite message.

"No pulse. No blood pressure. I had the restraints removed. He's been out five minutes tops," knowing that survival with CPR was twice as high during the first four minutes, and usually worthless after eight.

The assembled team swarmed like a flock of flamingos on a school of shrimp. Within a minute, all of the patient's life functions were being artificially assisted. CPR continued while an airway was prepared, then inserted and connected to an Ambu Bag; a cardiac monitor began cranking out information; two IV lines were started in proximal aspects of the ankles using cut downs, incising the vein and inserting a line—epinephrine, sodium bicarbonate, and calcium chloride were infusing as the defibrillator was readied, plugged in, tested; and set at 200 joules.

"Ready!"

"Clear!"

The paddles were placed in the standard arrangement, one to the right of the upper sternum, the other just to the left of the opposite nipple.

The patient's body jumped as the electricity coursed through him, though his viciously damaged heart failed to restart.

"Flat line! No pulse!"

"Let's go! 300!"

"Ready!"

"Clear!"

Humans and machines both reported failure.

Fredo was pacing frenetically behind the furiously working team, barking orders, reading monitors, adjusting IV lines like a football coach orchestrating a last-minute drive for a winning touchdown.

"Another milligram of epinephrine stat! And another amp of bicarb!"

"I want another set of blood gases! Start an isopoterinol drip!"

After applying more insulating gel to the paddles, one of the paramedics jacked it up to 400 joules—and got nothing more than a fresh set of burns on the patient's chest for his efforts.

Fredo moved up next to the supine man, pulling on a fresh set of gloves. "I'm going to try external cardiac massage," he said, and spent a full minute doing so, as a continuous feedback of negative vital signs were monitored and read to him. Finally, he too realized the futility of his efforts.

"I'm calling this one. There's nothing we can do. What's the time?"

The elapsed time (as recorded on the Code Clock on the cart) was a little more than 23 minutes. Real time was 0145, and was documented. Fredo signed the TOD (time of death) certificate.

"He's for the Medical Examiner now."

Tom called the Hospital Administrator who conference-called the Hospital Attorney for advice on how to best handle this extremely sticky situation.

All of monitors were flat lines, no heartbeat, no brainwaves, but the Code Team was still in an altered state. In their heart of hearts, the adrenaline rush was still working them, even in the aftermath of dancing a twisted pavane with

Death. Like compulsive gamblers, they lived for the wild ride, completely alive, up front, on stage. Many thought it was at least the equivalent of orgasm, some thought it better, feeling completely whole in one's skin, totally immersed in the moment with no separation, fed by the true lifeblood, the protein, the RNA, the very essence of Life itself, contained and defined by Death in all of its forms.

CHAPTER NINE
Who's Really in Charge?
September 22nd, 1988   0112

The seclusion room remained taped off, with a uniformed SFPD officer on duty 24/7. The aftermath of what had now been ruled a murder left The Unit bearing a distinct resemblance to the detritus of Dresden after the firestorm bombing. There were soda cans, snack wrappers, sandwich papers, ash trays filled with cigarette butts and cigar stubs, discarded cardboard cups with the dregs of tea or coffee, tubes, tape, bandages, blood-splattered gauze pads, broken handcuffs, paper cups, used syringes, wrappers, scraps of clothing, Kleenex, latex gloves, discarded laboratory vials, pieces of skin and nails, a broken restraint lock, scraps of paper, a shattered plastic spoon, and thousands of dust bunnies—all left in place in accord with the Medical Examiner's longstanding protocol, until he had officially "released" the body after having examined it extensively *in situ,* and declared it a "suspicious death in custody" (the 5150 qualified).

Everything else was left in place to molder if the forensic techs chose; left in place untouched until the end of time if they chose, because it was all potential evidence.

Immediately following the highly anticipated permission from the ME, the forensic techs, coordinated by the SFPD and Sheriff's Departments (jurisdictional dispute) from all of the major agencies swarmed over the room to gather countless samples from the passage of hundreds of individuals who had left visible and invisible traces of their journeys. The Tech people left a documented trail of their own of fingerprint dust (black and white), though they were more careful to not add to the enormous quantity of discarded and otherwise misbegotten potential evidence.

Paul felt torn emotionally, as if he were having a stroke. His brain ached (even though he knew it was physically impossible). He was simultaneously angry; depressed; frustrated; simmering with rage; confused; upset; nauseated; bewildered; spaced out; wanting to run, to cry, to smoke three hits of the very finest one-hit weed, to smoke some heroin, to smoke some free-base; to climb the highest mountain, and just sit there for about a thousand years contemplating the Universe; to cry for three years; to be held and comforted by a loving woman; to take a machete to a hundred random people; to puke and shit and fart simultaneously; to swim in the deepest ocean until his awareness ceased; to disappear in wafting waves of ever-increasing joy and wonder; to one day awaken from the long and tortured journey of his life to find it all had been a dream.

"And where were you when the death occurred?" asked one of the detectives, a hefty looking female Sheriff's deputy.

Paul asked what seemed to him a, if not the, most logical question.

"What time did the death occur?"

She dismissed his question curtly, and reminded him that they were the ones asking the questions.

It was such an inane question, that Paul had answered numerous times for three different people, ultimately commenting on the utter chaos that had happened on the unit just prior to the discovery of the body. As to time of death? How was he supposed to know? The seclusion sheet had been marked every fifteen minutes as required by law, up until the time the chaos erupted on the floor. Paul tried to clarify the details of the confusion and insanity in as much detail as he could, and wondered idly if the police thought they could actually trip up a potential killer by asking such an idiotic question—though he guessed they considered it to be tricky and ingenious. He grew exhausted with the amount of energy it took to repeat the same mundane details over and over; then he got totally bored, uninterested, and just shut down. Other than what he had witnessed, he had absolutely no idea what might have transpired—even if it was anything other than accidental. Fuck! With that asshole Hawkins, it could have been suicide! His way to fuck with them all even after he was dead (though he was careful to keep this remark to himself).

By the time he had been released, it was close to 0200. He had been interviewed three times (a uniformed officer, and then by two different sets of detectives). He felt completely unable to do any writing, drained of whatever creative energies he might have been able to muster secondary to the massive bullshit bureaucratic juggernaut that had rolled in to investigate to which he had been subjected. Consequently, he felt shitty, sluggish, constipated, leaden, bored, pissed off, distracted, homicidal, semi-suicidal, depressed, and emotionally bloated—as if he had emotional edema. He was pissed off at himself for not writing, for not turning the "incident" into grist for the mill (as Ram Das had always taught), for not feeling capable of turning to his own personal source of love and grace for confirmation of his existence and value in his life. His writing had always been his refuge from the world and all of the crazy people he had known (especially his wretched father). It always served as an outlet to keep him from overly criticizing himself and his personal salvation—as if authorship would or even could magically catapult him into a newer, brighter sphere of existence, one in which he was globally recognized as a literary icon and adulated for his brilliance. His writing had always been his very best friend, as if a doppelgänger twin, in whom he could confide everything without editing or oversight.

In his mind, he occasionally referred to his writings sardonically as his "scribblings," though he sincerely believed that the work of his lifetime, all of the adventures, the intensity of his personal work and the excruciating decades of therapy had the potential to become true autobiographical novels on the order of one of his literary heroes, Henry Miller. Conversely, his deepest and most private fear was that his imagination and life experience might not comprise the stuff of true literary value; might not be as vital, intriguing, or inspiring because they were based on his real-life struggles. He so aspired to be a literary figure, so wanted to be read and quoted by thousands, millions even—though he knew in his heart of hearts that the utter aim of his desire was to be heard in ways that he had never been ever in this lifetime—to attempt to satisfy the gigantic black hole in his heart, even though he knew that ultimately only loving himself could ever bring it.

In spite of what he usually viewed as his lack of worldly success, Paul would never have traded his experience for any amount of money. He was rich in his storehouse of memories that no one could take away from him. Never.

Even if he lived a hundred years, he could reflect on the adventures from which he had gleaned a glimmer of the Universal about which to write, to share the distilled essence of his journey, his passage on this Earth.

He had for so long lived for high-risk moments, the extremely altered states—admittedly seeking an antidote for the emotional wreckage of his childhood and the aftermath of the war. It was what had driven him both to working the moist dangerous psych units and to dealing drugs (initially only to supply his own needs without cost). By comparison, his everyday life now was rather boring, though he was grateful to have it. He still craved the fast women, though not so much the cocaine (though there were moments). This might be the greatest punishment of all—to have lived the highest highs, and carry the memories knowing he would never again do so. In this sense then he was in mourning now much as he had been when he returned from the 'Nam, the highest high of war, unduplicable, and one that he chased to this day.

Of course, he knew his dopamine receptors were still in rehab, given the amount of coke he had used. There remained the other possibility, given that highly altered states were just part of a vast spectrum of consciousness, that he might someday elevate his mental status enough that such numinous states would become ordinary one day—though he felt so very far from that goal. He'd always been attracted to stimulants and the high life, and the desire for more, ever more of everything. It paralyzed him sometimes, to the point when he just had to give in—grant himself a day in bed, reading, writing, and contemplating. It was one of the best treats he ever gave himself, a true day off from the world.

By the time he had been released and taken a Veteran's Cab home, it was well-nigh on to 0300 before Paul finally got to sit down in his favorite leather chair, put his feet up, sip a Drambuie from a crystal snifter, and unwind, contemplating as he made more journal notes toward a new novel. It always felt as if there would never be, could never be, enough—especially time—that mysterious quantity and quality that always seemed to elude him, always remained just out of reach. It used to be that when he was at the end of a five-day coke run, when many others complained of the come-down, and the post-adrenalized wastedness, he was able to revel in a strange sort of peace that came over him, mentally and emotionally bathing in a feeling of washed out desuetude that allowed him to just be without feeling he had to do anything else. In those moments, it was so tempting to do just a little bit more, to stay high and awake just a little bit longer, to not surrender to the forces of sleep and the need for renewal, to revel in that strange melancholia as he continued his vainglorious search for a permanent high.

He well knew the etymology of the word "enough" — "Adequate for the want or need; sufficient for the purpose, or to satisfy desire." As such, it implied sufficiency, adequacy, and a sense of even momentary completeness. Investigating further, he inevitably arrived at the understanding that such a state does or can exist only very briefly; and as such, could only be obtained in the moment, and had to be constantly renewed. It seemed impossible to attain any kind of permanent state of satisfaction. In his experience, it was one of the elements underlying all addictions—even (or especially) greed, the least spoken of, and most rampant, addiction of all. It seemed that there must be a connection to the original and most primary separation of human birth—what both Freud and Otto Rank had spoken of as being incorporated in that very first ontological moment of birth, "the most traumatic experience anyone ever suffers." Paul took it deeper, to the very first moment of the birth of the Universe, buried as a template holding the answer to the question every individual eventually had to ask: Who am I? And why did I come here? And ultimately, hermeneutically, what is the meaning of it all?

It was all related, of a single origin, but nonetheless a conundrum of the highest order—and one that could never be solved intellectually, emotionally, even therapeutically, though each of these approaches contained some element of the solution that tantalized him, left him craving more, needing more, wanting more. It seemed that the only answer lay in the silence buried in each moment, delving ever into the eternally unfolding and hidden nadirs of ineffable beauty, the numinous light shining through one and all, radiating through all Eternity. It was these rare joyous, ineffably peaceful moments in which he gloried, that passed all too quickly into the great morass of time. His brain switched gears as he thought about the police investigation, how much he absolutely hated the thought of anyone intruding on him, looking into the private details of his past, especially the idiosyncratic details of his present—just fucking hated it! Bastards! Just because the agents of a corrupt and dystopian society gave police plenipotentiary powers, did not mean he had to like it!

Part of that reflected his relative lack of power in the world, the lack of material success and money—and, in many ways, it boiled down to getting a better education, credentials, and social connections so that he could both feel better about himself and actually do more of the good he knew was buried in his heart. This was the recipe for Paul getting out of the trenches forever; that could provide forever relief from the grinding mental and emotional poverty in which he lived on a daily basis; from which he could embrace the more rarified air of a professional mental health practitioner! But how much more? A Master's? A Ph.D.? Maybe his goal was simply unobtainable after all. He'd always fantasized envisioned outcomes in just about every arena of his life, yet the results upon attainment invariably fell short of his expectations. This may be why Buddha called satisfying one's desire illusory, the only and ultimate result being more suffering. Maybe that was the Universal design, creating utter frustration so individuals would turn inward, to completely surrender striving, and the convert shame, pain, frustration, anger, and fear into the kind of peace that can only exist when one no longer harbors a desire for personal gain., when one becomes truly a servant of the Universe.

Paul rolled a medium-sized joint with a single Blanco y Negro paper, then took a deep drag, holding his breath until he breathed out empty air with a rush that exploded his brain case with a psychedelic array of purples, blues, yellows, reds, and greens, like a bag of spilled gemstones, and followed by a susurrus of wind and chimes. He sat back in his chair and let the emerging poem arise from the prehistoric peat bog in his head to be translated to his fingers.

In the wind and the rain,

in the fog and mist,

he walked

alone

as if destiny's call

received

on a wire directly to his brain,

that drove him

yet further along the illuminated path

set long before,

ordained by a will greater than his own,

a wisdom

far surpassing his meager fears and hungers,

directing him

on a path leading ever homeward.

CHAPTER TEN
Sturm und Drang
September 22nd, 1988   0325

Like a chain of demented dominos, the Ward Chief had called the Chief of Psychiatry, who called the Medical Director who called the Hospital Attorney (who called the District Attorney) and then the Mayor (on his private line) —who, in turn, called the Chief Medical Examiner and in his most politely demanding tones, told him that he wanted him to personally handle the "bizarre death" (refusing to call it a murder) in an adjunct County Hospital (soon to be annexed by UCSF).

"This is going to be a shitstorm! I do not want anyone being able to say that I didn't make the maximum effort!"

Morton Jahrlsberg (a distant relative of Count Vedel Jahrlsberg who created the cheese that bears his name) had been called "cheese head" in grammar school, but when he reached adolescence, no one any longer dared. He was a bear of a man, 6'3" tall with heavy body hair and a jowly face that carried a five o'clock shadow twenty minutes after he shaved. His disposition at this hour was ursine as well, growling and (some might say rudely) pushing his way through the throng of reporters, microphones and television cameras already gathered in anticipation of his arrival. How did these media vultures get the information so fast? He wondered to himself, then quickly reflected on the vast number of County, State and private employees who had been privy to the knowledge of the death; and even if each of them told only one other person...

As Chief Medical Examiner for the City and County of San Francisco, he had not had to take a middle-of-the-night call, but he bent to the Mayor's "request." He was ultimately responsible for the roughly 8000 bodies that passed through the portals of his demesne. Of these, approximately one-quarter required his office to determine cause of death. The law was very clear: Anyone who died in custody; from suspected Sudden Infant Death Syndrome; any "suspicious death"; or anyone who hadn't seen a doctor in the previous 20 days, were automatically remanded to him. He could routinely complete an autopsy in thirty to sixty minutes, while the far more detailed Medical/Legal Post Mortem could take as long as two full days, always mindful of yet another court appearance, and this was not counting the distinct possibility of a prolonged wait for detailed laboratory findings and reports, especially if it were for a tox screen asking for exotic poisons and chemicals.

A bright and alert staff member had taken the initiative to compile copies of the patient's records, Code Team Logs, case notes, and other paperwork. Since this incident had occurred on City and County of San Francisco property—and especially on the heels of the rather intemperate "request" from His Honor—he accepted the mantle of leadership for what might prove to be a very politically sticky situation.

He donned booties, a "space suit," and double-gloves to avoid cross-contamination whatever evidence there might be before entering the room where the body had been left *in situ*, as per his standing orders. His client's (always his client, never "vic" or "perp" or any other cop-speak) hands and feet had been covered in paper bags. The intravenous fluids had been discontinued, but the lines were still in place, and the bags carefully maintained for further examination. Protocol. Always protocols.

Although he never talked about it, he was always aware of energetic patterns associated with crime scenes that usually escaped others, and was able to factor in his intuitions when doing his clinical work and making judgments. He had the ability to take in the gestalt of a location in a single penetrating glance that registered all the minutiae, and was able to break it down later into mental photographs of single frames. He was able to use his eidetic memory to record images he would later compare with actual photographs, but it was almost always the ambiguities or discontinuities he could sense that led to more exacting conclusions. He immediately noted the gaping wound in, and burn marks on, the chest; the utterly pallid skin color; the extensive tattooing; the twisted, dystonic posture; the marked ecchymosis on both wrists and ankles; flushed, puffy cheeks; and glassy wide-open eyes staring into eternity.

Though the death had occurred in a medical facility, and under relatively close scrutiny with excellent documentation, he nonetheless made a small incision and inserted a thermometer into the man's liver. Then he produced a small ruler calibrated to measure the dilation of the victim's pupils

The photographer was similarly clothed and was methodically dashing around the seclusion room, shooting dozens, hundreds of shots from every conceivable angle, wide angles, close ups, micro-close-ups, macro shots, of every aspect of the room, even standing on a ladder hastily secured from maintenance and provided with its own set of booties so as to not further contaminate the scene.

Excess photos always satisfied the District Attorney who could invariably be counted upon to request an arcane angle, or possibly-unthought-of critical shot. The DA was an asshole anyway! He had made hundreds of court appearances, and had more than once "saved" the man's case with his thoroughness and the crisp clarity of his expert testimony.

The ME ordered paper bags be put around the patient's hands and feet, to retain intact any residue or fibers, soil or fluids under the nails, and any other cuts, scratches, or fresh puncture wounds. He wouldn't make a real pronouncement until he had the man on his table where the final truths were always told, but nonetheless...

The body was bundled into a plastic body bag, and transported to the Medical Examiners' Office (sometimes commonly referred to as "the morgue"), located underneath and behind the Hall of Justice. He marveled at the beauty of the facility that, in an emergency, could (and had) double as a surgical facility. Though the ME's ultimate instruments were his hands, a Crusader seeking the often obscured Grail of cause of death, here he was assisted by the wonders of modern medical technology. Here was a Mass Spectrometer, and Gas and Liquid High-Performance Chromatography— either capable of analyzing 40,000 drugs and chemicals.

He put two sticks of spearmint gum into his mouth, and started chewing them as if an antidote for the effused amalgam of odors that pervaded the cool, pale green-tiled room—disinfectants, preservatives, dyes, stains, burnt bone, even corned beef and cabbage cooking over a Bunsen burner—that underlay the sickly-sweet pervasive odor of human decay, an odor so pungent that it immediately imprints itself permanently and can never be forgotten, the neuroreceptors always recalling it, no matter that the air conditioning and the ventilators ran 24/7.

Working with human bodies in various stages of professional dismemberment and preservation gave rise to macabre jokes and disregard for decorum – a humor often thought vulgar or crude that served to soften the impact of the harsh reality in which they were immersed. It was very similar to those of combat soldiers exposed to the most grim and unmasked realities possible, completely misunderstood "civilians," those who had not experienced the hell of war. Or as Georges Santayana once remarked: "Only the dead have seen the end of war."

A crème colored ceiling reigned twelve feet above the waist-high tile line. Five stainless steel tables dominated the main room, each featuring a drain and a hose connected to a water source operated by foot pedals. A corner scale could accommodate up to six hundred fifty pounds, and a decontamination shower, including eye flushes, was located in every one of the working areas. He chuckled to himself, reflecting on how amazed would be a time travelling coroner from the 12th Century when the job was first established, who saw the wonders of his kingdom, a long way from being *custos placitorum coronae*, or "guardian of the Crown's pleas," charged with keeping local records of legal proceedings in which the Crown had jurisdiction, including suicide as a "crime against the State" for which all property would be forfeit, it being the duty of the family to prove otherwise. He would have also been required to raise money for the Crown by funneling the property of executed criminals into the king's treasury; and investigate any suspicious deaths among the Normans (assuring that deaths amongst the ruling class were not taken lightly). At one point, all criminal proceedings in England were the coroner's responsibilities.

Since he had been personally tasked with this examination, he took it upon himself to ask for his Chief Deputy Donald Betters (euphemistically referred to as "The Friar" because his male-pattern baldness had left him with a fringe of hair like a tonsured medieval monk) to assist, both providing another excellent set of eyes and hands and an excellent mind to boot. Though he had played professional football after college, he "quit the game before the game quit him." He had done a rotation with Mort, then a residency after medical school, and had worked with him ever since.

Benedict Moss had come in early to do all the things he did so well. He was Mort's favorite diener, though he so far exceeded the traditional definition of the term. The literal translation from the German was "corpse servant," and dated to the time before Christ when butchers, horse gelders and barbers did autopsies. Originally, the diener cleaned the rooms and instruments, and assisted the coroners whose essential task was to determine whether the individuals had committed suicide, in which case all of their worldly goods went to the local nobility. If there were such a thing, in Mort's estimation Benedict would be their patron saint. He was eerily able to participate Mort's every need and have instruments ready before being asked. He was also in charge of adjusting the volume and changing the audio cassettes, making coffee, and Mort considered him to be essential. He sometimes referred to him as the "Majordomo" of the autopsy suite.

Zack the Mack's body arrived unceremoniously, and Benedict quickly unbundled it onto an autopsy table. The ME assiduously washed his hands with disinfectant soap and a small brush, working from the elbows to the fingertips, then gowned and double-gloved (a necessary precaution since the advent of AIDS). Benedict had meticulously laid out the tray of instruments in Mort's preferred idiosyncratic fashion, having worked with him for so many years that it was like having two pairs of hands and eyes. He activated the microphone that hung above his head as he first performed an excruciatingly thorough external examination of the body, searching it with the intimacy of a lover, carefully scrutinizing every centimeter. He noted that the cheeks were sallow, almost waxy to the touch. From the head, he worked down the body with extreme care, inch by inch, the jugular and carotid, with deep ecchymoses evident bilaterally, then the axillaries, the crotch, and genitals. He noted the extensive scar tissue around the antecubital areas of both arms, behind the knees, as well as the hands and ankles, even between the toes.

"Subject is a white male who appears to be much older than his stated age from hospital records, proclaiming him to be 41; skin is leathery with multiple scars and pits as well as new abrasions as will be noted; height is 6 feet 2 inches; weight is 140.3 pounds. Subject apparently expired while face down in four-point restraints in a seclusion room on the Acute Adult Unit at Community Hospital. It should be noted for the record that the paramedics were called, and they attempted heroic measures. The pupils appear fixed and dilated. There is a scattering of what appear to be petechial hemorrhages bilaterally. He appears to be grossly malnourished, dehydrated, and cachectic. The skin is cool and dry. There are first-degree burns in the left thoracic area consistent with repeated attempts to defibrillate. There are marked ecchymoses on both wrists. The upper two ribs on the left side are fractured, consistent with CPR efforts. There are puncture wounds in the left mid-thoracic area consistent with injections of sodium bicarbonate ampoules. There is a tattoo measuring 8 centimeters in length, and 4.5 centimeters in width in the shape of wings covering both the left and right antecubital areas. 'Harley Davidson' is inscribed at the bottom of each, and is likely covering old scar tissue. There are cut down wounds on the proximal aspects of both ankles..."

When he completed his extensive external examination, including having the body flipped over so as to document the large variety of wounds that had been, over time, inflicted upon Zack's body, he then made the standard Y-shaped incision—running down from each shoulder, meeting the midline of the body at the solar plexus, and continuing as a single line to the pubic bone. He peeled back the skin and muscles in three flaps; widely incised the abdomen; and then removed the stomach and viscera as a solid mass. He used what looked like oversized garden shears to cut through and remove the rib cage.

He kept up a steady patter recording the details, placing the organs in stainless steel pans, that Benedict then washed and weighed them in the stainless-steel sink. He then examined them one by one, noting appearance and weight. Starting at the top with the thyroid, he cut it open and recorded no gross abnormalities, then set it aside for microscopic examination. He excised the trachea, and opened it all the way down to its bifurcation into the lungs. These, he noted on gross observation, were distorted with brittle, dark alveoli consistent with chronic cigarette smoking.

He excised the heart and placed it in a separate small pan, then worked his way down the gastrointestinal tract from esophagus to anus, finding nothing grossly abnormal—for a man who used alcohol and drugs in great quantities. Benedict used a bone saw to open the scalp, removed the skullcap, and the ME scooped out the brain—a procedure that was automatic in any case of "suspicious death."

He kept a private file, and numerous glass jars, of rare and unusual pathological anomalies, toward the day when he might finally sit down and write a book of strange cases he had encountered. Reflecting on the condition of the eyes, he opened up the neck. Knowing that compression of the carotid arteries, in any manner, produced a failure of the brain to get proper oxygen, he very carefully examined them, and noted that they were distorted and ecchymosed, consistent with compression. He already suspected either strangulation, wherein one often found the horseshoe-shaped hyoid bone at the base of the throat broken; or asphyxiation wherein such a finding was less common.

He turned to Benedict and said, "Unless this is an iatrogenic artifact related to trying to revive him, we have a homicide!"

CHAPTER ELEVEN
Another Level of Investigation
September 22nd, 1988   1109

Interviewing potential witnesses seemed at first glance to be a foregone conclusion, but the detectives hadn't counted on the legal quagmire into which they intended to walk interviewing the patients and staff. The Hospital Attorney called the City Attorney who, in turn called the Attorney General of California (a law school classmate). Extensive legal consultation (at $300 an hour) arrived at the opinion that the patients could be questioned if they consented, and were allowed to request their own attorneys, but that they could not be questioned about their symptoms or what might have led them to being hospitalized—unless for some reason it became relevant, and the patient signed a Release of Information. If the patient were to start discussing his or her personal peccadilloes for any reason, the detectives were expected to caution them about it, and, on a case-by-case basis, might need at that point to call in a Patient's Advocate.

Law enforcement, naturally, wanted access to all of the patients' charts, especially case notes detailing any actual or potential harm, or threat of harm. They also felt they should have the right to take patients' charts off the unit, or at the least, copy any sections which might prove relevant. The Hospital Attorney stood firm on confidentiality and demanded that any such copying be denied pending he and his staff rigorously argued against such a blatant breech in front of a judge. (Of course, the way it actually worked in practice was that the officers found out what they needed in conversations with, and the cajoling of, various staff members, especially those whose own attitudes slanted toward the rule of law, or who were potential "badge bunnies" (the groupies of law enforcement). It was amazing to see how far the power of doughnuts could go in loosening even the hardest heart, or the staunchest will.

Of course, someone called the Patients' Rights Advocacy Office, who claimed (incorrectly) that they had a legal right to be present during questioning; and that they were legally authorized to represent the patients' best interests, (true, but only if they had been asked to do so by specific patients for specific reasons or complaints). They were politely but firmly ushered out of the hospital as they voiced threats of lawsuits and going to the ACLU, and then promptly tried an end-around by calling the Office of the Ombudsman—all of them sincerely believing in protecting the confidentiality of the patients and their rights, even though most of the patients had been confined under the provisions of the Welfare and Institutions Code Section 5150 as being "a danger to themselves or others," or so "gravely disabled as to be unable to function and make appropriate decisions."

What law enforcement hoped might simply have been an ordinary police investigation, with the police literally sweating uncomfortable individuals under hot lights in small, airless, pale-green painted rooms, and asking them repeatedly to answer intrusive questions, often for hours, even days, instead it became a kind of circus conducted in several conference rooms and numerous offices crowded with representatives of half a dozen different agencies—SFPD assisted by the Sheriff's Department, State Bureau of Investigation, and the Highway Patrol—even the FBI offered to "help," but everybody knew what that meant, and they were politely told "No!" The police were tasked to keep meticulous records of each and every interview for further review, and the detectives were quickly dissuaded of the notion that they were in charge by objections and interjections from officials of every stripe, including the City Attorney who decided he had to become very visibly associated with this case for a variety of political reasons.

There had initially been bad, even tasteless, jokes made by the interviewing officers, many about extracting the truth out of "a bunch of loonies," and worse, some referring graphically to the scatological habits of some of the inmates. Each team was made up of a male and a female so that there was, first of all, a witness in case any untoward allegations were made as to inappropriate questioning or behavior—and as back up, should anyone go sideways.

From the beginning, they focused on the suspect being one individual, acting alone and with limited resources. The nascent investigation had a raw and unexpurgated power, as well as the administrative imprimatur to drive it, so that, within moments after being given the word, teams of detectives descended upon the units like hordes of proverbial locusts—eating and gathering whole virginal forests' worth of information; and writing reams of reports for superiors pressured for a quick solution to take the accusatory eyes of the press and the public (especially the Mayor's Office) off of them as soon as possible. There was a sense of enthusiasm, power even, that they would collectively resolve the case rather quickly.

Everyone knew that careers were made or broken with cases like this. No one involved would likely ever get another such chance to shine, illuminated and admired, promoted likely; or fall to the ground, broken into dust, if failure succeeded. But no one even considered they might fail. It might simply have been hubris that no one considered it, as neither did Daedalus nor Icarus before daring waxen wings to fly into the Sun. But, how could they? Why would they? They told themselves that they were the finest minds available, equipped with the latest of technology criminal investigative science had to offer. (Some wry observer compared their energy and preconceptions to that of the American military in Vietnam).

Each person involved in this investigation felt energized by two sources of power—pride in doing their very professional best; and a private—frequently considered, only occasionally expressed, and always deeply hidden—awareness that at any moment, any one of them could stumble across a seemingly irrelevant or overlooked fact or piece of information that could become extremely pertinent, that could even break the case. Such a one would be anointed as a future star when a successful prosecution ensued, featuring their evidence. No one envied the perpetrator of this crime—but then none of the investigators' wildest, most grandiose fantasies had yet stood up to the grinding, grueling footwork, paperwork, and voluminous interviews they faced, for which they would dearly have loved to have someone pre-screening the patients and the staff! Even the most veteran people quickly tired of being assaulted, insulted, or mind-boggled by the often long circuitous conversational routes that led nowhere. A relatively frequent comment overheard was: "I don't believe this. Can you imagine anybody coming to work here every day?"

Though it was bewildering for them, the detectives had all been briefed on using non-traditional approaches to interviewing psychiatric patients. They were not only off their home turf, but the plethora of behaviors exhibited by the patients was beyond the range of their training or experience. As much as possible, they were being assisted by the Psych Police team, and staff members who had already been interviewed. Even so, some of the patients took advantage of the situation to toy with the police: Some were simply annoying; some were truly frightened for real or imagined reasons—and therefore lied, confabulated, and obfuscated; some were outraged and angry; some felt maligned and even persecuted; some carried old grudges against the police; and some were simply being their ordinary psychotic selves. The task of sorting through all of the stories, hallucinations, delusions, and lies of the patients (not to mention the staff) without being overly intrusive, made the task Herculean, if not Sisyphean.

"I was out of my body visiting Alpha Centuri when it happened..." (From a 46-year old chronic schizophrenic).

"You must be fucking shitting me? Help you? You're responsible for me being here in the first place? Good fucking luck!" (From a 29-year old petty thief, a forensic overflow patient from SFGH, who had concocted a story about hearing voices to get here, and was now trying to recant just to go back to jail instead).

"OK. OK. I did it! Take me away!" (From a 37-year-old chronic confessor who regularly admitted to any front-page crime, and was glorying in the attention he was getting from the police).

Ben Fillarion, another of the personal messengers of the Jesus, who had most recently refused to vacate a lingerie shop on Balboa Street while "doing the Lord's work" reviling their customers as "unholy whores of Babylon." ("It's just proof of the power of Lord Jesus.")

"I don't remember anything..." (From a 76-year old demented man who'd been found wandering the streets naked, and fought with officers when they attempted to assist him).

Jonathan MacIntosh was a middle-aged engineer who had become suspicious enough of his wife's cooking that he stopped eating. Then he had installed a closed-circuit television camera in the kitchen, and suggested to the police that said wife may have "dosed" him with an unknown psychedelic. When the detectives arrived on the unit, requesting to interview him, it triggered his deepest delusions.

"I been telling you the police were after me! See? See? I told you so!"

He made a dash for the sally port, and was redirected and complied when asked to take a voluntary time out in his room.

Then there was "The Tin Foil Man," Reginald Horowitz. He was a balding, middle-aged Black man who had historically always dressed neatly, even nattily. His accounting procedures had likewise always been meticulous. One day, apropos of nothing else, he accused his supervisor of "stealing his thoughts," and of being "an alien disguised in human form." After everyone (but he) stopped laughing, he became an outcast in a middle management culture that did not easily tolerate anyone's eccentricity.

Both his work and his personal appearance steadily deteriorated until the day when he came to a staff meeting wearing an aluminum foil suit and hat to "protect me from those of you who are attempting to eat my brain." Detained by security and placed on a psychiatric hold, he was quietly fired a month later, after which time he became a regular habitué of the Bay Area's psych units.

During the course of a normal investigation, he would have been dismissed simply as another "loony." But when he had told the detectives that he had "inside information," and wanted "protection" before he would divulge it, they immediately assigned him a higher priority. After berating the original detective team as "incompetent fools" and "pawns of the oligarchy," he refused to speak except to a "supervisor."

"Are you a supervisor? Can you help me?"

"Yes, sir" answered Kube. "What kind of protection is it that you want?"

"I need you to keep me safe from the CIA!"

"The CIA?"

"Yes. It was them. They did it! They're out to get me!"

"How do you know?"

"What?"

"How do you know?"

"It was a political assassination."

"You think the victim was assassinated?"

"They know that I know! I have a transmitter in my head! They can read my thoughts!"

"And?"

"I've outwitted them! I know how to read their thoughts too!"

"I see," said Kube skeptically.

Seeing the look from the hulking detective, the patient hurriedly continued.

"Those damn fools won't believe me because it doesn't show up on the X-rays!"

"Why do you think he was assassinated?"

Voice hushed, and thick with conspiratorial overtones, he leaned closer after hypervigilantly scanning the surrounding area.

"He was a political prisoner. That's why he was here. He had information they didn't want him to reveal."

Kube took a deep breath, and stood.

"And what might that have been?"

"I need protection before I can tell you!"

"What might that look like, sir?"

"I need my aluminum foil suit back! They took it away from me!"

"Thanks very much, sir. We'll be in touch."

"Just because I'm a 'mental patient' doesn't mean I'm dumb!"

Kube had had very little contact with the mentally ill other than florid street crazies, so he was totally unprepared for the next patient to whom he spoke.

"Can you tell me what happened here yesterday? What you saw?"

When the man failed to respond, but instead covered both of his ears while looking around frantically, the detective felt as if he were lost in foreign territory without a map or compass.

Hervé Sanchez knew he was hallucinating. The Voice commanded

SPEAK AND DIE!

When the detective again asked in a quiet voice, Hervé saw it issue from his mouth in the form of a cartoon bubble.

DO NOT BETRAY ME!

The detective's face dissolved in a molten liquid plastic flow—first it became the face of his violent father, then, as layer after layer peeled off like rubber masks, other faces were revealed, other places, other lives—an Shawnee warrior in full paint; a young Portuguese girl in the 1400s; a Puritan minister hurling accusations of heresy; a naked-chested, black-masked executioner during the French Revolution; a Russian peasant grubbing for potatoes; a captured Phoenician chained to a rowing plank by Romans. Far too many images moved and shifted far too quickly for him to manage the whole montage. He lived entire lives compressed into nanoseconds. He screamed, feeling the pain and shame and violence of centuries, the reek of death in antiquity sharp and pungent in his nostrils as twisted hot wires penetrated his brain.

He ran to the closet in his room, in anticipation of yet another beating! And then the terrible voice of his long dead father spoke from inside of him.

I'LL KILL YOU IF YOU TALK!

One of the psych nurses appeared as if summoned silently by a potential crisis, and the detective turned to her as if seeking absolution.

"Holy crap! I didn't mean to upset him. I'm just trying to do my job."

"You'd better leave. Maybe I can ask your questions for you later."

"I really didn't mean to upset him."

"I understand, but you'd better go now."

Geraldine Wancko was a large woman in every way. She had a square face with irregularly cut bangs, and a long history of manic-depression. Released from the Mendocino State Hospital secondary to Ronald Reagan's edicts, issued ostensibly to cut costs (while the prime land was sold to his political cronies) she haunted The City's in-patient units. She was generally in residence at taxpayer's expense every three months or so.

She draped herself across the counter of the nursing station, whining that she "needed" a Valium. After days of relentless verbal campaigning, her doctor had finally written an order stating that it was to be given "at staff discretion," by which maneuver he had very efficiently taken the heat off himself, and passed it on to the staff—at least until they caved in, tired of hearing her litany of deficiencies.

As she spoke, it seemed as if her mouth had a separate existence from the rest of her face. No matter what emotion she purported to be expressing, the rest of her face did not move. Her skin was leathery, and a garish smear of bright red lipstick accentuated a collection of broken, stained, and decaying teeth that filled her mouth like ancient tombstones—the legacy of her longstanding methamphetamine habit.

"Can't you bastards just give me what I need? Nobody ever believes me!"

"You've been here every ten minutes since you woke up."

The order was actually written "for agitation," but the last time she'd been told she wasn't agitated, it took the entire staff and twelve Sheriffs' deputies to subdue her after she took a metal dayroom chair and laid waste to the entire unit like a modern-day female Attila.

"Motherfuckers!"

She spit the word like a sharpened dagger, and then walked away in a huff. She bumped into one of the demented older ladies awaiting placement on a less acute unit, and spun her around like a dervish dancer. Geraldine was considered so potentially volatile that the detective team decided to delay her interview as long as possible, and to conduct it in a seclusion room.

Perhaps the most disconcerting patient of all for the detectives was a creature called Dominica. It was difficult at first glance to determine if it was a he or a she. Political correctness demanded that he be called a "she," even though he still had his male genitalia, and was not allowed to use the women's bathroom, though she frequently insisted. Therefore, they called him a "her," and "she" was always given a room by herself when she was admitted, as "she" had been many times.

She was 6 feet tall, and had a very prominent Adam's apple that had not yet been surgically altered. She shaved her legs and chest. Her beard had essentially disappeared, and breasts had arisen due to more than two years of taking female hormones. Her voice was still husky, and when she went off on the staff, she packed quite a punch. Her body was covered with healed scars and actively healing cuts, mostly on the inner aspects of her arms and the insides of her thighs. She chronically threatened suicide, though the closest she ever had ever come was to mistakenly take an overdose of laxatives. Usually it was all histrionic threats, whining, crying, and attempts to induce shame in others in order to get her way. The psych staff knew this only too well, but Detective William Fiske was not at all prepared for a six foot "drag queen" (as he put it) wearing a floor-length, purple chenille bathrobe, bright red lip stick, and smoking a 101-millimeter cigarette.

"What is your real name?"

"Dominica Lawrence."

"I'm sorry, Ms. Lawrence, but according to our records your legal name is Daniel Lawrence Shipley."

Dominica rose to her full height with clenched fists and stepped threateningly toward the young detective.

"I don't answer to that goddamn male slave name anymore!"

"Please sit down—or I will be forced to cuff you!"

"Oooooh! That might be fun!"

"Please! Sit. Down!"

Dominica's eyes teared up immediately, as she put one not-too-delicate wrist to her right eye, and simpered.

"I'm so sorry. I don't know what gets into me sometimes. I try so hard to be ladylike."

"I...all of this is a little confusing for me...but let's just call you Dominica."

"It's those damn brute hormones."

"Pardon me?"

"It's that damn testosterone. It won't leave me alone, no matter how hard I try. I just won't be right until I get my surgery."

The detective blushed now, and leveled his gaze at the transvestite.

"I...um...need to ask you some questions about what happened...yesterday."

"It was exciting!"

"Exciting?"

"Oh God yes! I almost peed my pants!"

"What are you talking about? Why?"

"All that violence!"

"What?"

"All those men fighting. It was so exciting!"

"But what about Zack Hawkins?"

"I'm glad he's dead! He was a pig."

"Why do you say that?"

"He told me I didn't need the surgery because he'd gladly cut my cock off!"

CHAPTER TWELVE
A Simple Twist of Fate
September 11th, 1988   0827

The police were logically spending the bulk of their time interviewing the patients and staff of the Adult Acute Unit. More cursory, and hence superficial, attention had been paid to the inhabitants of the Detox Unit. This would eventually prove to have been a fairly substantial *faux pas*, given that one of those short-term transient visitors was, in fact, a San Francisco Police Department lieutenant who had run afoul of insurance mandates, and found himself temporarily housed under an assumed name. It was an attempt by his immediate superior officer to slip him through the system relatively unnoticed, so as to facilitate his return to duty as efficaciously as possible. In and of itself, it was not that egregious. The fact that he might make an excellent witness would eventually prove to be both far more deleterious and rewarding.

Samuel Xavier Smith was a drunk. No question. His daily intake of alcohol far surpassed that of his consumption of food, water, or any other nutrients. He drank in the morning (only after his wife Camille and the kids were out of eyeshot); he drank on his lunch break (again surreptitiously so that his fellow officers, especially his subordinates in Auto

Theft, didn't see him); he drank after, often instead of, dinner; he drank whenever he felt any sense of shame, fear or anxiety; whenever, for that matter, he felt anything at all. Alcohol was his redoubt, his safety valve, his refuge from the inner raging world he carried around and in which he was lost—even though he managed to function in the "real world" of law and politics in San Francisco, or at least functioned marginally well, even with increasing amounts of alcohol, until fairly recently.

"Function" though, was a relative term, depending on whether one counted the number of detoxes he had had, the state of health of his medical insurance, and the number of "incidents" on the job that had been covered up and/or conveniently "forgotten" in order to not "make waves." His home life suffered equally, if not worse, with Camille having taken up residence in the spare bedroom, and the kids increasingly less interested in interacting with him. He always acted as if he were actually functional, though more and more his behavior had degenerated to the point where he had become so sloppy that he had become either an object of pity or disgust amongst his fellow officers who considered that he had stepped over the invisible line that had stood between him and his status as "special" and "protected," that had previously allowed him to feel that he was above and beyond the laws he was sworn to uphold. He had become, in actuality and in effect, guilty of a living a constant felony. The insatiable craving for drink had proven to be stronger than what he had previously believed to be his implacable dedication to law enforcement.

The day he was arrested and subsequently hospitalized had started out in a rather unspectacular fashion. Feeling somewhat grumpy and irritable, and needing an eye-opener, he went to the false seam in his walk-in closet where he had hidden a half-pint of Bushmills. It was only a third full, but even so, the beautiful brown liquor slithered down his throat wiping away all his pain and sorrow. It was almost better, more soothing, more fulfilling, more exciting than the liquid fire that had he had withstood under fire in Vietnam.

He swallowed the contents in one hot, burning bittersweet rush, and then started ransacking the house looking for more. He tore through cupboards and caches, looking for concealed stashes, hoping against hope that he had not eliminated them all in one of his religious frenzies during which he decided to get sober, and made wild grandiose promises to himself and Camille—after which Camille had systematically eliminated all of his hides. He tore through the laundry hamper and his toolboxes. He threw olive oil, soy sauce, salt, cardamom, tarragon, and corn flakes onto the kitchen floor. He considered drinking the cleaning fluid, could not find any Sterno, and then, at length, rejected aftershave too.

He'd been in the process of shaving when the urge hit, his face half-covered with shaving cream. Then he, like the good cop that he had previously been, strapped on his shoulder-holstered service revolver before heading out to the liquor store, and slung a gray herringbone jacket over his bare chest and shoulders while the obsession of his one true purpose seared through his mind like a vision of the Holy Grail.

He did not stop to rub the shaving cream off his face, but drove rapidly from his house in St. Francis Wood to the Tower Market shopping complex on Portola and O'Shaunessey near Glen Park. He parked sloppily in a handicapped zone, failing to note that his former favorite bottle shop was under new management.

Looking very unlike a man on a mission for God, this knight-errant's demeanor was sloppy, eyes red and wild, and mouth foaming like a horse run too hard. The newly-minted Asian proprietor eyed Sam warily. He smelled the alcohol on his breath as soon as he came through the door, and could not ignore the half-shaving creamed face and the lack of a shirt. He seriously weighed his need for revenue against the law that prohibited selling to intoxicated customers. When Sam's coat flared open and the owner saw his gun, he immediately started praying to his ancestors, then pressed the silent alarm that rang through directly to Taraval Station. He'd had it installed when he decided to keep his newly purchased business open until midnight every night, remembering the ancient Bedouin saying "Put your faith in Allah, but tie your camel to the post."

Sam set his bottle of Bushmill's on the counter, and reached for his wallet. Then he started cursing.

"Goddamn the fucking luck!" Sam screamed while continuing to search futilely through his pockets. When he turned to the profusely perspiring and thoroughly frightened man, Sam articulated each word as if it were a sentence, in the exaggerated manner of one who believes that the listener does not understand English.

Sam mimicked having a police badge.

"I am a policeman."

He now turned his back pocket inside out.

"I forgot my wallet."

Next, he made a rolling motion with his hand.

"I will pay you for this tomorrow."

The owner placed his hands flat on the countertop, eyes filled with fear.

"Please don't kill me!"

"You don't understand!"

"No! You crazy man! Take whiskey!"

A huge burst of rage wracked Sam as he grabbed the frightened proprietor by the shirt front, and started shaking him, trying to get him to understand. The front door burst open and two uniformed policemen entered, one carrying a pump shotgun, the other officer bent in a shooting stance, with both weapons aimed directly at him.

"Freeze, mister! SFPD! Put your hands in the air!"

CHAPTER THIRTEEN
The Revelations Continue
September 22nd, 1988   1033

Sam was not feeling any emotional attachment to the passing parade of people and events on the day of the murder, but he clearly remembered. He'd still been too sick, too immersed in his own misery, to have been able to either consciously file away what had happened, or attach any significant meaning to what he had witnessed. He was still being triggered to tears by maudlin television commercials. He'd been immersed in the constant looping scenes of his plagued past, like a berserk montage that had yet been so real, so vivid and visceral, that he had been tempted to dismiss them as hallucinations.

He couldn't tell anyone. He just couldn't tell anyone. He was so afraid of being put on neuroleptic drugs! He'd seen too much of that on the unit, and all the so-called side effects—eyeballs rolling back into their skulls; tongues lolling; fingers rolling; ceaseless pacing; neck tendons cording frozen and merciless—until they were given yet another injection. Jesus! None for me thanks!

He could no longer hold at bay his awareness of how damaged he had been by alcohol; how infused by the kind of virulent emotional deprivation that reigned supreme in his family. He was slowing being rejuvenated by the rigorous program here. It was pasting his head and heart back together—two AA meetings a day; private therapeutic contact every shift; and a host of "occupational therapy" activities.

He felt himself burning with the desire to re-capture the beauty he had surrendered to the violence and chaos of surviving his childhood, the tender wonders of his own truth that had been sacrificed like a lamb to slaughter to meet his father's aberrant needs. He understood better now that his parents had been severely damaged, and that they had nonetheless used his relative weakness to make themselves feel stronger and more powerful. Now was gradually coming to realize that he had been a parent to both of them. They had coerced and tortured him for his love, like the little beetle (*Platyrhopalopsis melyi*) kept captive by ants, who secreted a sweet, sticky, possibly psychedelic substance from his back side when stimulated by its keepers rubbing his belly.

CHAPTER FOURTEEN
Questions and Conundrums
September 22nd, 1988   1400

Mondays and Thursdays were the days on which the staff usually met to discuss the patient load. Every incoming patient was sent to whichever of the teams was up on the rotation. Each team had a Staff Psychiatrist as its head, and he or she supervised all of their assigned residents. The murder and its reverberating aftereffects were still one of the hot topics of conversation before they formally launched the meetings.

The administration had arranged debriefing sessions for the staff that, for the most part, most of the staff avoided, considering themselves to be consummate professionals, and thereby unmoved by the traumatic event on the unit. The patients had been "encouraged" to take extra time to rehash their needs and feeling vis a vis the death on the unit, even though some of them would have been harsher in their descriptions of the manner in which they were gathered for extra group sessions.

The day shift Techs had gathered the charts of all the patients, and taken them to the Conference Room—centrally located so as to be accessible to staff of all units yet separate from them. There was a large round table in the middle of the room around which the psychiatrists and residents had found places. The periphery was left to the Techs and the rare private therapist who came—and was where those who arrived late were relegated, literally the outer circle.

The Ward Chief (aka the Medical Director), was a brilliant, punctilious young doctor named Edward Sanderson. Though only thirty-one years old, he held both an MD and a Ph.D. It was rumored that his IQ was in the high 190's. Also, that he would likely become youngest Chief of Psychiatry in the history of the University of California system—if he were not lured away by an astronomical salary, or sultan-like benefits, by Kaiser or some other HMO.

He was well connected in many circles Citywide. He swam well in the often-cloudy waters of hospital politics, and acted as if with insider information in advance of any important power play, and invariably aligning himself with the element that most favored his position. He could be assertive, even aggressive—yet knew when to hold his fire and ire. He invariably wore a starched white lab coat, in spite of the longstanding protocol that all staff wear street clothes to lessen the sense of separation and class stratification. Minor infractions of the dress code were totally insignificant to him. His spies had failed to inform him that today, of all days, his immediate superior, the Chief of Psychiatry herself, would be attending the meeting, intending to ambush him. She was the only person who had the chutzpah to criticize his sense of superiority, and hauteur.

"Do you still wear that lab coat on the units? It's such an affectation!" she said, standing tall and proud in a sharply tailored dark brown gabardine business suit, and

crème brûlée-colored linen blouse, over which she, of course, wore a starched lab coat.

Spreading his hands in mock resignation, he put on what he believed was one of the best of his winning smiles.

"It comes with the territory, Doctor la Tourre."

He wore khaki slacks (pressed, of course), and a black cashmere turtleneck sweater. Since doctors traditionally wore a shirt and tie, he was in contradistinction to the unwritten protocols on at least two levels.

"You'd look less threatening without it."

"*Au contraire, ma bon docteur.* I believe the patients need to see someone solid who models positive authority, since they have such poor boundaries."

They smiled falsely at each other, having had this discussion many, many times before. There was never a clear winner in their emotionally-tinged ongoing battle of wits.

Given that it was a teaching hospital, patients generally had to endure endless rounds of interviews (cum interrogation), and risk death by torture via boring and stereotypical questions from a never-ending stream of psychiatrists, psychologists, psych nurses and Techs, occupational and music therapists—and the residents, trainees, and the assigned interns of each of the above. This made for a very odd dynamic. Some of the more constituted patients would give different answers to the same question from different people; or would choose to either lie or withhold information in a kind of power struggle that they were ultimately destined to lose. Then there were the patients in the throes of delusions or florid hallucinations whose answers were sometimes completely idiosyncratic. Staff members usually scrutinized every bit of data given with a skeptical eye—and generally took only half of that as even approximating the truth. The staff was relatively inured of non-sequiturs and neologisms.

Most of the staff embraced the principles of biological psychiatry—the concept of the "broken brain" to be repaired by neuroleptic chemicals. Most had read Freud, Jung, and Adler. Ergo, patients were invariably asked repeatedly about the dynamics of their childhoods by those mandated to interview them.

This type of intrusive questioning could become so predictable, even boring, that only someone deeply immersed in a compelling personal crisis might easily choose to answer honestly. Anyone else, psychotic or otherwise, might find any number of creative solutions to avoid such uninformed and insensitive questioners.

Conversely, Sam Smith seemed baffling to the young practitioners-in-training. He would answer their questions before they asked them, or volubly share his internal process, and the remarkable yet labyrinthine path he was taking to recovery. Though when he was questioned about his personal life, he adamantly refused to divulge a single syllable.

Every level of staff found him infuriatingly obtuse, or selectively mute—and were therefore constantly driven to attempt to pry beneath the surface of his semi-hardened carapace. In their esteemed opinion, failing to reveal himself utterly to their specious ministrations equaled the potential for serious mental illness.

"He's obviously hiding something relevant," complained one of the young female residents. "Anytime we mention something even remotely personal, he shuts down. He practically becomes obtunded."

Frank Schapiro, Sam's assigned resident, spoke up next.

"Get him talking about recovery. He absolutely shines."

"And why do you think that might be?" asked Dr. Mark Sanders, playing the game of being pseudo-interested in others' opinions so that he could eventually, and condescendingly, spew the facile answers with which his own brain was brimming, those that he could barely contain, so anxious was he to unleash a torrential display of what he considered to be his underrated brilliance.

Frank Schapiro believed that he was witnessing one of the most remarkable recovery trajectories he had ever seen. In the last two weeks, he had watched a man who had come in barely able to walk, who managed to get up on his feet and maneuver his way through the collapsed maze he had created of his life. Frank had personally developed a great deal of respect for the man, but as a clinician, he knew he had to view him as a puzzle, a clinical conundrum to crack quickly, in order to shine in the eyes of his colleagues (after all was said and done, it was still a highly-competitive environment filled with really bright minds). Whatever incredible gifts the man might have—if he were allowed the opportunity for his recovery to unfold more naturally—was stifled by the concept of "patient progress" by which senior staff was judged. If it weren't for Sam's utter unwillingness to divulge his personal details, Frank felt perfectly willing to send the man home. But given that, he voiced his opposition.

"What do you suggest then, Frank?" came the question from Dr. Martin Fawlkes, the Staff Psychiatrist in charge of Gold Team. They had bored of Black and White, Silver and Blue, and were now embracing Gold and Red, the World Champion San Francisco Forty-Niner's colors.

"I hate the thought of putting him on meds, though I admit he might have a low-grade psychosis hiding behind his alcohol dependence. And he seems to be recovering quite quickly. But Alcohol Dependence as an Axis One does not support prescribing neuroleptic meds!"

"Anyone have evidence to the contrary?"

"His guardedness could be seen as suspicion, even paranoia."

Mary Sampson was a young Shoshone woman who wanted nothing more than to complete her residency and return to the reservation to help her people. She was generally reserved with expressing her opinions, but she felt very strongly about psych meds.

"Frank, what if you had been dragged in here by the police—never mind that they allowed him to sign in voluntarily—and you were just a garden variety drunk. And you wake up on a psych unit surrounded by a whole bunch of certifiable lunatics. Wouldn't you be inclined to hide your personal information? And refuse to take strange drugs offered to you in the vain hope and vague wish that they might work?"

"But he's so open about everything else."

"Maybe he's a criminal? A hit man!"

"Next thing you're gonna say is that he killed Hawkins!"

"Has he been drug seeking?"

Now Violette spoke up.

"I'd like to say something about this fellow." She went on to recount her encounter with him earlier that morning. He had "inappropriately laughed" when she had asked him about "hearing voices."

"Do you think he was hallucinating? Or maybe he was just playing with you?"

"He might be Manic Depressive. He certainly has gone through a lot of mood swings since he's been here."

"What do you expect—the man's been coming off an alcohol level three times the legal limit. Is he still taking the Valium I prescribed?"

"No. Not since early yesterday morning."

"He is voluntary. And unless I'm missing something, he does not meet criteria for a 5150. Anybody else?"

"I heard he might think he's a cop, maybe even here undercover. That could be a delusion, or even an aspect of a paranoid personality. We could consider calling him a

Paranoid Personality, even as a Rule Out, but that's still Axis Two. We need a solid Axis One that meets criteria if we want to force meds on him. I don't think we can justify that."

"Let's keep him a few more days. Keep observing him. Let's make sure the floor staff makes detailed notes," said Ed Sanderson in a very snide manner, drawing grimaces and shared glances of distaste from those who labored mightily "in the trenches."

"Imagine yourself in his position. Would <u>you</u> want to discuss your personal life in great detail?" asked Mary Sampson in an understated voice.

CHAPTER FIFTEEN
Another Long Day
September 23rd, 0730

The detectives expected cooperation, and yet were more than willing to use force to the extent necessary to assure it. Their interviewing techniques were intrusive, tending toward the abusive (depending on which end of the interrogation one happened to be). Many of the staff seemed to feel that the level of their education granted them a god-like presumption of entitlement, and thus was inversely proportional to their willingness to cooperate.

Generally, the staff had a strong reaction to the intrusiveness of the questioning, probing into the most personal aspects of their lives; and leaving many of them reeling, feeling that their civil rights were being abused, if not abrogated outright. The potential political implications went unmentioned during the extensive questioning that seemed to be demanding more than a simple uncovering of facts, ostensibly "for their own good." The heavy-handed approach, under the aegis of the law, eliciting only opposition, anger, and a marked lack of cooperation.

Sean Hartley was a second-year intern, doing his Psych rotation. The ragged edges of his crash from amphetamines, combined with the lack of sleep accumulated from his routine hundred-hour weeks and general lack of nutrition, had seriously fogged his brain. It also gave rise to his inability to maintain his equanimity, and his reactions were typical—he was testy, stressed, and severely irritated with the intrusion. His ire rose precipitously as his perspiration released profusely.

"I'll sue you, the university, and the city if you persist in asking these questions without my attorney being present!"

"We can go downtown right now, and you can make an official statement with your attorney present; but my understanding is that Dr. Winters ordered all staff to cooperate with the investigation."

Even though he'd been on the last day of another over one-hundred-hour week, and had simply stopped by to sign off orders for the day the murder occurred, the detectives honed in relentlessly on the young doctor, repeatedly battering him with the same questions as if with their fists.

"Yes. Yes. I know the Deputy Chief of Staff," he said resignedly. He had a cellophane twist of amphetamines melting in his jacket pocket, and couldn't wait to get away.

"Just a reminder, Dr. Hartley. Now. Shall we try again?"

"Look, it's like I told you, the man was already dead by the time I got to the seclusion room!"

"And then?"

"One of the nurses had me start writing PRNs!"

"PRNs?"

"As needed meds. The place was a zoo! Everybody was getting extra meds! The staff could have used some too!"

"Oh? Like who, for instance?"

"I just meant that some of the staff looked pretty upset too. It was a fucking mess, trying to control all the patients; and deal with the police."

"So, you didn't see anyone enter or leave the seclusion room?"

"The guy was already dead by the time I got there!" he said, indignantly. "Look. I'm awfully tired. You've got my numbers. Call me later, huh? Like tomorrow. This is my only day to get some sleep."

"Just don't leave town. OK?"

Compounded by the drugs he had taken, his arrogance overrode his suppressed emotions, and his irritability sparked as he spread his arms wide and bowed toward the floor.

"As Allah commands," he said, then turned and walked away.

———————

Kristi Waring had been on the Alcohol unit that fateful day. Today she had come to work at the "request" of the police.

"I'm not happy about being here. My little girl is 6 years old, and in day care," she said. She looked at her watch for the seventh time since the interview started only ten minutes earlier. "I pay double the regular rate for every fifteen minutes I'm late!"

Detective Second Grade Tommy Welch said, "I'm very sorry about that, but we need to talk about your statement."

"When will I be allowed to leave?"

"Just as soon as we're done here."

"I have to pick up my daughter. They wouldn't even let me call!"

"We're restricting all outside contact for right now; and asking that you please not talk to the media."

"Why not? It's a free country!"

"If you do, you might become criminally liable."

"That's outrageous! What's this country coming to?"

"Ms. Waring," said the detective, who had been castigated earlier for calling her "Mrs.," "did you witness anything suspicious, in or around the seclusion rooms?"

"As I told you before, detective," she said, making it sound like she was describing a new kind of bacteria, "I was nowhere near the seclusion rooms. I was at the other end of the wing, involved in the takedown."

Tommy decided he would definitely need a drink, or three, after this day. He certainly didn't envy the poor schmucks who had to interview the patients! What a zoo that must be!

———————

Eduardo "Fast Eddie" Chacon was an émigré from Los Angeles. He was newly hired and this was his first assignment, awaiting his license examination. He was neatly dressed with his flannel shirt buttoned up to his neck and exhibited a small, wry smile when he entered.

Kube sat and looked at him for a moment, then asked, "Where were you when Zack Hawkins died?"

"I don't know. What time did he die?"

Kube smiled, and said, "I'll ask the questions here. So, where were you when Hawkins was discovered dead?"

"We had another patient who went off and we had just put him in the seclusion room when we got the word that he might be dead."

"'We?' Who's 'we'?"

"Paul Marzeky, the Senior Tech he was there. And Tom Sutton, the Nursing Supervisor. There were others, I can't remember them all."

"And then what?"

"What do you mean?"

"Did you ever enter the seclusion room?"

"No, I was assigned to the front door, to direct the Code Team, and make sure none of the patients escaped."

"And then?"

"What do you mean?"

"Then what?"

"What did I do then?"

"That's correct."

"When we got orders to medicate everybody, I was part of one of teams. We gave all of the patients meds."

"You personally?"

"No. I don't have a license yet."

"What did you do?"

"I... We call it 'show of force.' Just standing there, looking intimidating. In case somebody goes off."

"I see. And then?"

"By the time we got everybody settled, the Medical Examiner was here. And then, you guys all showed up."

"That'll be all for now, Mr. Chacon. We will likely want to talk to you again."

"Why?"

"Just routine questioning, sir."

————————

Dr. Andrews St. John stood haughtily, in the commanding presence of Gloria Flores, a seasoned investigator from the California Bureau of Investigation (CBI), who addressed him as if he were a very annoying combination of a young boy and a demented elder. He had originally refused to answer even the simplest questions of a uniformed officer, and then those of two different pairs of detectives, looking at them as if observing alien artifacts under a microscope.

"Why do you need to know?" he snidely replied.

"We can talk here, Doctor, or we can go downtown. Your choice."

"Who do you think you are to speak to me like that?"

"You've refused to 'divulge any information' as to your whereabouts at the time of the murder. Now I'm going to ask you the same questions again."

"You impudent bitch! How fucking dare you!"

Then he stepped forward and grabbed Gloria's left forearm.

"I'll have your badge, you…"

Gloria gabbed his hand, pivoted, and twisted it behind his back. She quickly pulled out her handcuffs, and very efficiently locked his hands behind his back, and pushed him into a desk chair facing her desk.

"You are under arrest for assaulting a police officer! You have the right to remain silent," and continued with the Miranda warning, raising her voice to be heard above his increasingly strident tones.

"Let me out of these restraints immediately! You have no fucking right!" he screamed, attempting to twist from side to side, rattling the cuffs.

"Wait until my attorneys get a hold of you!"

No one moved to assist the twisting, ranting man.

"Fuck off! You have no right to detain me!"

Gloria kept her distance, as the angry man's scarlet complexion started turning purple.

"Doctor. Putting your hand on me constitutes assault on a police officer. That kind of behavior will not be tolerated. Do you understand me?"

"I...I didn't mean any harm!"

"Nonetheless, you committed a crime."

"Goddamn it! Let me go!" he screamed, the razor-sharp creases of his expensive linen pants wilting, and his double-oxford shirt soaking with perspiration as he continued to resist his captivity.

"What do you want us to do, ma'am?" asked one the uniformed officers.

"Put him in one of the seclusion rooms, and guard the door until we can find transport downtown."

"You can't do this to me!"

"I can and I will, Doctor—unless you answer my questions. Right now!"

"Let me out of these handcuffs first!"

"No. You answer my questions first! You are under arrest. If you wish to call your attorneys before questioning, that is your right."

CHAPTER SIXTEEN
Attempting to Stanch the Lava
September 23rd, 1988   1234

Paul had been having a resurgence of the flames that had erupted when he had first had returned from the 'Nam in 1969 There was revolution in the air. You could feel it just walking around the streets of The City, and especially at the concerts and poetry readings done old school with jazz music accompanying, at Stephen Gaskin's Monday Night Classes at the Straight Theater on Haight. It was the days of free concerts and spontaneous gathering like at Speedway Meadows or the Polo Grounds in Golden Gate Park. All the hopes and dreams of newly blooming lives were proclaimed by the Jefferson Airplane, Country Joe, Santana, Creedence. All of the bands were political because the personal <u>was</u> political. Everyone knew that the revolution was coming. It was inevitable. His generation was going to build a new world that would sweep away the corrupt and venal institutions, and the evil machinations of the previous two thousand years. The change was so palpable, so available, so visible in their smiles and the stoned eyes. His generation was going to re-make the face of the planet, distribute love and wealth everywhere, feed all of the hungry and put an end to forever war!

From the perspective of almost two decades later, it all seemed extremely rich and juicy yet delusional. He was tempted to judge it as an enormous waste of time and energy, their having attempted to turn back the tides of a vicious and violent history woven by the hearts and minds of those who had epitomized the peaks of cupidity and separation; who had repudiated all of the tenderness and glory of humanity that he and his ilk had taken so very personally. He wished he could simply renounce the whole goddamn tragi-comedic drama created by countless generations of numb and thoughtless individuals, crafted through time by the black magicians and blood priests who derived power from harming others, turning them into zombies and slaves, cogs trapped in the wheels and gears of the Great Machine driven by Social Darwinism, the specious Cartesian-Newtonian gift holding no empathy, no conscience, who cared for nothing but money and power to feed the growing insatiable needs and greed of the corporatocracy, the icon for the "New World Order" (with totalitarian connotations dating back to the Nazis of the 1940's, and George Orwell's dark visions of the 1950's).

Ronald Reagan totally epitomized spectacle politics, promoting vacuous theories of economics accompanying a totally shallow understanding of spirituality and a unified inner life. Though some called him "Teflon," he was all surface with no depth, no character. The emptiness of his vessel made it easy for his wife and political handlers to manipulate and disseminate the desired propaganda for the public to lap up. Everybody wanted the glamor without having to sweat, to do the real work of transformation.

Smiling Ronnie Ray Gun was the puppet of the free market economy, with the USA run by "Mommy" Nancy, H. W. Bush, Deaver, Jordan, and Poindexter—a venal bunch of thugs and creeps under the specious guise of "the new federalism" —creating spectacle events, and instant video bytes designed for public consumption to convince they were to consider themselves blessed by the pseudo-patriarchal hands.

Paul would always vilify Reagan for his many crimes, but destroying the mental health benefits the Carter administration had implemented was the most profound. The media ludicrously promoted cold tubs, insulin shock, and electroshock "therapies" as "more humane," though that was only compared to mental health treatment in the Middle-Ages! His "cost saving" measures caused enormous misery for thousands of people, not to mention his "brilliant" closing of three State Hospitals in California when he was Governor, dumping three thousand people on the streets with no care or provision. (Of course, the media never spoke of the fate of the suddenly "liberated" properties now worth billions of dollars that quietly slipped into the hands of RR's avaricious real estate developer "friends").

Paul considered this as yet another of the tortures imposed upon him by dint of his participating in so called modern life, and having to live with the barbaric lineage and practices that passed as "normal," that so impeded his personal journey toward greater spiritual wholeness and integration. It was so difficult to not blame the external, the proximal cause of all that he found so hurtful.

Where was the true transformation, the one he briefly saw in moments of his highest illumination? Where was the truly humane global treatment he believed should be rendered to all who suffered, the kind of beneficent treatment he knew he could give, had given, embracing those magical moments when he had been able to set himself aside, step away from his own prejudices to allow the healing energies to flow through without disturbance? He had been blessed to have had such experiences that allowed him to keep believing in himself, in his nascent abilities, to heal himself and manifest himself as a healer, having magnificently passed through the fire—giving the healing flow of love and empathy to those who hungered and thirsted, who cried and died, for that perfect gentle touch of heart and soul; who would, in turn, use their altered energies to uplift the lives of yet others, and contribute to glory of the planetary awakening.

Paul really believed that continuous work on improving himself was the only way to change the world; to bring about the kind of enormous shift in consciousness he knew was not only possible, but utterly necessary. He could see this other world as clearly as this one, sometimes even more so—a world where everyone lived in the awareness of, and cooperation with, the entire of Nature and all of her children; where all citizens related to each other as brothers and sisters, in the way that the indigenous people had always taught—we are all relatives. He was ashamed to have to admit that his Indian friends were right—being White was a disease, and having to learn what is so self-evident to indigenous people was extremely hard work, far more difficult than managing some kind of mindless corporatocracy gig.

Even so, it seemed impossible to change some of his own long-held beliefs and understandings. Paul knew that most people tended either to fall into patterns or be molded into them through repetition, even if the fit wasn't quite right. He had seen so many individuals stay in a bad relationship simply out of inertia, creating a situation in which it seemed as if one were unable to move or leave or change—or as

Bradshaw once noted, they had become inured of the "terrible familiar."

Which, of course, allowed many people to embrace the bland, the banal, what he called the "beige," as a primary emotional tone. The illusions of the world, what most often were termed "realities," were upheld and promoted by the "law and order" advocates, those who were the most vociferous and demanding of attention to "the rules." Paul was frequently at odds with such people. He found them irritating in the extreme, and avoided them as best he could. Away from San Francisco, he always seemed to meet less people with whom he could easily associate. Some had called him an "elitist," and perhaps rightly so. He had always been a genius and had the paperwork to prove it. It rankled him that so many people bandied about the word when true genius by definition comprised less than one percent of the planet. Now that he had the paperwork, he thought he might become unbearable!

He really did find most people boring! He found being alone to be far preferable to being with anyone not *simpatico*. Feeling alienated seemed inalienable to him, as if it were his natural born state. He did secretly believe that he was originally from the Pleiades, as if he were an alien squeezed into human form. He resonated so much with Van Morrison's line: "I'm nothing but a stranger in this world."

After the nuclear wasteland of his childhood, renewal had become his ongoing quest, convinced that he had some small part to play in the upliftment of humanity that was unfolding, a process that he decidedly knew was coming in the fullness of time, in divine right timing, though that was far slower than he could have imagined or certainly desired, at a pace set by Creation itself.

He was changing, being illuminated, gradually transformed by the alchemic process of shifting the base metal of his leaden shadowy emotions into the far more precious gold of truly embodied spirituality. He had, somewhat reluctantly he had to admit, come to the conclusion that the only way to change the world was to become a living agent of change, holding the energy of a higher dimension within himself, radiating it, living it in every muscle and tendon, and thereby having an amplified positive effect on everyone and everything around him; lifting, shifting and expanding a more positive sphere of influence that radiated out to change ever-deeper circles of Life living itself through him, the trees, the birds, all creatures. Ergo, when he changed, the Universe changed. It was never a matter, ultimately, of changing the Universe itself.

When he wrote he felt like a hollow bone, a tube through which energy moved most strongly through him, felt on a cellular level most in touch with this other, higher energy that used him in the most positive, loving way. Words and phrases just came on their own; characters shone, plot twists appeared, and the flow deepened, dialogue sparkled—and he felt illuminated like one of the prophets of old talking directly with Creator.

He phrased it as his soul reaching out to be heard. Once when J.D. Salinger was asked about "writer's block," he responded by saying "Write your way out!" If you were not just a poseur, a wannabe, a pretend writer, or one of the many who said: "Oh anybody can do that!" as if that line were a brilliant critique of deep and intuitive understanding, as if they had managed to plumb the depths of human understanding with a flick of their indifferent wrists whilst he had spent decades slitting open his belly and plastering his entrails on paper just to begin to approach the realm of authorship. If one were a real writer, an actual writer, then there was no question about how much time, energy and devotion one might commit, how many late nights and early mornings one might spend to get one's daily minimum down before having to deal with the inconvenience of "making a living" in a world that essentially shuns art except as an investment. Erich Fromm, the brilliant psychiatrist, once commented that:

> All great art is by its very essence in conflict with the
> society with which it coexists. It expresses the truth

about existence regardless of whether this truth serves or hinders the survival purpose of any given society. All great art is revolutionary because it touches upon the reality of man and questions the reality of the various transitory forms of human society.

He had heard it said "Everybody has at least one novel in them. Write it, then throw it away, and then write the second one." That second novel was the true sign of a writer because it showed strength and perspicacity; will and drive; desire and willingness, to struggle to earn, to own, the title "writer," so exotic to the uninitiated, for those who had not spent uncountable decades poring over misbegotten manuscripts attempting to keep the ship afloat on the written page, correcting errors, syntax, grammar, increasing the depth of narrative and the quality of dialogue.

He lived for those incredible transporting moments, filled with joy, lightness, and completion. It was so energizing, always left him feeling stronger, clearer, richer, better. It often felt as if he were fitting the final piece into his personal jigsaw puzzle, and everything were finally making sense! As if he had reached an apex of consciousness from which all Creation unfolded, and to which it all must inevitably return. It was the closest he ever came to feeling that he really belonged. He often found himself so moved when re-reading his own work that he would sit at the keyboard and simply weep at the beauty and wonder of the work having come through him. He believed that, if there really were such a thing as enlightenment, full absorption in consciousness where all of the ebb and flow of sensation and perception were rolled into one gigantic whole, indivisible and total, it was in these fleeting states that he came closest. For him, the incredible words of Anais Nin succinctly defined his true purpose:

> We write to taste life twice, in the moment, and in retrospection. We write, like Proust, to render all of it eternal, and to persuade ourselves that it is eternal. We write to be able to transcend our life, to reach beyond it. We write to teach ourselves to speak with others, to record the journey into the labyrinth. We write to expand our world when we feel strangled, or constricted, or lonely. We write as the birds sing, as the primitives dance their rituals. If you do not breathe through writing, if you do not cry out in writing, or sing in writing, then don't write, because our culture has no use for it. When I don't write, I feel my world shrinking. I feel I am in a prison. I feel I lose my fire and my color. It should be a necessity, as the sea needs to heave, and I call it breathing.

CHAPTER SEVENTEEN
Boiling and Roiling
September 23rd, 1988   1414

The seclusion room was still taped off. The continuing police presence had created a much more highly-charged atmosphere, even though there were not as many detectives visible. One of the earliest questions asked was of each staff member to show their #1, or Master key (clearly stamped with "Do Not Duplicate"). To date all staff had complied and been checked off the list. Paul had been questioned initially, and was told he likely would be again.

He groused that it really sucked to have total strangers rummaging through his life as if he were a set of dresser drawers. He thought it especially ludicrous when they couched their intrusions in terms of "safety and security" to frame some of their inane questions.

"There's a killer out there. Don't you want us to catch and punish him?"

When he considered that the vast majority of "Americans" completely and conveniently ignored the American Holocaust that had killed 120 million Native people that was considered to be "necessary" to steal the land called "USA," Paul could not help but feel that that same fascist principle was still at work in continuing to erode of the stated principles upon which the country had ostensibly been founded. He could not discount the fact that most of the "Founding Fathers" had been slave owners, drug addicts, alcoholics, and pre-corporate fascists at heart. The grand design they had always included private ownership and exploitation of the land as the very center of its machinations—pre-cursing the permanent war economy. A far more pristine vision had been lost, fueled by the specious "wisdom" of Social Darwinist thinking that would eventually create, according to the United Nations statistics, eighteen thousand children dying every single day from starvation, three thousand in the US alone.

Paul sometimes felt as if he were immersed in the deepest, most dank bardos of the modern world, so constricting that he felt almost unable to breathe freely—constrained, overwhelmed by the complete banality and inanity of superficiality that was presented, sold, and lived, internalized, and digested as "normal." It was believably frustrating that he just wanted to fucking leave the planet; or alternatively dampen down his awareness so much that he did not have to feel so very, very much, or so deeply. He was always reminded of the last line of a song called *Four and Twenty* by Steven Stills: "And I find myself wishing that my life would simply cease."

When he realized that he had been standing in the same spot, spacing out, he shook his head. Bob Dylan would have said "Lost in his own dream."

It was in this moment that he remembered that Ryan and Kubicek had returned to the unit and re-contacted him, wanting to "run through his statement again." Jesus H. fucking Christ! What bullshit! What total bullshit! Three times already by three different pairs of law enforcement personnel, and now this! What a fucking bunch of crap! And now he was going to have to leave work to go to Mission Station to talk to them! Jesus! At least he didn't have to go all the way downtown to the "Hall of Injustice."

He didn't really have any hard and fast statistics, but he just knew that people of color were far more at risk from the "forces of law and order" than were White folk; and the richer you happened to be, the safer you were from law enforcement. Laws were made to protect the rich and their private property by so called "elected representatives," lawyers, and lobbyists who only wanted greater power and more money for themselves—who sat in Congress, and defended genocide, assassinations, and toppling foreign governments that did not agree with the policies that had mythologically "made this country great," created by the shadow government about which Orwell had so long ago warned us, of double speak and government controlled media oriented to grow the "national product" at the expense of the environment and the populace! The biggest hypocrisy of all was the fucking war on drugs! What a massive lie! Prohibition of alcohol had only made millionaires out of all those who dared flout the "law of the land" by manufacturing and selling it; and made criminals out of every ordinary citizen who took a drink of the "demon rum!" What utter fucking bosh! Of course, those same brain-trust assholes were now imprisoning regular, ordinary citizens for marijuana, one of the least harmful, most innocuous substances in the world, while allowing the continuing manufacturing and taxation of alcohol, a proven killer, racking up some 300,000 deaths a year versus zero for cannabis! Totally ridiculous! Absolutely ludicrous!

The Egyptians used it medicinally more than three thousand years ago, and hemp fiber imprints have been found in pottery shards in China over 10,000 years old. But Paul knew only too well the story of how this ancient healing plant had been demonized for profit by those who would benefit by its being made illegal in 1937.

When DuPont Laboratories first created nylon out of petroleum in 1929, and wanted to replace all of the uses to which hemp fiber had been put for centuries—rope, rigging for ships, sacking, carpets, webbing, cloth, nets, string, non-toxic diesel fuel, paint, varnish, detergent, ink and lubricating oil, even paper. The originals of both the Bill of Rights and the Declaration of Independence were all written on hemp paper with hemp ink. From 1776 to 1937, hemp was a major American crop, and textiles made from hemp were commonplace. There had always been serious questions about hemp being put into a Category I status (along with heroin and LSD, as having no legitimate medical use"). For Paul it was insanely suspicious that William Randolph Hearst, Andrew Mellon and the Du Ponts had all been linked with the campaign leading to its prohibition—promoted by the very first drug "czar" Harry J. Anslinger, Andrew Mellon's son-in-law.

No matter what was promoted and/or supposed to be the "truth" about such issues, it always boiled down to some kind of power equation. And here he was, being summarily called to yet another stupid fucking interview! What a bunch of crap! He had at least half a dozen witnesses as an alibi. Tom Sutton was right by his side. What the fuck more did they need? Assholes!

CHAPTER EIGHTEEN
Aftermath
September 23rd, 1988   1657

Two days after the death on the unit, Eddie had decided that he should be making some extra money for all of the hassle The Voice put him through. He thought Maria Conchita was a very tasty on television. Maybe he could get paid more than just the money.

"Hello? Is this Maria?"

"This is Maria Conchita Corazon."

"Maria. My name is Eddie Chacon. I got some information maybe you can use."

"Who are you? Why are you calling me?"

"Do you pay for information? And keep it confidential?"

"Who are you?

"I work at County Hospital."

Maria brightened. Maybe this wasn't a kook caller after all.

"Reporters have what is called a 'shield law' that protects me from having to give up my sources."

"I got something really hot."

"So, give it up."

"I want $200."

"You been smoking too much weed."

"No, I'm serious."

"You better have something really outstanding."

"I do. I saw you standing out there in front of the hospital tonight. Bet you'd like to know what's going on inside?"

"And you'll tell me, exclusive, for $200?"

"You bet, Maria."

"I'll have to get it approved, but..."

"Where should I meet you?"

"Are you on the level? No bullshit."

"Square business. Meet me at the Asimakoupoulos Café."

"Where's that?"

"Potrero. The Greek restaurant at 18th and Connecticut."

"When?"

"Half hour."

"How will I know you?"

"I'll know you. And be on time. I'll only have a few minutes."

"OK."

She arrived, looking as glamorous as she did on air, but she was accompanied by a tall, good-looking Caucasian man. Eddie was disconcerted, and almost rabbited. He got up from his seat, crossed the blue-and-white tiled floor, and motioned them to his booth in the corner. The lure of the money was too strong, more important than anonymity.

"Are you crazy?" he asked, "bringing somebody else here?"

Drawing herself up imperiously, she said: "I have no idea who you are, or if this was real. I certainly wasn't going to come here alone."

Eddie felt appropriately chastened, and mumbled "You're right. I didn't want anyone else knowing who I am."

"So, what you told me is for real? Do you know what's going on? Was it a homicide? We can't get in."

"I'll only tell you, not him," Eddie said, with resentment lingering.

"He's my producer" she said. "He stays."

"No deal."

"If you want the money, you have to tell us both. He's my source of validation, in case we get sued. He'll keep you anonymous too" she lied adroitly as she fanned the stack of twenty-dollar bills.

Eddie rolled out what he knew (not about The Voice!). He told the pair all he knew that pertained to the arcane series of events that had culminated with the death of Zack Hawkins.

"I need more detail. This guy Hawkins, what was his background? Any witnesses? Any suspects? Was it a staff member?"

Eddie was clearly overwhelmed by her tidal wave of questions.

"Look, I've told you all I know right now. If I find out more, I'll call you."

"OK, Eddie, I'm going to trust you on this" she said, and slid the folded pile of bills across the table to him.

"But it's gonna cost you again."

She smiled a weary smile at him, and said: "I kind of figured that."

CHAPTER NINETEEN
Information Overwhelm

September 24th, 1988   0654

Ryan addressed the gathering of detectives, and stated, "I know it wasn't any of you, but somebody had leaked inside information to the media. It's likely some 'he said, she said' kind of thing, but Maria Conchita had a big splashy piece last night on Channel 7's evening news. Just another headache of which we need to be aware. Kube?" he nodded for the other senior detective to carry on.

Extensive background information about the staff had begun to pour in, collected from a wide variety of databases, including from the National Crime Information Center (NCIC).

"Ralph Myers, 33, Caucasian, 5'7" tall, 185#, brown and brown. Psych Tech. Licensed since 1971. Arrested in L.A. in 1967: Possession of dangerous drugs—LSD, he had 100 hits. Charges dropped due to improper search. Arrested 1968 at the student takeover at SF State. Charges dropped. Arrested 1969 in Berkeley at People's Park. Fined $25. Arrested 1971: Possession of cocaine. Charges dropped due to improper search. Since then he appears to be clean. Nothing else in NCIC."

"And?"

"I don't know. There's something kind of...off about him."

"Let's re-interview him! Next!"

"Alysha Greene, age 42, Black, 5'8,"145 #, black and blue. Registered Nurse, all psych since she got her license in 1961: St. Mary's, Presbyterian, and now here. Previously worked at Agnew's, and Santa Clara County Hospital on Two South. Two kids, both boys, both married, living in the Bay Area. One prior for Disturbing the Peace."

"What's so hinky about that?"

"The charges against her were reduced from Assault with a Deadly Weapon."

"What?"

"She was married to a cop. He used to beat her. She hit him with a cast iron frying pan."

"Why the charge then?"

"She started screaming after she hit him. He hadn't assaulted her that night. It was some kind of weird plea bargain. But that's Hollywood for you. Her husband was charged, lost his job. Killed himself two months later."

"Whew. Quite a crew, huh?"

"You bet."

"Who else?"

"Got a kid, name of Chacon, Eduardo. Goes by "Fast Eddie." 22, Latino, 5'4" tall, 125#, brown and brown. He has a huge sealed juvenile file. Might have been a "banger" in LA. No adult sheet. But I want a Spanish-speaking officer to interview him next. The guy seemed clean, but he was nervous. Elusive"

"Next!"

"Art Therapy Intern, Anna Boskin. 24, Caucasian, 4'11, 97#, blonde and green. No record. She was late for work and couldn't enter the hospital that day. She seemed...strange at first, like she was holding back. She finally she told Detective Washington she was, get this, 'meeting a girlfriend at the Meat Market Coffee Shop'—on 24th between Castro and Diamond."

"What's wrong with that?"

"Turns out her girlfriend is her supervisor. They were both late because they were dawdling over their coffee drinks. They're probably lesbians."

"Next!"

"The supervisor, Mary Thursday, is a serious dyke; calls herself a 'separatist,' thinks the world would be better off without men. 42, half-breed Caucasian and Papago Indian, 5'6" tall, 200 #, tatted up. Drives a big Harley hog. Two arrests for Possession of Marijuana—diversion on the one, DA refused to prosecute on the other. But," Kube paused for dramatic tension, "she got popped for assaulting a guy at the Café Flore. According to her, the guy 'hit on her girlfriend.' The vic refused to testify—guess he felt like an idiot. Claimed the girlfriend was 'hot and sweet.'"

"Why is she on the list?"

"Turns out our Mr. Hawkins was pretty indiscriminate. He used to hit on all the women, staff and patients. A few days ago, he hit on Anna Boskin, who had to fend him off. She was rescued by Mary Thursday, who told the creep she would 'kick his ass if he ever even talked to her friend again.'"

"Wow! Anybody else?"

"I know he seems to have a good alibi, but this guy Marzeky, Paul. 6 foot, 235#, 02/07/47. Caucasian. Brown and brown."

"Yeah? But?"

"It may be nothing, but he had a Court Martial in Vietnam for AWOL."

"So?"

"Well, he was working as some kind of Psych Consultant or other."

"And?"

"Seems like he skated. Had some psychiatrist testify in his favor. Got him off with a slap on the wrist."

"Again, so?"

"I decided to dig deeper. He's had a number of negative write ups and complaints, different places he has worked."

"Violence?"

"'Excessive force' alleged. Disobeying direct orders."

"Alleged?"

"It looks like a 'he said/she said' kind of thing."

"And?"

"I asked him to come in for another little chat."

"He shouldn't mind if he has nothing to hide."

CHAPTER TWENTY
Reiteration or Mitigation?
Phu Bai, Viet Nam, April 1969

"Specialist Marzeky has been subjected to a great many mortar and rocket attacks. He has been shot at during helicopter flights undertaken while performing his duties. He has experienced what we call 'vicarious stresses' as a result of interviewing and intervening with many men coming directly from intense combat, who have poured out their turbulent emotions and their stories onto him. As a result, he has experienced symptoms similar to those experienced by those who have actually been in combat."

"What is the relevance of this?"

"The charges that have been levied against Specialist Marzeky for Absent without Leave grow out of, or are a result of, his having suffered significant psychiatric injury—directly as a result of his performing his assigned duties."

"So, his are the psychiatric equivalent of a Purple Heart wound?"

"Your Honor..." the Prosecutor was up again.

"Sustained. There is no Army regulation covering psychiatric injuries and the awarding of the Purple Heart."

"Thank you, sir."

"Let me re-phrase. So, doctor, would you say that this 'psychological wounding,' as you're calling it, was sustained in the line of duty?"

"Absolutely!"

"And would you further submit that this injury was one of the root causes that gave rise to an otherwise good soldier—with no previous military or civilian offenses—to act in an aberrant manner? "

"Yes, I would."

"And would you further state, for the record, that in your considered opinion as an expert," and here he looked at the extremely frustrated Prosecutor, "that this soldier's acting out, contrary to orders, was out of the range of expected response, given his injury?

"No. Not at all."

"And therefore, doctor, just to be totally clear—do you believe that this man deserves to be punished for behaviors consistent with the aftermath of trauma and stress incurred in the line of duty?"

"No, I do not."

Soon thereafter the verdict was announced: Paul was to be reduced one grade in rank, fined $584, and sent home by the most immediate transport with an Honorable Discharge.

Command Sergeant Major Hoxley's had pushed for Paul to be prosecuted as "an example to the other young troopers."

He wanted him sentenced to Long Biên Jail or even Leavenworth. Hearing the verdict, his face imploded. His eyes went wild with suppressed rage, and his skin had turned bright red like a blown ammo dump. He looked like a demented three-year-old having a tantrum. I simply raised an aching middle finger in his direction, and saluted him with it.

The Prosecutor completely lost it at this point, screaming shrilly and profaning me, my family, my attorney, and his entire lineage—and declaiming Captain Martin Browne as "the Anti-Christ!"

San Francisco May 1983

After a stretch of six days in a row (with two doubles), Paul was having a real day off. He cursed as he woke up depressed as if he couldn't stand a day off! A tremendous headache began to arc across the vault of Paul's brain case, fragmenting like the hundred branches of a lightning tree across the sky. Jesus! He absolutely needed this day off, and fervently hoped it would help him calm down a taste since the usual intensity seemed to be diminishing slightly. He had experienced so much worse, especially a memorable shift at the Santa Clara County Medical Center Crisis Clinic when they had had thirty-five admissions on the night shift, during which he had participated in five takedowns (all with injectable meds).

Lately he had really begun to feel the burden of imprisoning people against their will, even though he got a certain exhilaration, power even, that allowed him to feel less crazy than the patients. It was part of the price he had to pay was getting to be too high, allowing himself to feel more, to be more, that had led to the acute awareness that he himself was not as pristine as he had always believed himself to be; that many of his complaints about and discontents with the world were rooted in his personal responsibility, not the proximal cause of the world itself. This was especially so when he realized that he had to stop painting those he despised—the power brokers, high ranking military and businessmen, who he considered to be crude and barbaric, greedy and violent to the core, uncaring, insensitive, and displaying all of the absolute worst traits of humankind—as a separate species that he disowned, as if he were somehow set apart from or above everyone else. This realization hammered at him when he sank into an episode of abysmal depression, and he found himself envying the rich and famous, the overseers, wanting to be the whip hand for a change to shake him out of the craggy reaches of his mental quagmires. Despite this occasional fantasied journey, he always felt a simpatico *with the patients, that went beyond his required duties.*

He had been a part of many discussions with other professionals and para-professionals about forcing meds on unwilling patients, or the truly barbaric practice of Electroconvulsive (shock) Therapy (ECT), sending jolts of electricity through people's brains and calling it "therapeutic" because these folks lost their memories and stopped exhibiting "symptoms" for a few days or a week. This was directly related to the concept of the Therapeutic State that "granted (Paul always believed subsumed) to the government to make determinations about who was unable to consent to treatment "for their own good," and stepping in like a fascist step-parent (in loco parentis*). He had always questioned the basis of their making this determination in the first place; and further, at what point was one considered reconstituted enough to make appropriate decisions, especially if those decisions included deciding not to take psych meds any longer? There had been numerous court cases where people were court-ordered against their wills to have ECT, even when they were lucid and cognizant enough to describe the aftermath of the "treatments," and declare in open court their desire not to participate!*

Paul especially hated it that patients were now called "consumers of mental health services!" True Orwellian double-speak!

He was the PM Med Nurse, and Andy was the AM Med Nurse on the unit on which they'd been working. They had gone beyond being working confrères and started smoking weed together with some regularity. Once during a stoned rambling conversation, they had started discussing the provisions of the State of California code concerning their job description. Andy invited him to a meeting of the Network Against Psychiatric Assault (NAPA). They became convinced that they had not only a right, but a legal obligation to tell all of the patients exactly what their medications were, but also precisely what the possible "side effects" were.

Their actions had a profound effect on the patient population. Within days, more than half of those prescribed brain-damaging chemicals were refusing to take them, especially in light of descriptions of: akathisia; oculogyric crisis; dystonia; pseudo-Parkinsonism (including "pill rolling tremors"); orthostatic hypotension; weight gain; sexual dysfunction; torticollis; seizures; tardive dyskinesia; and even Neuroleptic Malignant Syndrome. These were just a few of the possibilities. Others were called "tongue lolling" *behaviors (permanent and uncontrollable), as well as stroke and heart attack.*

Within the week, he and Andy had been called in to the Head Nurse's Office. The Hospital Administrator, James Corcoran, M.D., was ranting and pacing the floor as they entered the room. The Director of Nursing, and their immediate supervisor, the Head Nurse, Violette Anders, were sitting and smoking cigarettes while glaring at them. Paul and Andy exchanged an immediate, telepathic look and turned simultaneously to ask why they had been summoned to the meeting. The Head Nurse started talking to them, in a barely-controlled voice humming with tension, about "ethics" and "appropriate practices." Then she asked rhetorically whether they were conversant with the concepts. They both smiled, and nodded.

"And have either of you committed any acts that might be considered to be 'unethical' during the course of your duties on the units?" she asked barely suppressing a sneer.

They looked at each other again, and then answered with straight faces.

"No."

The Hospital Administrator stopped his frenetic patrolling, and suddenly made as if to charge at them from across the room. His face was twisted with a barely suppressed rictus of rage and disgust. Then, gritting his teeth, he started wildly gesticulating and shouting.

"You're both fucking lying!"

Andy and Paul looked stunned, then smirked, looking at the wild man still shouting at them.

"What do you mean, doctor?" asked Andy.

"We have signed statements that you two have been telling them not to take their medications!"

"Excuse me?" they both exclaimed.

"You heard me!"

Andy took a deep breath before he replied.

"That is patently untrue!"

"I agree!" said Paul.

Dr. Corcoran immediately grabbed up a small sheaf of paperwork, and started reading from them.

"Pauline Stretter (brain-damaged alcoholic) says..."

"John de Loquand (multiply hospitalized schizoaffective) told us..."

Paul and Andy had blank looks on their faces as he went on. At some length Jane peremptorily shushed the flushed, frenetic doctor's bombast. He, in turn, looked confused, then sat down, still holding the paperwork.

"Let me re-phrase what Dr. Corcoron was saying. Have either, or both of you, been telling the patients what the possible side effects of their medication might be?"

Paul and Andy looked at one another, smiled, and nodded.

Dr. Corcoron jumped up, triumphantly pointing his forefinger at them in an extremely theatrical manner, as if he were a villain in an ancient melodrama, as if he had caught them stealing atomic secrets. Paul and Andy thought he looked extremely comical, and started giggling, then burst out in full belly laughter.

Then Violette Anders spoke.

"You are not allowed to give the patients that kind of information!"

Paul exploded, having reached his limit for bullshit.

"You. Are. Totally. Wrong!" enunciating each word as a sentence, and stabbing his finger at her to reinforce his contempt.

Sputtering, and shocked that she had been so summarily rebuffed, all she could say was "What?"

Andy took up the cudgel, and replied.

"According to State Regs, and our job description therein, it is not only our duty to provide medication information to patients, it is our obligation!"

"But you have been telling them not to take their prescribed meds!"

"No, ma'am! We have been using the drug company's own description of the meds and side effects—and telling the

patients what the true meaning of all those medical terms is."

"But that's sabotage!" Corcoran.

"No, sir, it is the law. It is our duty! Read the job description in the California Administrative Rules!"

"I am forbidding you to continue to do that!"

"You cannot do that! That, sir, is illegal!"

"Then I'll fire you!"

Now Andy exploded.

"Try it! Just fucking try it! We'll go to the media!"

"We'll sue you!" Corcoran.

"Great! Head on, asshole!"

Violette jumped up, and spread her hands wide.

"Whoa! Let's all calm down!"

"He's threatening us! We're just doing our job!"

"You're subverting treatment!" Corcoran again.

"We're advising the patients about their rights!"

"You're disobeying direct doctors' orders!"

"We have an ethical responsibility that is spelled out in the State reg! Many of the patients, being more fully informed of what they were being asked to take, have simply decided that it is not in their best interest."

Violette jumped in again. "Wait a minute! Wait a minute! Maybe we can reach some kind of compromise!"

"There is no comprise. We're just doing our job, and we are within legal guidelines!"

Corcoran again. "I'm going to tell all the doctors to write 'give injectable if refused' orders!"

"You can't do that!"

"Yes, I can. And I will! State law allows it! And I will do it!"

Paul and Andy had been completely unprepared for this tack. They were, in fact, nonplussed.

Corcoran smirked at them, then crossed his right leg over the left, simply waiting, as the two Techs simmered in the poisoned juices of their own arrogance, and the delusional confidence it had inspired.

Andy found his voice, as Paul continued to seethe, totally fucking pissed at being outmaneuvered by a bureaucratic asshole!

"So, what do you want?"

"You stop 'informing' the patients about the nature and quality of the medications—and I will not write for 'IM if refused.'"

So, the deal was struck, even though it was violated as soon as he and Andy changed jobs. They found out later that an unsubstantiated complaint filed for unspecified "inappropriate behaviors" on the unit was filed by Violette, co-signed by Dr. Corcoran, and placed in their files.

CHAPTER TWENTY-ONE
Resurgence
September 23rd, 1847

Like every seasoned investigator, Timothy Ryan thought he had seen it all, but this case had taken him beyond any of his previous experience. He marveled that the staff—a group of such seemingly well respected, well educated people—could count amongst themselves so many alcoholics, a vegetarian body builder who preyed on underage girls, drug abusers (cocaine was so popular these days), underemployed genius Psych Techs, religious fanatics, and a married couple who swung primarily with partners of their own sex. She was somewhat notorious for inappropriately hitting on other women, and he proudly displayed golden butterflies connected by a golden chain through both nipples. The odds seemed stratospherically impossible for there to be such a mix! What a place! And these were the guardians of the mental health of The City, his city, where he had grown up having such a relatively normal life! It was growing more and more difficult to meet a native San Franciscan who still lived here!

They were anxiously awaiting entry into the luxury high-rise condominium of the erstwhile psychiatrist when he was summoned to the radio net.

Milt Krasborne, a CHP detective, had discovered some new information.

"Holy shit, Sergeant!" he told Kube. "We might have something hot here!"

He had uncovered reports of "excessive violence" that had been filed against Paul Marzeky through the years, on an obscure State of California Board of Licenses database, accessed by a tech using one of the Department's first computers.

CHAPTER TWENTY-TWO

Furor

September 24th, 1988   1643

The media had been repeatedly told to direct all inquiries to the Public Information Officer (who was, of course, not giving out anything of substance). Every staff member had been besieged by phone calls from reporters from as far away as Minnesota and New York, wanting interviews.

The City itself had come under vast public scrutiny and media attention too. Sensational stories filled with innuendoes and outright lies appeared in all kinds of publications designed to stir up the reading public's attention. The media had declared it a homicide before the ME even ruled. The Network Against Psychiatric Assault, the Patients' Rights Advocacy Office, and even the American Civil Liberties Union were deluging the city, the county, and the state, not to mention the hospital itself, with thousands of phone calls and letters, even telegrams—and applying vaingloriously for court orders. Splinter groups with their own agendas, who generally saw benefit in rabble rousing of any sort around any topic, clamored for more public attention too.

Paul knew several staff members who had been approached with offers of "untraceable" cash to tell their side of the story, as if the death of a patient had a "side," or as if individuals had been named as culpable. Paul had been screening his telephone calls, and simply deleting any that had no personal connection to him. Fuck the media! They were a vicious bunch of intrusive, greedy jackal assholes who wanted to aggrandize themselves through, and profit from, the misfortune of others. They could all fucking rot in hell!

He was really pissed off and purposely arrived fifteen minutes late for his appointment. He had refused to rush to get there on time, having first showered and carefully shaved while keeping his mounting rage under wraps as much as possible. He was greeted semi-politely by the gruff-looking desk sergeant who told him to "take a seat" while he made a phone call. Paul propped himself up in a corner with the 1934 Dashiell Hammett novel *The Thin Man*. Most of those waiting in the lobby were handcuffed to steel rings arrayed around the walls. The cloying scents of human rot and human waste allied with unbathed funk, cigarette smoke, alcohol fumes, and utter despair, all warred with the disinfectant fumes, and resembled nothing so much as the odors of Battle of the Somme. Although it was not at all appropriate, the phrase "Black Hole of Calcutta," kept running through Paul's brain. He put a clean handkerchief to his nose to filter out some portion of the offensive odors.

Whether as payback or by design, he was kept waiting fifteen minutes longer, growing increasingly restless and irritated. At length, he told the burly man at the desk that he was going to step outside for some fresh air. He started to protest until Paul asserted himself and asked "Am I under arrest?" When he received a negative reply, he went immediately to the door and let himself out. He hoped that his actions—based primarily on his not wanting to endure the miasmic odors—would get the ball rolling a little quicker. He had far, far better things to do than hang out at a shitty ass police station!

The oppressiveness of the situation weighed on him, and he cast his thoughts into the wind like a fisherman's hand net. All he caught for his efforts was yet another glimpse of the myriad twisting pathways that branched and re-branched like a tree of neurons, as he ever sought a solution to issues that seemed far too large and convoluted to be approached; that might not be approachable until he left his body and was no longer tormented by the everyday details of embodied life. It seemed impossible to solve the problems of the world that were so deeply intertwined with and inseparable from all that was good. And yet there had to be a way to be at least 99% true to oneself and still manage to live in the world, perhaps even live well, enjoying good food and drink, having fun, with exciting, inspiring friends and lovers, and still not lose one's spiritual path, not lose one's way home, not have one's internal/eternal compass permanently shattered.

"Mr. Marzeky? Won't you come in?"

The polite approach and the seeming gentility of the words belied the appearance of the man addressing him. He was five foot six inches tall with a thick, bushy moustache that did not completely hide a razor-thin scar that ran from his left ear to the tip of his chin (possibly a souvenir of his days as in undercover narcotics).

The energy went downhill from there. Paul was shown into a small, airless, stench-drenched, pale-green painted room that was already occupied by Detectives Timothy Ryan and Ladislaw Kubicek, who did not get up from their chairs facing the door, and looked at him quite skeptically.

"What? What? Why are you looking at me like that?" asked Paul.

The two detectives shared a glance, but said nothing.

"Why am I here? What do you want?"

Still no response.

Paul felt the deeply encysted well of his rage bursting open as he raised his voice even higher.

"If I'm not under arrest, I'm fucking leaving!" he said, and turned to the door which was, of course, locked.

"Let me the fuck out of here!" said Paul slamming the door with his right hand, and then kicking it brutally twice.

At this point Kubicek approached him in a very threatening manner, arms spread wide, grim look on his face—just as the door opened and three uniformed cops entered with threatening postures.

"Motherfuckers! Leave me alone! I didn't do a goddamn thing!" he said as the whole world turned red, and he thrashed as ten arms and legs attempted to restrain him. In his mind, he was trapped and unable to move, stuck under a bookcase when he was five years old, a memory that still haunted him, and being reactivated right in that moment. His paranoia index shot through the roof, and his claustrophobic rage erupted through the top of his skull. They held him tightly, and he started screaming incoherently, fighting for his life, and then disappeared swirling into the blackest black hole in the heart of the Universe.

He floated in a dark void populated with billions of stars. He was lost all consciousness of being a separate being with semi-osmotic membranes. After an interminable amount of time, Paul became aware of having fingers and toes, then started feeling the vague outlines of his body re-appear as he began to appraise the artifacts of the "he" that "he" might be infiltrated through the flimsiest translucent veil. When next his eyes flickered open, the most horrible stench he had ever encountered assaulted him, surrounded him. He was handcuffed to a hospital bed, and had had leg chains attached as well. His head was bursting like a beach ball overinflated with helium. His entire body ached, every muscle, tendon, and thew. Rippling waves of pain and intense nausea shot through his body no matter how miniaturized, how minimalized, the motion. Then he started shouting, shouting, shouting—until his voice croaked hoarsely.

"Somebody! Help me!"

He heard a rumbling and clanking in the distance, but could see nothing, so he tried again and again, as loud as he could after clearing his throat several times and spitting twice.

"Hey! I need some help here!

A uniformed sergeant looked through the peephole of the door, and walked away. Very shortly, Ryan and Kubicek entered, and, standing as far back as possible, observing him as if he were a laboratory specimen.

"What the fuck am I doing here?!" he squeaked.

"Maybe you should tell us that." Ryan.

"What the fuck do you mean?"

"You freaked out in the interrogation room. We had to restrain you for your own safety." Kubicek.

"Fuck that shit! I want a fucking lawyer! I'm gonna sue your asses off! I didn't do a goddamn thing wrong! You motherfuckers are harassing me!"

Ryan stepped closer, and said, "Well, Paul, you came in voluntarily for further questioning, and then you started screaming and fighting before we even had a chance to talk to you."

"That's bullshit! You fucking locked me in a room, and then took me down and put me in handcuffs!"

"I have the statements of five police officers that contradict what you just said."

"I don't give a fuck! That's bullshit! I want a lawyer!"

"You're not under arrest, so that means you will have to call one, and pay for engaging his services."

"If I'm not under arrest, then what the fuck am I doing in handcuffs? And why in a jail cell and not a hospital? You fuckers triggered me! I had a flashback!"

"We considered a 5150 for 'Danger to Self' and 'Danger to Others,' but we thought we'd give you a chance to regain your composure, maybe talk to us."

"About what? I've already answered your fucking stupid questions four or five times! At least a half a dozen people saw me at the time you claim the murder happened! So, let me the fuck out of here!"

"Murder is a very serious business. And it happened at your workplace."

"It's not my fucking job to figure out who did it!"

"We thought you might like to assist the police in their investigations."

"Fuck you! This is harassment! I want a lawyer! I want Shirley Stephenson!"

Ryan raised an eyebrow at the mention of the name. She had represented a number of people who had successfully sued SFPD, The City and County of San Francisco, and the State of California for a variety of infractions related to civil liberties violations—and won handsome settlements.

"So, you know Miss Stephenson?"

"I want to call her! She'll be really interested in what's happening to me!"

"I guess that means you'll have to get out of cuffs first," said The Kube, laconically.

"Fuck you! This is bullshit!"

"Until we're reasonably sure you won't harm yourself or anyone else, you're staying in cuffs."

"And how would you determine that?"

"Your attitude and willingness to cooperate."

"With what? Goddamn it, I have answered the same-same fucking questions, over and over! I'm not a fucking dummy! I know you fuckers are trying to pin this one me!"

"Why would we want to do that?"

"Because you fuckers don't have a clue, and you want a quick solution!"

"You been reading too many detective novels, Paul."

"Fuck you too! I been in a whole lot of worse situations than this and survived!"

Ryan stepped closer, and said "In the 'Nam?"

"What do you know about the fucking 'Nam?"

"I was an MP! 196th Infantry Brigade. 67-68."

"No shit?" Paul asked, in spite of his resolve not to cooperate.

"No shit! I have no reason to lie to you."

Paul burst into tears as if a large frozen wall of ice had just melted the glacier of his heart; as if all of his pent-up rage had been spent; as if he could finally surrender to a higher level or measure of himself that had lain hidden, emerging out of the dark mists to reveal real clarity. He sobbed and sobbed, eons of anguish washing away. He felt as if he might be dying as wave after wave of pictures and images flashing. He felt as if he might be dying, memories of his entire life from his very first moment flashing like neon signs from the time even before he was supposed to be able to remember. He felt as if his hippocampus were releasing fleeting sketchy pre-verbal images of the deep, deep past, as if all of the prohibitions of his limbic system were collapsing in response to the hormonal flood triggered by the pituitary gland at the base of his brain.

A sudden fluorescent brightness flared behind his closed eyes, and he separated from his body again, the body that no longer struggled against the metal restraints but simply lay there melted, unresisting, in thrall to the greater forces of the Universe, as still more gouts of healing tears fell unimpeded, as if from an inexhaustible well, as if he himself were only the tears, impelled by Creation's providence even *in extremis*, giving him an ally, a brother who had been there, done that—no matter that he had been responsible for being restrained there in the first place. His prayer was that someone might actually be listening, might potentially believe him, and might even be willing to add some force to his continued assertions of innocence.

He was grateful.

CHAPTER TWENTY-THREE
The Saga Continues
September 24th, 1988   2219

Paul lay awake, eyes closed, deep, deep in thought dreams; far, far away from where he lay, now in a bed with sheets and a blanket. He intuitively felt that the door was unlocked. He had absolutely no idea where he was or how he had gotten there—no sense of time, lost in the warm, gentle, undulating currents, the nurturing unguents that flowed all around him, through him, transporting him to times and places and spaces he had never before seen or imagined. Something frantic and shameful had flown free like a wild bird from his chest, a weight, a yoke, a millstone, a cangue, an ancient curse that had haunted him through many lifetimes. Was he dead? He wondered: Was this a past life review? Was he coming into yet another lifetime?

During all the years of addiction, he had run so hard that he had allowed himself only very fleeting glimpses of the amazing depths of what felt like an unapproachable, impossible-to-attain wholeness. He had felt for the longest time that such intimate awareness was only, could only, appear when he was blasted out of his brain. The eerie, seductive obsession without cessation had pursued him even in his writing, until he was enraptured, caught up so completely in the rising and falling rhythms and rhymes of his thoughts, that used him and his fingers, his hands, to translate a music that came from far beyond his tiny little brain, used him to become alive, take breath and sing, become real and vibrant without provocation or prevarication, with no need to achieve or succeed, to live vibrantly for a brief time with love and fullness of spirit and in inner harmony—until he looked up at some point and noticed the page count, always marveling that he had been the source through which had flowed such prose, such beautiful poetry and amazing pictures; blessed that he had been chosen to transmit, to channel, such lilting melodies of the heart and soul; that he had been granted the privilege of being the instrument through which such celestial inspiration could flow. It was as if, as Anais Nin had so beautifully put it, he got to live his life twice, to redeem himself from the agony that had stolen his heart. It was what defined his art and writing, the intensity of his suffering tempering and being tempered by, the raw material of his consciousness in order to discover the extraordinary gold that had been buried under gigantic mounds of dross for what seemed like countless ages and eons.

When he finally felt inclined to open his eyes, he found, unaccountably, that no matter how otherwise uncomfortable he might be, he was no longer restrained to the steel bed frame. Detective Ryan stood in the doorway, silently observing him.

"What happened?" asked Paul, croaking.

"Maybe you can tell me," Ryan said, handing Paul a hot steaming black cup of coffee from Homicide's urn.

"What time is it? Fuck, what day is it?"

"It's still Thursday, about four hours since we last spoke."

"Why the fuck did you treat me so badly? I've answered all of your questions! At least four times!"

"It sure as hell freaked you out!"

"What the fuck?"

"You first."

"You guys treated me like shit!"

"We didn't say a word!"

"I...guess I had a flashback! You reminded me of the 'Nam!"

"Is that an answer? We still have a lot of questions."

"What the fuck do you want from me?!"

"Let's go make this official. I want this on tape."

Paul's head had stopped throbbing, and he was actually in his body again by the time they reconvened in the interrogation room. Kubicek came in, and stood quietly, observing.

"What do you want? I am fucking sick of the same fucking questions!

Kubicek spoke, gesturing to the chair in front of the desk.

"Inspector Ryan is cutting you a lot of slack here. If it were up to me, you would still be in the fucking cell! So, shut up and sit down!"

"If you're gonna be like that, I want my attorney present! Your attitude sucks!"

Ryan jumped up and spread his hands wide in a conciliatory gesture.

"Let's hold up here, both of you!" he said, and then looked at Paul.

"We have some information to confirm that may be relevant to the investigation, and we need your answers. If you still want your attorney, we can read you your rights and place you in custody!"

"Or if you don't read me my rights, I will assume that I am not under arrest, and will walk the fuck out of here! The next time we meet will be in Shirley's office where I have some protection from this kind of bullshit!" Paul said, looking directly at The Kube, whose thick Slavic features visibly tensed as he suppressed his rage, his long, thick fingers tightening into fists.

"We've gathered some information from a routine background check we'd like to talk to you about. OK?"

Paul was practically somnolent when the next question was asked.

"What 'information' are you talking about?"

"When we did a routine search of everyone's credentials, we found something related to you. And we were wondering what you might tell us about all the 'excessive force' complaints in your file, the 'failure to obey direct orders' accusations."

Paul jumped up out of his chair as a streak of phosphorescent rage seared through his brain in a nanosecond.

"That's the crap you're hassling me about?"

"No, it's not crap. It's a matter of record."

"Bullshit! None of those...First of all, the women who filed those goddamn complaints weren't even in the room when the alleged incidents happened!"

"'Alleged incidents?' Sounds like legal talk to me!"

"What, you think you're the only one who watches television?"

Kubicek made a move toward him, and Paul made ready to stand up.

"Sergeant, maybe you better wait outside."

"But Inspector..."

"Just go! OK?"

After he left the room, Ryan looked at him and said, "You'll have to excuse my partner. He gets a little heavy-handed sometimes. It's that 'old country' shit!"

"It's OK. I wasn't gonna talk to him anyway."

"So, what's with the 'alleged incidents'?"

"None of those fucking bitches was in the room when the stuff they 'reported,'" said Paul, making air quotes with his fingers, "supposedly happened!"

"But they're in your file."

"Had to be. They filed them!"

"So, you're telling me that you have never used excessive force on a patient?"

"That's right! The way the law reads, I am allowed to use the level of force necessary to keep myself and the patients from harm."

"Including choke holds?"

"We don't use them anymore!"

"You've never used one?"

"I've seen them applied."

"You didn't answer my question!"

"No, I have never used one. I have never liked them, even before they were outlawed. I never like choking guys out!"

"Never?"

"Never! Though I must admit that there were some for whom I thought it was a good idea."

"Zack Hawkins?"

"He was an asshole! But I did not choke him out!"

"Ever?"

"Never!"

"And you maintain that you were not in the seclusion room when he died?"

"Are you saying that he died of a choke hold?"

"I can't answer that. Just answer my question."

"How can I answer that? I don't know when he died."

"Let's say that he died on or about the night he was discovered dead."

"What time was he declared dead?"

"After the end of your shift that night."

"Well shit! It could have been any of us! I'd been in and out of that seclusion room dozens of times!"

"So, you wouldn't be surprised that we found your fingerprints in there?"

"Not at all."

"How about on the bed?"

"My prints?"

"Yes."

"Not surprised at all. If you read the incident report about how he ended up in there, you wouldn't be either."

Ryan switched tacks so quickly that it caught Paull off-guard, but not unguarded or unprepared for any hint of perfidy.

"So, what about the Court Martial?"

"Just another bunch of shit started by an asshole lifer who wanted to 'make an example out of me!'"

"I read the transcript of the testimony of Dr. Browne."

"So you know."

"You saw a lot of shit, huh? In the 101st?"

Paul shook his head and laughed.

"Nice try, Detective. I been expecting this."

"What?"

"You saw the records."

Ryan simply spread his hands.

"That asshole Hoxley tried to have me sent to LBJ (Long Biên Jail) over that petty shit!"

"'Desertion in the time of war?' You could have been shot, or sent to Leavenworth for life! Not so petty!"

"You don't know any of the backstory!"

"So, tell me."

Paul took a deep breath, and contemplated what and how much to reveal. The paperwork was the paperwork, and then there was the unwritten stuff. But he believed in his own righteousness, and, despite his earlier outburst about being framed, he sincerely had confidence in the truth as a defense against whatever malignancy might be afoot.

Paul decided to tell at least a portion of the unadulterated truth. He related some of the historical backdrop—Qui Nhon, Evans, Brother Arrow, R-and-R.

"I was pretty burned out by the time I got a chance to get the fuck out of the 'Nam."

Paul stopped, dropped eye contact briefly, took a deep breath, and then re-established his gaze.

"When I came back from Taipei, I just took a little extended vacation to see some friends around the country!"

"You were charged with AWOL!"

"You got the Court Martial records? I thought they were sealed!"

Ryan simply kept his gaze and waited.

"OK. That's true, but it wasn't any fucking thirty-eight days! That motherfucker Hoxley made all that shit up!"

"The Command Sergeant Major of the 101st Airborne Division lied?"

Paul jumped up, and said vehemently "Goddamn right! He was a fucking lying lifer asshole. He wanted to 'make an example' of me—because things were going to shit after Tet of '68!" He slashed the air with his hands as he continued.

"Because a whole bunch of guys were getting sick to fucking death of getting sent out to be killed for bullshit reasons! The whole fucking war was a fucking lie!

Ryan had kept his composure, and simply sat at the desk during Paul's diatribe.

"But you were gone? Correct?"

Paul sat down again before answering.

"So, tell me something. Am I cutting my own throat here, telling you the truth?"

"You can't harm yourself with the truth."

"That's the same kind of shit my father used to say! He'd force me to sit in a fucking chair in the middle of the kitchen, and get fucking interrogated for hours while he paced back and forth in front of me! I'd tell him the truth and he'd give me some old shit about 'Telling the truth will make you feel better!' When I insisted that I was telling the truth, he'd start in on me again. Then I'd finally lie, so I could finally get to go out and play baseball!"

Paul adjusted himself on the chair, and his face suddenly lit up.

"What?" asked Ryan.

"I just had a flash! Your fucking partner there reminds me of my father! He's Bohemian too!" said Paul, referring not to the underpinnings of a Beatnik or Hippie lifestyle, but to an area of Eastern Europe that had been annexed to help create Czechoslovakia after WWI.

Paul had been staying with his parents for a few days before he was going to move to California. When he stumbled into the house at 0500, reeking of two days of perspiration, alcohol, weed, and uppers, his father's brooding, unpredictable behaviors surfaced.

"Where have you been?" His father asked in an extremely surly voice

"Out" Paul said as he moved to the bathroom to piss. When he stepped out, his father's stale, musty breath slammed into Paul's face like a surge from a rotten coffin. Paul stepped back and waved his hand at the foul smell.

His father staggered yet again, a lightning bolt of hatred and disgust flashing in his eyes.

"Where were you? We we're worried!"

Thunderheads rose in a dark mass in Paul's brain, and he whirled on his father.

"I just got back from fourteen months in Viet Nam! I can certainly handle a few nights in south St. Louis!" he answered in the most surly and disrespectful voice he could muster.

"We almost called the police!"

"That's it!"

Paul lashed out, grabbed the older man by the collar, and started dragging him out of the house. Layers and layers of old traumatic memories like slices of an MRI slashed through his mind's eye, and he contemplated stomping the shit out of him with great relish.

"I've had a lifetime of your shit, old man! Now I'm going to fucking kill you!"

His mother came flying out of her bedroom wearing a slip, and literally threw herself between Paul and his father, inserted herself between them like well-sliced meat into a sandwich.

"Please! Please! Don't kill your father!"

He was laughing to himself at the memory when the detective pierced his reverie.

"What's so funny about that?

"You had to have been there! 'Please don't kill your father!' It was fucking hilarious! Broke my trance."

"Do you think that explains your reaction to my partner?"

"Absolutely! I am telling the truth. If you want any more 'conversations' with me," he said, again making air quotes, "it will have to be with my attorney present... unless you are planning to arrest me right now?"

"You're free to go—at this time, though we may need to speak to you again."

"Next time, attorney. I'm going to put her on retainer today, just in case."

"You are, of course, free to do anything you like."

As Ryan stood, Paul offered his hand for a dap. After slapping palms, they slid into an open-palmed handshake.

"Thanks for earlier," said Paul.

"Don't mean nothing."

CHAPTER TWENTY-FOUR
The Work Goes On
September 24th, 1988   1634

There were teams of detectives using many of the offices and conference rooms, as well as the basement of St. Paul's Catholic Church on 29th between Church and Sanchez, a beautiful Gothic style building where the incident room for the investigation had been set up. One detective wryly commented that he felt like he needed a program to tell the patients from the staff!

"Sam Smith" seemed to be dozing, sitting up on the dayroom couch—yet he remained alert, his mind processing massive amounts of data, much of it a review of his previous life's triumphs and tragedies. In another small other part of his split-up self, he was feeling a deep regret that he had lost his way, the path of his heart. He envied the detectives the beauty, the clarity, the focus, and the vast energies they were able to utilize and pour into the investigation. He envied the energy and exuberance they embodied, the purity of their desire and ability to focus on what they perceived as a noble undertaking.

To an objective observer, his consciousness might have appeared to be akin to a virgin mass of marble awaiting the master's touch to awaken; but he was awake and aware enough as he watched from a perch somewhere deep in his mind, almost in a fugue, this latest journey of his roller-coaster life—and was briefly aroused as pictures of the murder unrolled as a series of perfectly crisp frames of images in his inner cinema, although they seemed almost completely devoid of meaning.

CHAPTER TWENTY-FIVE
Solitude, or Isolation?
September 24th, 1988   2047

Sometimes Paul like to work the Detox Unit better. It was, in some ways, usually easier duty, except when they got an admission who was on the verge of delirium tremens (DTs), in which case that client might require close supervision as well as personal assistance to prevent falls. Convulsions due to rapid onset of alcohol withdrawal, and may be accompanied by shaking, shivering, irregular heart rate, and profuse sweating. Some individuals may experience visual or auditory hallucinations, even the sensory experience of having insects crawling on their skin (formication). Occasionally, a very high body temperature or seizures may result in death. Since the dose margin between the anticonvulsant and hypnotic effect is small, paraldehyde treatment usually resulted in sleep. This was given after initial injections of thiamine and folic acid, both depleted by chronic alcohol abuse.

Most of the patients were gorked out much of the time. Many slept their time away, their bodies slowly recovering from years of arduous abuse. Some were in a coma-like state purposely induced by the paraldehyde they were given to "snow" them, to keep the potential for the severe seizures of delirium tremens from becoming the continuous seizures of *status epilepticus*. Later the detox protocol of benzodiazepines (Librium, Valium, or Ativan) worked to keep the seizure threshold suppressed, as well as the patients' overall mental status. Duty there often involved a lot of housekeeping. Detoxing drunks were often impaired in their ability to get to the bathroom on time. Then there were the mandatory Alcoholics Anonymous meetings twice a day, with staff expected to sit in to provide a sense of solidarity.

Paul endured these as part of his job description, but was never really able to get deeply immersed in their process. He agreed with the primary principles—surrendering to a Higher Power, rigorous honesty, making amends and forgiveness—but he differed strongly on two main points: he completely disagreed with the idea of always identifying as an addict (no matter how clean and sober, no matter how grateful), and the idea that total abstinence was the only and singular way that a recovering addict could ever hope to navigate his or her life forever.

Paul had explored addiction deeply, especially in light of his own many encounters with addictive substances. He heartily disagreed with the defining medical model, the established ideology that drove most theory and treatment. It was much too rigid and didactic, the established ideology of addiction dictated that the addict was deviating from an otherwise sane norm, and as such was to be seen as deficient, lacking in something essential that could only be temporarily fixed by total and permanent abstinence. In order to maintain sobriety, the recovering person had to live a life of rigorous honesty, and to clean up the dysfunctional path that had driven him or her to use. The accepted medical model also postulated that one could never completely recover, and that the alcoholic was eternally doomed to be morally deficient and corrupt. Paul, conversely, maintained that society itself was dysfunctional, and addicts were the living artifacts of attempting to live in alignment of the essential insanity promoted by government and media as "proper" and "correct." Paul believed that such a position left no room for ambiguity or authenticity; or for personal growth beyond the arbitrary boundaries set by an economically-driven and spiritually bereft society.

Most of the "talking heads" who promoted themselves as experts were themselves completely inexperienced with either use or recovery, so when they spoke, it was always to promote the party line, and, of course, for the money. What was so hypocritical about the whole process was the incredibly warped standards by which public officials were expected to present themselves as straight and narrow, bland, and sexless creatures who lived in Jesus' pocket—in total denial of true human nature, and the pursuit of personal upliftment and empowerment.

He thought of addiction and recovery as a spiritual journey of reclamation. True recovery was the redemption of the self, and one had to go far more deeply and more pithily than what he had experienced through Twelve Step programs, and the recommended (usually cognitive) therapy formats that had been given the imprimatur by "experts." All of them essentially avoided what to him was essential—the redemption of the essential self through releasing all of the emotional impediments that led to adopting the addictive process initially. No one chooses to get strung out because it's fun. The entire development rests on the avoidance of the tremendous avoidance and suppression of traumatic material that is not released and integrated. There were a variety of therapies—Holotropic Breathwork and Primal Therapy amongst others— and other deep, personal work aimed to ameliorate the initial damage that led individuals to take on and foster obsessive/compulsive behaviors as a ward against the raging inner fires. Paul had carved his own path through the murky morass that had formed the foundation of his lifetime of addictions. He hoped one day to be the man he had always wanted to be. Recovery for him was always and ever the promise of a new and shining life.

CHAPTER TWENTY-SIX
Information Flow
September 24th, 1988   2143

Kube complained, "Almost everyone either has an alibi, was too impaired, or was otherwise indisposed!"

Ryan replied, "What about the staff?"

"There's a few I'd like to question some more. That young doctor's been reported to his supervisor for possible drug use. Dorothy Boskin's been reprimanded for being late that day, and her supervisor, Mary Thursday, had been given a written reprimand for non-specific 'inappropriate activities.' She's appealing. But I'd really like to talk to that guy, Eduardo Martinez."

"You just got a hard on for him because he used to be a drug addict!"

"Hawkins was a drug addict too!"

"That's just 'guilt by association' shit! Besides we have nothing linking them!"

"It's either too much or not enough," complained Kube.

"What else do we have on the vic?"

"NCIC sent us a shit load of info. No prison time. His name is Hawkins, Zackary NMI (No Middle Initial). Born 12/31/54 in Pittsburgh, P-A. He's got dozens of arrests for everything from petty theft to Assault with a Deadly Weapon, and between the two coasts—New York, Philadelphia, Cincinnati, Dallas, Santa Fe, several in Southern California. Every time he's been busted, he's been remanded to psych units. Even when he was state committed, he never served a minute. The guy has a long—I mean long—psych history, and he's been non-compliant with aftercare every time he's been released."

"And?"

"I notified his parents."

"And?"

"They refuse to identify the body."

"Why not?"

"They haven't seen him in ten years. They disowned him a long time ago."

"Jesus."

"Father said he just wanted to be absolutely sure he was really dead."

"Wonderful!"

"They didn't seem sad...more like relieved!"

Switching tacks, Ryan spoke again.

"OK, so the vic was a bad guy. Most of the patients, even the staff, had opportunity. Maybe we ought to look deeper into motive. Who might have had the best possible motive?"

"It's always one of the big three—money, love, or revenge" cited Kube, repeating what was almost a mantra for homicide detectives.

"The guy was homeless. And he was a well-known asshole. I've not heard one good word spoken about him. In fact, almost everyone said they were glad he was dead—even the staff!"

"Anyone could have hated him enough to kill him!"

"There has to be something, Kube!"

Kubicek could not help but reflect on how he might have handled things when he was still a policeman in Prague, tactics that might have quickly resolved the confusion, and netted them a suspect. But then it was those very tactics that had driven him from his native hometown just before the almost-revolution of Prague Spring in 1968.

"Anything else on the staff backgrounds?"

"Ralph Lee Myers. Drugs and radical politics when he was young. Turned his life around after a stormy youth. Says he has found Jesus, but then discovered that he was gay. He's still in the closet, so he was reluctant to admit it earlier. Seems clean."

"Gloria Greene is remarried, to a doctor," continued Kube. "She admitted that she was 'extremely nervous' when she was being interviewed because she 'has a new life now,' and her new husband doesn't know about her old one. Her being part of the ruckus in the dayroom was verified by at least 3 other staff members. She's clean."

"Dom Flores asked 'Fast Eddie' Chacon why he was still using his old nickname when he claims to have given up his gang ties. Stupid little shit! Thinks he's some kind of stud. He told me he thinks the 'chiquitas' like his gang tag. I still got a feeling about him, but at least two other witnesses gave him an alibi."

"I had a female officer talk to Anna Boskin. She admitted she resented having to talk to Washington, says he was 'ogling her breasts!'" He raised his eyebrows like a pair of furry caterpillars, and said, "It happens." He scratched the back of his head, and continued. "Checked at the Meat Market Coffee Shop. She and her girlfriend are regulars. It was the owner's birthday, and they brought her some home-baked pastries."

"Mary Thursday, aka Marianne Okell, admitted that she has a 'very serious thing' for our Ms. Boskin. Also admitted that she had threatened Hawkins, but swears it was just the heat of the moment; swears she would never have followed through. I think she's capable, but she seems clean. Both of them do. Solid alibis."

"But we still have no motive. None!"

"Could it be one of the patients? Maybe the motive is just crazy!"

"I just wish the fuck we knew!"

CHAPTER TWENTY-SEVEN
Operant Procedures
September 24th, 1988   1812

The law required that staff chart case notes with a certain ambiguity. Unless an event had unfolded directly in front of one's eyes, you were told repeatedly only to chart "seems to be" or "appears to be," as you were not a true witness. Even if this latter requirement were fulfilled, as for example, a staff member actually saw a patient talking to herself, that staff person could only chart "She seemed to be talking to herself," not "She seemed to be hallucinating." That way, if subpoenaed, the nurses' notes were vague enough not to be legally actionable. Cover Your Ass (CYA) was the first rule. It always paid to take the extra time to voluminously document any dialogue or interaction, especially if the patient had been threatening or verbally abusive. Manic patients were especially prone to call Patient's Rights Advocacy to complain about being abused or badly handled.

There was only one, albeit very passive-aggressive, outlet through which staff could discharge anger, frustration, and other, often inappropriate emotions and judgments maintain their relative sanity or garner a kind of revenge for real or imagined insults. It was called "The Mad Book," a large, black 3-ring binder that lived on a corner of the Unit Clerk's desk. It was available for anonymous comments, opinions, drawings, whatever—from the state of the unit to the state of the union, management, or simply the mood *du jour*. Management tended to "overlook" its presence though some of the comments were either obscene, directed at them, or both. Many of the anonymous writers critiqued official policies that were detrimental to patients or staff; or went contrary to the lived experience of those who worked the floors. Some of the entries were the stuff of frequent conversation amongst the staff.

"Hey! Do you remember that crazy Ward Clerk who used to work days? You know, the one that used to shoot coke?"

"Oh yeah! Crazy motherfucker! Can't remember his name."

"Me either. But I remember he made up a fake patient's ID so he could order syringes from Central Supply!

"That was him! What was his name? The made up one?"

"Raz Whoozits!"

"That's it! That's it!"

"And all the weird shit he used to put in the 'Mad Book!'"

"But it was when he started writing those comments about 'Svelte Charlene,' and the drawings."

"I'll never forget him coming in so toxic every Monday morning! He had the biggest, reddest eyeballs I ever saw. Looked like a raccoon."

"I heard he used to lay in his bathtub all weekend shooting coke and jacking off!"

"He used to brag about it! Weird guy!"

They both laughed.

"But then he threatened to kill the Assistant Medical Director when he woke him up, crashed out at his desk at 10:30 in the morning!"

"And then they put him on a 5150 as 'Danger to Others.' Where'd they take him? St. Francis?"

"No. No. Out of county. Either Seton or El Camino. I heard he had track marks all over his body."

"And he never came back."

"I heard a rumor."

In spite of their being completely alone, Paul looked over both shoulders before continuing.

"I heard he walked into one of the shrink's offices, and caught him having anal sex with one of his male patients!"

"No!"

"Yeah!"

"Wow! What happened?"

"The guy had a lot of pull! Admin covered it up!"

"Jesus!"

"It could have just been one of his delusions!""I don't think so!" He had heard and did not mention that a certain doctor donated a quarter of a million dollars to the new library fund around that same time.

Psych units flourished on rumors and hearsay. There was always something strange and odd upon which to feed. The sense of humor on psych units rivalled that of the Emergency Room for twisted and macabre. There was not a clinician he had encountered through his many years who did not, at one time or another, admit "Thank God I'm not as crazy as the patients!"

CHAPTER TWENTY-EIGHT
Yet Another Layer
September 25th, 1988   0103

The night had been exceptionally quiet on the Acute Unit. There were only a couple of patients awake, and out of their beds. One was quietly snoring in a chair by the window with The Big Book spread open on his left thigh. The other was a man who had recently been transferred from the Alcohol Unit. He looked to be older than his years, and who seemed to be recovering from his battle with demon rum. He had spider angiomas around his nose and eyes (indicating potential liver disease, maybe even cirrhosis), though they were fading. His skin had a pinkish glow (increased blood flow); his pajamas were clearly too tight (recent weight gain); a sparkle in his eyes (secondary to increased activity in the medulla). He was sitting watching a replay of the Giants' losing battle with the Astros, though his attention seemed to be far away. Paul decided to speak with the man, perhaps actually do something therapeutic for a change. It wasn't too often that Detox staff got a real chance to interact with the patients in a meaningful way. Usually by the time a patient got to where he or she could hold a decent conversation, they were discharged.

"Howdy. You're Sam, aren't you?"

"That's right."

"I couldn't help but notice that you're looking better, though still a little wasted."

"Thanks a fuck of a lot!"

"No, come on man, have you looked in the mirror lately?"

"I've been looking in my inner mirror far more than I ever have in my life!"

"Well that too, I guess. I was referring to a regular mirror. You look like you had a rough ride this time!"

Sam was silent, attention again turned inward for a long pause. Then he sighed, and replied.

"I'd say that was an understatement."

"I didn't mean to be rude. It's just that I been there, done that myself. For me it was cocaine."

Sam's eyes suddenly sharpened, and he cocked his head to look more closely at Paul.

"No shit?"

"Square business."

"Do they know?" said Sam, inclining his head, referring to the ubiquitous "they," to include administrators, boards, and management, perhaps even the whole straight world out there that would condemn him for working as a recovering person without their explicit permission.

Paul was tempted to launch into one of his notorious rants about the history of addiction laws and prohibitions, specifically about the deeply racist nature of them—opium being prohibited specifically as an act against Chinese immigrants use thereof; and marijuana proscription originally as a backslap at Blacks. But this was not the right time. He wanted to build rapport. This guy might turn out to be an interesting patient.

"Not really. If they knew, they'd never let me work here where I can do the most good. They'd freak out. They believe that only somebody with an armful of degrees, and no real-life experience is qualified. Most of them have no idea what it means to be addicted, and to come back from the abyss. A lot of them are addicts themselves, only they're in denial!"

"You really believe that?"

"Why the fuck would I lie to you?" Paul was feeling a little salty.

"I don't know. Maybe you're just trying to jolly me up!"

"And why would I do that?"

"To be superior! To get off on my pain! I don't fucking know!" Now Sam was in an equally querulous space.

"Well I'm not! I don't do that moral superiority shit!"

"Most of these people do."

"That's an acute observation!"

"Are you mocking me?!"

"You sound fucking paranoid! I thought you looked like you might have something intelligent to say."

"Sorry, man!"

"Part of my recovery is giving it away! Just because I'm not public about it yet doesn't mean that it's not fucking real!"

"Guess I'm feeling victimized tonight."

"I'm tempted to say 'Sin loi, motherfucker!' but you might take it the wrong way!"

"'Sin loi'?' Are you a vet?"

"Damn straight! 101st Airborne '68-'69!"

"Fourth Infantry!"

"No shit? When?"

"August 68 to November '69."

"Did you extend to get out early?"

"Damn straight! Fuck CONUS (Continental United States) after being in the fucking 'Nam!"

"What's you do?"

"RTO (Radio Telephone Operator) in the bush for four months, then they pulled me out for some secret shit because I had high test scores!"

"Boo-coo good luck!"

"No shit! How about you?"

"I did psych. Interviewing people getting kicked out mostly, though every once in a while, I got to help a brother in need. Anybody getting kicked out as 'undesirable' had to have a Psych Eval. I would do what we called 'pre-interviews'—social, medical and military histories. Then the shrink would come in once a week, and see like a forty guys in an afternoon, basically rubberstamp my shit, though he tweaked my 'provisional diagnosis' before he signed."

"No shit?! I knew a guy name of Danny Leggo in the 4th who did that. Ever hear of him?"

"Short guy? Sandy hair? From like, Iowa or somewhere like that?"

"That's him!"

"Oh, my fucking God! What a small world! We were at Fort Sam together!"

"Good fucking guy! I talked to him when I got my first 'Dear John' letter!"

"'First Dear John letter?' How many did you get?"

"Two! But the weird thing is we're still together. Well sort of. My drinking... Fucked me up with the kids too!"

"I hear that!"

"I'm...trying to get...a new start. But it's so fucking hard!"

"I understand. The first two weeks—seems more like months actually—after I finally kicked, were brutal! (He pronounced it broo-tahl). I was sleeping like eighteen or twenty hours a day! But that was after years of five-day coke runs!"

"Boy! I hear that!"

"It sounds like you tried to do the normal thing with the wife and kids and all. What do you do for a living?"

"You know what they always say—with an alcoholic, the job is the last thing to go. With a drug addict, it's the first thing!" Sam replied, attempting to skillfully avoid the question. He paused again, and took a deep breath that seemed to suck all of the oxygen out of the room.

"Well, let's see. Is this conversation confidential? I mean do you have to write notes about it or anything? Do you have to report me?"

"Only if you're planning a murder; or you have serious suicidal intent with a plan. Or if you tell me about child or elder abuse."

"What if I falsified my personal information?"

"Only if you didn't do it with the intention to defraud—at least that's what they tell me."

"No, it's none of that. But Samuel X. Smith is not my real name. And all of the information you have for me is false."

"Jesus! Are you a Federally Protected Witness or some shit?"

"No. But there is a reason. I'm trying to protect my job."

"Hmmm. What the fuck?"

"I...can't tell you anymore. I won't tell you anymore, unless you absolutely guarantee my confidentiality."

"Well, as long as you told me the truth about why; and you're not in conflict with any of the ethical guidelines I laid out, then sure, yes, I will totally protect your confidentiality!"

Sam drew a deep breath, then nodded his head as if he had made a commitment.

"My name is actually Samuel Q. Jones. I'm a cop!"

CHAPTER TWENTY-NINE
Revelation?
September 25th, 1988   1031

As the thousands of hours invested in the investigation became ten thousand hours, overtime budgets got expanded by the hand of elite financial operators—who were pushed by hospital administrators, who were pushed by city officials, who were pushed by the mayor, who were in turn pushed by large scale contributors to political funds and causes. As a seeming sidebar to all of this frenetic activity, one of those just dumb luck occurrences happened, the kind that no one in law enforcement was really willing to admit actually happened, even though they had all heard stories about miracle witnesses or critical evidence just showing up— though they were all congenitally wary of eyewitness testimony, the most unreliable of all, even when given by cops who were supposed to be "trained observers."

In this particular case, the investigating officers assigned to re-interview a young woman patient who had originally denied seeing anything, and then been subsequently discharged from the hospital, were told by a talkative and poetic staff member flirting with one of the detectives that this particular young woman had been re-hospitalized at

UCSF Langley-Porter Neuropsychiatric Institute, with her "garden of delusions and hallucinations blooming." Her therapist was an ex-psych nurse, and firmly shut the door on further interviews—never mind that it was "just a few questions" —claiming her client was "too fragile." Besides the young woman had already told detectives that she "hadn't seen anything." Terrier-like persistence, and an agreement reached at the highest pay grades, had resulted in permission being granted for a re-interview, but only with the concerned therapist present.

———————

Alice Twillin had a private practice as a Licensed Clinical Social Worker (LCSW). She stood 5'7' tall with long brown hair to the middle of her back. She considered herself to be a "gym rat," usually working out five or six days a week. Her client, Sophia della Torre, had been hospitalized following one of a series of regressive episodes related to breakthrough memories of debilitating childhood sexual abuse; and a severe claustrophobia that grew in the snake-filled forest of her traumatic memories.

She had had a session with Sophia on the day she had been discharged, and Alice had been concerned that maybe she had been released too soon. The very next day, Alice had decided to go "bed shopping," hoping to get her re-admitted immediately to either Pacific Presbyterian or St. Mary's, because of her extreme fragility and lability. Alice had been unable to connect with a doctor at either facility to admit Sophia. Even though she did the bulk of the work, she did not have admitting privileges. That golden perk was reserved for MDs only.

Having failed to have her wishes met, she nonetheless gratefully agreed when her need was fulfilled, and Alice was re-admitted to her old unit.

When Sophia looked at Alice, there were tears in her eyes.

"What's wrong?"

"I'm afraid to tell you! You won't believe me!"

"Of course, I will."

"No! No, you won't!"

"Try me, Sophia!"

"You know that nasty guy that died?"

"You mean Zack Hawkins?"

"Yes."

"I...might know something."

"'Something?'"

"About him."

"What do you mean?"

"I think I saw somebody go into the room."

"When?"

"During the fight."

"You think? Or you did see somebody?

"I was...there. I... was...watching."

"And?"

"I saw someone. I know I did."

"Can you describe him?"

"Oh yes, Alice. I can."

———————

Alice noticed a female SFPD standing duty outside of Sophia's half-open door, along with a pair of plain-clothed men she assumed were the ones about whom Sophia had called her. As she got closer to the door, she overheard a snatch of conversation, so she stopped for a moment to listen while holding up her hand palm out to the detectives.

"Don't you want to just take your medication? The doctor ordered it."

"I already told you 'No!'" Sophia voice was whining and soft.

"But you're obviously upset about something." More insistent, harsher.

"Go the fuck away!" Petulant, but not regressed the "little girl" voice. This one was hard and clearly angry.

"You shouldn't talk like that!" Authoritarian, chiding.

"I don't trust you! And why are the police at my door?" Even stronger now. Demanding.

"She's just here to make sure you're safe." Almost baby-talk cadence.

"Right. And I'm the fucking Easter Bunny." Definitely forceful.

This last was said with such skepticism and vehemence that Alice laughed out loud, then stepped forward, and addressed the police officer.

"I'm her therapist. Maybe I can help."

When Sophia heard Alice's voice, her entire demeanor changed. She instantly looked less ferocious, and her voice expressed relief.

"Alice! You're here!"

Alice looked directly at the nurse, and asked: "What's going on?"

"Who are you?"

"I'm her therapist. Sophia paged me."

"She has medication ordered, a PRN (as needed). I brought her a milligram of Ativan, and asked her to take it. She refused."

"And you were trying to convince her to take it?"

"Well, yeah."

"Did you ask her first if she wanted it?"

"She refused."

"So, you just walked in here with your little pill cup, and asked her to take a medication without telling her what it was. And expected her to do it?"

"The PRN was ordered!"

"'As needed,' not 'At staff discretion.'"

The nurse's face turned red and ugly, and she said: "Let's talk about this outside! Please?"

Alice turned to Sophia and said: "I'll be right back."

Melinda Torrance was a psych nurse who had worked there for a year. She had a forceful, borderline disrespectful, manner with the patients; and tended to be rude with anyone who did not recognize her authority.

"Who exactly are you to question my clinical judgment?" she snarled as she turned to face the uppity person who had the temerity to question her.

"I'm her therapist. I've been working with her for two years. She doesn't react well to intimidation."

"I wasn't trying to intimidate her. I just wanted her to take her meds."

"She's a voluntary patient. She has the right to refuse!"

"So? The PRN is ordered!"

"I know how difficult it must be, working a full unit, especially with all this chaos. But what if she continued to say 'No'? Would you have put her on a hold so you could force meds on her?"

"What do you know about any of this? You've never worked on a psych unit!"

Alice smiled, her eyes suddenly transformed from holding pure compassion to a fierce pair of BBs floating in oil.

"How exactly would you know that?" Alice asked in the quietest of voices.

"It's obvious that you're overly involved with your patient. You probably let her get away with anything she wants!"

"Because I don't try to coerce her to take meds when she clearly doesn't want them?"

"For starters. And now you show up here pushing your weight around!"

Alice scrutinized her name badge, and then said softly, in a tone so softly that Melinda at first was not sure Alice had spoken—until the import of her words penetrated the thickness of her consciousness, and struck here like a fist to the jaw.

"I worked this unit for five years as an RN while I was getting my MSW. Don't you dare try to tell me about what's you think is happening with my client!"

The other woman stepped back, seeming to shrink as Alice bored in further.

Alice stepped after her, and continued.

"Did you even bother to read the order? It says 'at patient's request!'"

Now Alice filled her voice with steel newly smelted.

"You have neither the training nor the sensitivity to make judgments about my relationship with my client."

Alice contained her outrage and sincerely wanted to slap the woman, and call her a "Bitch!"

"Your behavior and attitude have been rude, angry, and inappropriate. I'm filing a complaint with Noah Biederhoff, Chief of Psychiatry! Now get out of here, and let me see if I can repair some of the damage you've done!"

"Oh Alice, I'm so glad you're here!"

Alice smoothed her client's long, curly black hair, then sat in the chair next to the bed and held her right hand. She had flawless creamy-looking skin and striking features, but she exuded the aura of a much younger woman. Many of her mannerisms and speech pattern too, gave lie to her appearance.

"I'm here, I'm not leaving!"

She paused for a moment, sitting in the silence.

Alice could not avoid seeing the prominent scars on both wrists from Sophia's two previous suicide attempts. She also knew about the many scars on her inner thighs self-inflicted to relieve her rage and anxiety. Alice thought of her as a very old soul, and likened her inner world to a worn vessel filled with contaminated contents.

She pulled the Release of Information form out of her briefcase. "The police are here, and they want to talk to you." Then she placed the form on top of a recent copy of *Vogue*, and handed her a pen. "Signing this allows me to talk to them. It also allows me to intervene if they get too scary."

Sophia had always had a strong negative reaction to men who were attracted to her beauty, which was just about any man with a pulse, even some who were gay. When any man tried to touch her, even casually, she reacted with a horror that transcended the phobic. She had the stiff attractiveness of a porcelain figurine, though she had a vibrancy that was simultaneously very sexy and extremely innocent. Her eyes were deep green, her hair was long, black and curly. She had what men would describe as perfect melon breasts, a flat belly, and long legs that carried most of her 5'7" frame. She had heard it suggested that Sophia should have either orange or yellow and black coloration to broadcast a warning, as if she were a snake.

"Please Alice! They won't believe me!"

"I can maybe put it off."

"They won't believe me!"

"Don't worry about that. Just tell the truth."

"Nobody believed me...about my father!"

"Did you really see somebody?"

Tears ran down from Sophia's bruised eyes, and Alice reacted immediately.

"I didn't mean it that way," said Alice. "I just want to make sure you...that you weren't just remembering your father."

Sophia's voice shifted again, into a smoky, deep contralto not unlike Lauren Bacall's.

"No, Alice. I know the difference now. This was real. It wasn't a flashback."

Sophia initialed the Release of Information where Alice had highlighted it, and signed her name at the bottom. Alice then signed as witness, and went to the door to invite the police in.

Ryan and Kubicek entered, accompanied by a police woman named Jane Thurmond who was on special assignment. They were all in mufti, though the stiffness of their postures and the uneasiness with which they carried themselves gave them away. Sophia initially startled at their presence, but relaxed again when Alice took her hand.

The detectives introduced themselves, and clustered themselves around the bed opposite Sophia, giving her plenty of space, and unfolded chairs so as to be on the same eye level with her.

Ryan reached into his gray cashmere sport coat, and produced a small 3-ring binder from an inside pocket, flipped it open to a book-marked page, and turned his attention to Sophia. Kubicek laid a small tape recorder on the bed and positioned the microphone. Alice followed suit with one of her own.

"We're going to need to ask you some awkward questions."

"I don't remember anything!"

"Miss della Torre, please! We need your help!"

Sophia turned to Alice with her arms open, and eyes pleading.

Alice turned to the detectives, and said "She's still having some gaps in her memory."

Kubicek and Ryan exchanged a look, then Ryan tried to open the questioning again.

"I need to ask you a few questions about when you were in the hospital recently." His voice was mellifluous and a deep baritone. He had been told that his manner of speaking put people at ease. Usually.

"Is that OK?"

Sophia looked from Alice to Brian to Jane to Kube, and back again before nodding.

"Did you know Zack Hawkins?"

Sophia lowered her eyes, and then spoke, sounding very much like a little girl.

"He wasn't very nice."

"Why was that, Sophia?"

"He...came into my room one time."

"Did he touch you?" asked Jane.

"He...tried to, but May Beth—she was my roommate—came in, and he left."

"Did he say anything to you?"

"No."

"Did you see him any other time, Sophia?"

"I didn't like him."

"Did you see him during the...trouble on the unit?"

"No."

"Did you see anybody who looked like they didn't belong there?"

"Lots of people. I was scared."

"Did you see anybody near the rooms at the end of the hall?"

"I don't know. Maybe."

They waited, feeding the silence, knowing it could be the most effective technique sometimes.

"There was a man—he looked a lot like my father."

Brian and Jane exchanged a look. Oh boy! Here we go.

"Really?"

"That's why I remember him."

"Where did he go?"

"Into the one of the locked rooms."

"During the big fight?"

"Yes." Very softly.

"And what did he do?"

"He went in."

"Then what?"

"I don't know."

"Would you know him if you saw him again?"

"Maybe."

"You said he looked like your father. Is that true?"

"I told you they wouldn't believe me!" Wailed Sophia and reached out to Alice, and started sobbing. She reached up and tangled her arms around Alice's neck like a pair of jungle vines.

Alice looked at Jane, and whispered, "Can we do this later?"

"It sounds as if your client may have seen somebody no one else saw." Kubicek.

Quickly disengaging from Sophia, Alice calmed her, and directed her to "Do her deep breathing exercises."

"We're going to step into the hall for a few minutes, Sophia. I'll be right back."

Outside the room, she joined the detectives, and said, "You just touched on the crux of the matter. On the other hand, she may just be having a flashback. Let me take the lead. I'll see if I can get you what you want!"

When they re-entered the room, Sophia's beautiful face looked as if it were a mirror shattered by a hammer. She was pacing wildly, and emitted a short, almost canine bark of displeasure when they came back. Then she started to sob.

"I saw him! I saw him! I did!"

"She's very fragile right now" said Alice.

"If she 'saw him,' I need to know who it was."

"She...sometimes...believes things have happened..."

"I knew you wouldn't fucking believe me!" Sophia half-shouted with tears still in her throat. She threw herself onto the bed, and looked at them fearful and angry, her face flushed darkly, the blood flooding her face like the leading edge of a storm. Then she jumped off the bed, and stamped her foot, as if she were indeed just a young and petulant girl.

"I did too see him! I am not hallucinating! I can make a drawing of him!"

CHAPTER THIRTY
End or Beginning?
September 25th, 1988   2201

Ever since the 'Nam, Paul had been affected by loud noises and sudden movements. They always reminded him of sitting hunkered in bunkers, shivering and shaking as mortars and rockets thundered down; or being a moving target every time he flew on a chopper (always sitting on his steel pot); remembering "Gooks in the wire!" at Long Biên and at Evans, chaos and disorder raining death and destruction, not only then, but for many unforgettable decades to come, infiltrating his dreams both night and day, continuing to alter him in many and intimate ways forever, trailing streaming remnants of harm and damage through multiple generations (and Paul gave thanks once again that he had decided never to have children); creating countless lines of self-destructive and addictive behaviors, suicides and homicides in their wake; abandoning multitudes of homeless vets to practice "field expediency" to survive on streets and in the jungles of the world. He shared symptoms with all combat vets everywhere, especially Vietnam vets, a connection throughout time, one so special that he was always willing to extend his hand in support of brother vets.

His conversation with Sam had set off a train of recollections, and ignited his desire to assist in ways that he had been previously dunned as "inappropriate" because he had treated patients as if they were equal human beings—and had been lectured and hectored about the absolute necessity of always maintaining the proper "therapeutic distance" in order to better facilitate "treatment." He, of course, had always held an opposite opinion, firmly believing in the power and necessity of the human connection for healing the often-jagged vagaries of the past.

While doing his rounds, Paul found Sam still awake, and decided to continue their conversation.

"So, you're a cop?!"

At first Paul believed the man might be in the throes of a vast delusional system. It was a pretty audacious pronouncement to declare himself a police officer. Nonetheless, he scanned his encyclopedia of psychiatric symptomatology, and decided that perhaps the man might be experiencing Korsakoff's syndrome, that he was confabulating to make up for gaps in his memory. After all, he had come from the Detox Unit, even though, according to the Progress Notes, some thought he might be harboring a low-grade psychosis!

"Depends. Are you going to keep your word about confidentiality?"

"I told you I would. But you gotta be straight with me too! Are you still having tremors?"

"No, I'm not! I been here five days already. No tremors, no faintness, no more vomiting or diarrhea. I've been eating at least twice a day. No temperature, and I'm actually sleeping pretty well, only getting up two, maybe three times a night. How's that for compos mentis?" Sam laughed.

"Pretty fucking good, man! Pretty fucking good!"

"So, answer my question!"

"What's so important that you need assurance about that?"

"I...I'm having a conflict, and I need to talk to someone about it. But I can't have my true identity exposed right now. I can't risk the consequences! I've probably told you too much already!"

"Tell me again where you were and when in the 'Nam."

"Are you questioning whether or not I'm a vet?"

"You gotta admit that this is a pretty fucking strange situation we're in, you and I!"

Sam looked deeply inward, eyes glazed for a few moments, then looked up with a deep sadness in his eyes, and said "It sucks that you don't believe me!"

"Think about my position! I buy your story, help you further your investigation, or whatever, and administration finds out, I'll be fired before my next breath!"

"Ok! OK! US 56 738 977. Fourth Infantry! 1968-1969. RTO. Plei Trap Valley, Fire Base Gold, Dak To, the Oasis, Kontum, Pleiku, Ben Het, An Khe. Then I got pulled for a 'special assignment' that I can't and won't tell you about! More than that—Fuck you!"

Paul knew that the Tactical Area of Operations (TAO) of the Fourth had included all of those places. He hadn't had a blip from his built-in bullshit detector, and immediately felt inclined to give credence to what Sam had said. Observing his face as he recited his personal litany had convinced Paul that Sam's rap was genuine.

Paul held out his hand to shake vet-style.

"Welcome home, brother!"

Sam almost cried as he took the proffered hand and shook.

"Thank you, man! You too!"

Paul took a deep breath, then started a Mini-Mental Status Exam, and asked Sam what day it was.

"You fucker! I thought you believed me!"

"I believe you're a brother vet. I believe that you have some kind of amazing story to tell. I also know from your case history that you have significant alcohol history. So, I'm concerned, just as anyone official you end up telling this story to. I need to document your progress, to see exactly how damaged you are!"

Sam answered most of the questions perfectly, including a wry comment on what an asshole Ronald Reagan was, but was two days off on what day it was.

"I'm a little confused around that, but I'm telling you truth—I know what I experienced the night of the big upset here! I. Am. Not. Fucking. Crazy! Hiểu không?

Sam had asked in Vietnamese if he understood, though the bastardized pidgin had usually been "Cong biet," or even "Cong bic?"

It was the last brick in the wall for Paul, and he reminded Sam of the parameters within which he would and could keep confidentiality.

"No, I've got it. I'm not contemplating suicide or murder. I'm not a child molester and I am not harming elders. OK?"

"Shit! This is fucking tough! I've never had anybody ask such a thing before!"

"So, brother. Your word?"

Paul breathed deeply, and sighed again.

"OK, but remember the guidelines! I can't afford to lose my job!"

"Cool."

"So, what the fuck is so important? What are you doing here? Are you really a cop?"

"Yeah, I've had one too many detoxes—even the Betty Ford Center. None of them has ever stuck! My insurance benefits wouldn't cover another one. So, my Captain had me sent here under a false name. This is what we call 'Duffy's.' Officially I am on vacation."

"Wait a minute! Wait a minute! This is all a little too much for me!"

"Believe me, it's true."

"And, what do you want from me, exactly?"

"I need some help here. It's been hard enough for me to get sober. On top of that, my wife has asked me, through channels, not to come home when I'm released from treatment."

Paul breathed out, relieved that it was something workable, more-or-less within the realm of his assistance. He started to go into his spiel about available social services, support groups, private therapists and the like when Sam smiled at him, and held up his right hand, palm out.

"Thanks man, I appreciate that. But that's not what I need to talk about!"

"O-K!" Paul breathed out slowly, enunciating each letter separately, awaiting, as it were, the punch line.

Sam's face twisted with the effort as he internally struggled with material that he was attempting to dredge up from the detritus at the bottom of the ocean of his soul.

"I...I'm not sure how to say this!"

Paul smiled benignly and went into full therapist mode, and leaned back in his chair. Then he spread his hands wide in a beneficent gesture like an obese sultan granting a quasi-divine favor.

"Just tell me. It's OK, really."

Sam took a deep breath, sighed again, and looked directly into Paul's smiling, open face.

"I...I saw the murderer...coming out of the seclusion room!"

Paul's entire world shifted on its axis and crashed. His mouth fell open agape, tongue slightly protruding as he stared goggle-eyed at this patient, who, he rightly still questioned, might be delusional.

"Are you fucking shitting me?"

Sam smiled, and said a bit ruefully, "I'm tempted to say: Hell no, you're my favorite turd!"

"Jesus! That sounds like fucking grade school!"

"Maybe we're brothers from different mothers!"

"Wait a minute! Wait a minute! You 'saw the murderer?!'"

"Yes, I saw her coming out of the seclusion room!"

"'Her?' A woman?"

"Looked like it to me—long hair, tits!"

"Did you see her face?"

"No. And she disappeared into the confusion before I could!"

"So, you don't really know who it was?"

"No, I don't."

"Have you told anyone else?"

"Fuck no!" said Sam vehemently.

This answer sent Paul fleeing inward, seeking firm ground upon which to stand, upon which to base a satisfying answer, any answer, to what he had just heard—trying to balance all of the disparate elements involved: ethics, responsibility, the law, his license, Sam's responsibility, his safety if such information were to be revealed! What the fuck? Now what?

Sam watched the play of emotions across Paul's face, and accurately perceived the confusion radiating from him. He decided to jump in, and throw him a life preserver.

"I have some ideas!"

"Who you gonna tell?"

"Fuck that! Totally! This stays between me and you! It goes no further! Understand? Otherwise I will completely disavow it, and they'll think you're delusional!"

"Fuck you, man! You just laid this gigantic shit bomb on me! And now you've got the fucking balls to threaten me? Fuck you!"

Sam immediately spread his hands wide in a placating gesture.

"Wait a minute! Wait a minute! I'm sorry man! I didn't mean it as a threat!"

"Well, it certainly was one!"

"Look! I'm sorry!"

Paul looked at him for a long moment, seething—and waited until his level of emotional magma lowered sufficiently to not erupt in a volcanic rush all over the man.

"OK. Let's look at this again."

"OK."

"So, you really did see someone, what, going in, or coming out, of the seclusion room?"

"Coming out! It looked like a woman, I swear to God!"

"OK. Are you, or were you, able to identify her?"

"No. Just black clothing."

"Pants or dress?"

"Pants. And a black shirt."

"Did you see her face at all?"

"No! I just caught a side view. Saw her tits!"

"And you didn't see her going in?"

"No. There was total fucking chaos. And...I must admit that I wasn't feeling very well...kinda spaced out."

"'Spaced out?'"

"Yeah, you know, drifting away mentally. Mainly because I was sick, nauseated, kind of sleepy."

"Did she see you?"

"I don't think so. I would have seen her face if she had."

"Whew! What a giant fucking pile!"

"That's why I gotta talk confidentially. I can't go to SFPD with this. It would blow my whole arrangement here."

"I understand. But what the fuck are we going to do?"

"'We?'"

"Yeah, 'we' Tonto. You brought me into this, and I gave my word to help you extricate yourself."

"Thanks, brother!"

"That may be the only reason I'm willing to do this!"

CHAPTER THIRTY-ONE
More to Come
September 26th, 1988   0842

Sophia felt safe, finding the hospital to be a far safer womb for her than her mother's house where the emotional cross-currents could be so vicious and disorienting. She knew her personal history was still unfolding, still being revealed, especially the emerging gap in her memories of her father, who her mother always called "tainted."

Her memories of him were always of anger and violence—and always wanting to touch her. Her mother had always beaten her, frequently lashing both her and her father with her sharp tongue and the unfailing tyranny of her imperious manner. He mother had always treated he as a speck of dirt, a scurrilous micro-dot, valueless no matter her age or achievement, the small waif who even now lived trembling and quaking inside of her belly.

Her body was such a mystery to her. She only very rarely felt that the voluptuous container in which she lived actually belonged to her. It sometimes felt like she were living inside a robot. She had told Alice about her inner community, all of the selves that lived within her—protectors, defenders, warriors, placaters, soothers, manipulators, negotiators to manage the real insanity of what was called the "real" world, the crazy world—sometimes a little girl, sometimes bold or tenacious, even violent and vindictive—a girl, a woman, a nasty boy, a wild variety of animals.

Alice told her she was "dissociative." The abnormal psychology book she'd found at the school's bookstore verified her symptoms, though she wasn't yet able to wrap her mind the concept or healing its psychological outgrowths. She became acquainted with the idea of "traumatic memories," and how heavy the weight accumulated in a child's mind, who had few, if any, defenses. It had led her to searching for her own memories, that had led her to resisting her mother's violent overtures. One of her hospitalizations came about when she hither mother with a cast iron frying pan when she herself was being attacked, and her mother told the police it was "unprovoked"—and they did not believe her! That had been two years earlier and marked the last time her mother had attempted anything more violent than using her sharp tongue.

She continued to be haunted by memories, at least she thought they were memories, they felt like memories, but it one of the worst parts for her was she couldn't factually verify the information she felt to be true—even when they sometimes came in the night and she awoke screaming. The dreams seemed to arise on their own, came to ambush her, calling to her to remember, no matter the pain and shame, to free herself from the stick tentacles of her mordant past.

Try as she might—she had done so valiantly so many times—she could never remember her mother being gentle or kind or loving in any way with her. Search as she might, there was absolutely no gentleness or affection anywhere in her memory banks. Her earliest recollection of her mother was at age three, but why she would, or even could, remember such a terrible time was beyond her comprehension.

San Francisco June 1966

Her mother had dressed her for the party. She was wearing the same dress as Mommy. She got hungry. She found the chocolate syrup and it was delicious! She really didn't remember getting a drop of it on one of her nine crinoline petticoats.

But she would never forget the flaming waves of hatred and disgust that radiated out to her when Mommy first saw her, searing, burning her even from across the room. And then Mommy wound up and slapped her face with all of her force. It was much worse than when she fell off her tricycle onto the concrete driveway.

"Filthy, filthy child!" she said, yanking her arm and shaking her to her feet.

"Stop, Mommy! Stop! It hurts!"

"You think that hurts? Wait 'til I'm done with you!"

"Stop, mommy! Please!"

She slapped her again, just "for crying!"

"Shut up!" she muttered. "Dirty little heathen bitch!"

Then she slapped her again and again as the water filled the bathtub, then tore off every stitch of her clothing.

Her mother slapped her again and roughly picked her up, moving toward the steam-filled bathroom.

"No, Mommy, no! Don't! Please!"

She screamed and wriggled, but her mother's grip was tighter than an anaconda's.

"I'll be good, Mommy! Please!"

She screamed, again and again, then a released a wild shriek as she was deposited into the scalding tub, scrabbling with her tiny hands to get out, but to no avail.

Her mother thwacked her with the back side of a long-handled scrub brush, and then grabbed the container of Ajax cleanser.

Sophia's world ended right then, as she felt some essential part of herself slip away and left her body behind to endure the indescribable pain that wracked her. She went mute, unable to speak, in deep shock. She could no longer even scream as she watched herself from the corner of the bathroom ceiling. Her mother repeatedly attacked her now-unresisting body again and again, scrubbing her with a stiff nylon brush, muttering "Filthy little bitch!" over and over.

As she sat in the steaming tub, eyes blank and unseeing, her mother's rage rekindled as she went to the bathroom cabinet and walked back toward Sophia with a holocaust in her eyes.

Grabbing her by the scruff of the neck, her mother screamed at her again before she assaulted the sweet little bud of her tiny vagina with both the brush and her vile attention.

"This is the source of your filth! Dirty, dirty little pussy!"

Sophia was far, far away, feeling nothing, seeing nothing, hearing only her mother's last words.

"Let's just see if your father enjoys you now, little bitch!

CHAPTER THIRTY-TWO

Progress

September 26th, 1988   1335

"More information on that goddamn Hawkins!" exclaimed Kube as he entered, carrying several thick stacks of faxed pages stapled together in piles in his right hand, and handing them out with his left.

"Good! Maybe something in there will give us something more solid."

Kube had immersed himself in the life of one Zack Hawkins, and had found every second of it to be torture, albeit vicarious. The more he read about the ostensible victim of this crime, the more compassion he had for any and everyone who had ever had contact with him. Kube felt as though a particularly virulent microorganism had invaded his immune system, and left him gasping for fresh air, as if he needed to take a shower on the inside of his body.

"Hawkins was the third child of three. Alcoholic mother. Father unknown. Mom claims it could have been one of seven guys. She was investigated when he was born because of potential injuries to the first child, but they called it 'postpartum depression' and CPS (Child Protective Services) let her go."

There were groans all around. Gloria Flores muttered "Bitch!"

"Just wait folks, it gets better! Second child dies under mysterious circumstances—Mom claimed the child 'must have crawled under her when she was passed out drunk,' and suffocated. She was almost prosecuted that time."

Kube drank a huge glass of water, and wiped his forehead on a white handkerchief he produced out of his left rear pocket.

"Third time's the charm. Along comes our Zack. Diagnosed "Oppositional-Defiant" when he was age four. Wouldn't obey Mom who claimed she 'only whipped him when he deserved it.' He became increasingly violent at age six when he assaulted a teacher with a ruler after she refused to allow him to run around the classroom screaming. He claimed he was 'bored.' At age eight, he started routinely attacking other children and spitting on them. A school psychologist diagnosed Attention Deficit Hyperactivity Disorder (ADHD), but because it was considered a 'stigmatizing diagnosis,' it was not officially applied. But they put him on methylphenidate."

"That's damn Ritalin! No wonder he developed a meth problem!"

Kube continued mumbling, shuffling through the papers as Gloria Flores picked up the narrative.

"He was 'removed from parental care numerous times;' in and out of foster care where he was described as being 'unmanageable.' A social work type early on called him 'difficult to nurture.' Jesus! What a thing to say about a little child!"

She read a few lines further, and then quoted, "'Unable to pierce his shell,' and his 'seemingly unnatural interest in matters sexual' (Dr. George Hall, MD, 1962). It had also been noted for the record that young Zack had 'seemingly vast untapped reservoirs of rage' (Valerie Reynolds, RN, School Nurse, 1964). Every social service evaluation since the age of eight has practically condemned him, like he was the son of Satan!"

Ryan now jumped in, having read slightly ahead.

"Sent to a juvenile detention facility at age 13 when he almost killed an older boy who had been bullying him. The report says Hawkins 'not only beat him unconscious, but also repeatedly kicked him.' Then he reportedly said, and I quote, he was 'extremely proud' of having done so' because 'the son of a bitch will think twice next time.' A Pre-Trial Adjudication Report (New York State Social Services, 1968) reported that he had shown 'no remorse' and 'would do it again if he had the chance.'"

"In the old country, we would have straightened this kid out quick. He would never have lasted very long," said Kube, reminding them all of his "old country" philosophy and the often rough-handed justice that was routinely meted out to children there. It was a stance that frequently found support among the police rank-and-file.

"The list of major and minor offenses goes on for pages. He was held until the legal limit under juvenile statutes. When he turned eighteen, his parents legally disowned him, refusing to have anything further to do with him, even refused court-ordered mediation. Our boy Zack managed to coerce some dumb lawyer to represent him on a contingency basis and had his juvenile record sealed. Then he sued his parents who ponied up a substantial payment to keep their names out of the public records."

Gloria commented, "No wonder they won't fly out to identify the body. They only called back to make sure he was really dead."

Ryan continued reading, "As an adult, he racked up offenses on both coasts and in between: attempted fraud, all kinds of violence that seemed to fall beneath felony requirements; suspected of robbery and strong-arm robbery, witnesses recanted numerous times; rape and attempted rape, dropped for lack of evidence. The net result, boys and girls," said Ryan in a rare show of sarcasm, "is frequent psychiatric hospitalizations. In Oklahoma City, while being held for trial, he instigated a riot that caused damage in the six figures!

And get this, he was 'released due to pre-existing psychiatric condition.' I'll bet they gave him a plane ticket and told him to never come back! Bastard!"

Thereinafter it seemed that Zack kept getting hospitalized in the vast majority of jurisdictions who had developed an attitude (if such were possible) that it was in Zack's (and their own) best interest that he be hospitalized instead of prosecuted.

"Oh Jesus," moaned Kube, "here's a whole other page of charges!" and went on to annunciate some of the dozens of arrests that had not been pursued: petty theft (many times); intimidation of a witness; harassment (a woman he claimed had "come on" to him, and then repulsed him); possession of marijuana (many); soliciting undercover police officer (female) for the purposes of sex; and possession of dangerous drugs (18 tubes of airplane glue). There were allegations of other more violent crimes, though they were somewhat blithely dismissed as 'disturbance with another inmate,' or other, often vague and unnamed, violence while in custody or hospitalized. His drugs of choice usually ran to marijuana and amphetamines, from which he had apparently garnered a secondary source of untaxed income. He had done half a dozen short stints in county jails for possession with intent, all of which had been dropped apparently when authorities had gotten a glimpse of his psychiatric records.

Gloria picked up the thread. "Oh, check this! Hawkins is 'disabled!' At least according to Social Security! No wonder he's been in and out of hospitals all this time! Our tax dollars have been supporting that son of a bitch!"

"Let's see here. 'Oppositional Defiant' and 'Conduct Disorder' as a child; then he graduated to 'Agitated Depression with Sociopathic Traits' in custody, and finally to 'Manic-Depressive Disorder, Mixed' as an adult. A whole bunch of fruit salad, you ask me," grumbled Kube.

Gloria spoke again, more quietly, nose buried deeply in a folder.

"At least one child; wouldn't marry the mom...what else? Anything on his most recent trip to the East Coast?"

"Social work types tell us he was 'tormented,' maybe 'hearing voices'; that we should have a mercy on him because of his 'poor childrearing.' I don't care! This punk son of a bitch got himself killed—and we're stuck having to figure out who did it! I don't really care how fucking 'disabled,' or 'disadvantaged' he was!"

Ryan commented, "Maybe this just a crime of opportunity? It almost has to be a staff member! They all had Number One keys!" (These were issued to all staff, and, of course, opened most of the relevant doors on the unit. Med Room keys were separate, and handed off from shift to shift by whoever was passing meds).

Kube slapped his forehead.

"Jesus! I know we checked the line staff, but did anybody check the doctors' Number One keys? Maybe somebody's missing theirs!"

CHAPTER THIRTY-THREE
An Image Emerges
September 25th, 1988   1239

Alice shivered involuntarily when she looked at the picture. Sophia had perfectly portrayed the glassy emptiness of the eyes of someone deeply callous and calculating. Alice was immediately concerned that Sophia had projected her own desolation onto the man, maybe even identified with him in a twisted kind of way.

Sophia had claimed not to have seen the perpetrator's face, but the image taking shape on the artist's pad under the nimble fingers of her young client very much resembled an early photograph of Sophia's father, especially the glaring, mean look in his eyes.

"I don't know. I just have this feeling that's how his eyes should look."

CHAPTER THIRTY-FOUR
Gathering Steam
September 25th, 1988   2347

The whole time he was pulling another grueling double-shift, all Paul could think about was getting home to write. As soon as he got there, he started a pot of strong coffee brewing. Then he sighed and sought the respite of his favorite chair. It was an old, leather captain's chair with brass rivets rescued from an office supply store that had gone out of business in Oakland in 1970.

As he sat back, exhaustion slammed into him like a Montana blizzard and he flashed to a memorable triple shift once during the Asian flu outbreak in 1969. The Head Nurse signed out a ten-milligram Dexedrine capsule as "wasted," and gave it to him as a kind of bonus for staying on duty. The third shift was straight triple time, but they were still getting a bargain at his base rate of $2.03 an hour!

His mind started gaining momentum, and he started tripping about being almost six years clean this time after turning loose of the demon cocaine. He had been clean seven years, and thought he was exempt from the "sucker line rule," that he could get away with having one line, one little line (whereas a thousand would not be enough). Fuck! He remembered it so vividly, living in a very quiet apartment house on Jackson between Fillmore and Webster while he was working for two different registries, attempting to make it in the straight world while not having adequate emotional tools or academic credentials.

February 6th, 1979

The night before his seventh anniversary clean, he had had the hubris to brag to his apartment manager about it. The very next day, on his birthday, he was summoned to his front door by a resounding knock on his front door, drawing him out of his reverie. He spent a lot of time those days, flashing back to Vietnam and the terrifying undercurrent of the wild and crazy 411 days and nights he had spent there, underlined by brilliant euphoric recall of all of the drugs and the adrenalized adventures he had lived.

BAM! BAM! BAM!

His apartment manager, JT, stood there grinning, arms hidden behind his back. I invited him in, and turned my back to go the kitchen get him a cup of coffee. By the time I returned, he had placed a large mirror on my dining table, and was holding a squat glass jar with a huge white crystal rock in it.

He smiled at me through his sparse reddish beard and said, "Happy Birthday!"

"Didn't I just tell you yesterday that today I'm seven years clean today?"

"Yeah. So?"

I was filled with a mixture of irritation, perplexity, and a mounting rage.

"So, why the fuck <u>are</u> you bringing cocaine into my house?"

He gve me a pseudo-innocent smile that bespoke his utter indifference.

"I thought it was long enough. You surely can have one line."

In Alcoholics Anonymous they called it a "sucker drink," the first one that is too much followed by the thousand that are not enough. I still drank immoderately on occasion, but did not consider it to be a problem. JT, on the other hand, was here to introduce me to the "sucker line."

I dithered and dawdled as he shaved a shimmering slice off the veritable iceberg of flake, chopped it finely into a robust powder, all the while chattering away in his best huckster's patter.

"After all this time, you can't have one little line...just to celebrate?"

I must admit I was salivating. When I opened my mouth to protest, fluid shot out of my parotid glands as if from a venomous snake. JT kept chopping, and laughed at me.

"If I don't do a line, does that mean I owe you a hundred lifetimes?"

Chop, chop, chop.

"Something like that."

Chop, chop, chop.

Paul always felt transformed when he was high on stimulants; relieved of the constant burden of shame; no longer fearful about talking to women, amazed actually how easy women really were, especially when you offered them a line; filled with a virility and manliness of one who had lived the types of adventures about which he wrote; felt saturated as if a magic epoxy had filled all the cracks and crevices in his personality, and glued him together in a smooth and seamless way.

By the end of the night, Paul was practically assaulting JT to keep the lines coming. The next morning, terrifically hung over, Paul managed to get to work, where remarkably, miraculously, another employee turned him onto several lines to get him through the day.

December 24th, 1982   Sausalito 11:35 PM

It was a party to which he had been hesitant to attend, especially as it would be attended by former or current customers and friends of a former connection and still current friend. He'd gone anyway, with a firm resolve to avoid the big bag of cocaine that would assuredly be there. Perhaps arrogantly, he believed he was strong enough, with almost three months clean, to tolerate nefarious company for a few hours.

No sooner had he walked through the door than he was offered a giant whack. Of course, he had immediately eyed the big bag enviously, but declined the offer. Every other guest was using freely, some even making extra lines and offering them to him along with different tooters, including one that looked like a miniature Hoover vacuum cleaner.

He did have a small snifter of Remy Martin XO, but sipped it very slowly, savoring the nose and flavor. He made it last for the better part of an hour as the bacchanalian atmosphere grew in intensity and former friends and contacts came and went. During the next several hours, he was offered cocaína *many more times. After his continual refusals, almost everyone just let him be as he played several games of chess in a quiet corner of the hillside house overlooking Sausalito.*

He had been fighting silently with himself —self against self—all night long, battling to resist that "one little line" —self against self—wanting just a little taste, a line of what was the undoubtedly the finest in the world (just like he used to sell), and fearing mightily that he might succumb to the offer of just "one little line."

Finally, approaching midnight, and exhausted with the battle; terrified, raging and uncertain about his own ability to choose wisely; and staring at the glistening crystal shards of mother cocaína, he took a rolled hundred-dollar bill, inserted it into his right nostril and inhaled.

And it burned the shit out of his nose! Disgustedly, he threw the tooter down.

"Fuck this! I will never do this again!"

September 26, 1988 0131

So far, he hadn't.

He roused himself and immediately went to his keyboard, wanting to get his thoughts organized and stored, his minimum daily requirement of a thousand words. He had decided to go to bed as soon as he completed thoughts, but a flash of wild, vivid color splashed across the television at the end of the program he'd been watching, and it started a new flow that quickly turned into the new day's thousand.

He longed to release his healer's soul to the greater work to which he was felt called, to which he had always been drawn even as he fell asleep dreaming of doing more, to fulfill the promise that lived within himself, one that could never be satisfied, yet always hinted at a vast magnitude of glory always just out of reach, as if the great black hole that lay at the center of the Universe had taken up residence within him.

CHAPTER THIRTY-FIVE
Tightening Up
September 26th, 1988   1134

Brian returned Alice Twillin's page and asked her to come to the command center. Gloria Flores and The Kube were both there when she entered, somewhat timidly at first, and then with increasing confidence when Gloria welcomed her.

"I understand your client believes she saw our intruder."

"I believe she did, Ms. Flores."

"Ms. Twillin, I can be Gloria if you'll be Alice. Is that a deal?" said Gloria, and smiled.

"Works for me, Gloria. I have the drawing Sophia produced. She's very clear right now. I believe she saw what she says."

They gathered around Bryan's desk and looked at the drawing of a clean-shaven, swarthy, possibly Latino or Native American-looking man. Sophia had drawn eyes that looked quite sinister, even though Sophia had originally described the man as potentially wearing tinted glasses.

"I asked about that too. She drew the eyes from intuition, but somehow, they look right."

Kube, of all people, seemed most enthusiastic, seeming to agree with her. Gloria Flores held her tongue and her judgment. Tim Ryan pondered the possibility of this good fortune, while still considering the likelihood that his "unwitting witness" was simply hallucinating.

CHAPTER THIRTY-SIX
Yet another Step Closer
September 26, 1988 1800

On his second day on the unit, Sam had met an old man on the unit, "just an old fucking drunk," he'd said. He had bat-shit breath, but his message was so clear and powerful that Sam listened to him about Alcoholics Anonymous. But the part about" rigorous honesty" was so depressing it almost curled his skin. He told Sam that he was "forever grateful for his serenity," and the fact that he "got a second chance at life" when he quit drinking. Fucking unbelievable!

Sam had met "Tony T., a grateful recovering alcoholic" at an AA meeting on the unit. He asserted that he'd had a profound spiritual shift after he'd lost his wife, his job, and his kids—and woke up with his house stripped completely bare. Sam thought he was fucking nuts!

Sam felt moved to speak, but he couldn't raise more than a squeak. His thoughts were jumbled, and his emotions were playing him like a bad song on a cheap guitar. The speaker's words awakened him from the mistral of his shame and failure to the dark treasure within him.

"It's kind of magic. I can't really tell you how it works, but for the first time in my life, I know, I truly know, that 'someone' is listening, twenty-four/seven. My Higher Power and the people in these rooms have saved my life. I am changed forever. But I still have to practice these principles in all my affairs. I have to constantly admit that I am powerless over alcohol every single day. And with this great grace I have been given, I stay sober one day at a time!"

There was a stunned silence that Sam thought was the kind of vacuum created by a bunch of hospitalized drunks and assorted crazies from the bottom of the heap.

But then, as if collectively awakened by the same gentle hand, first one, then all of those assembled there stood and began to applaud, smiles of joy and hope spreading across all of the ruined and damaged faces. Staff members appeared in order to check out what the commotion was, ready to start issuing meds and putting people into seclusion. Then they left, confused and shame-faced to see a bunch of "drunks" standing around smiling and having exuberant conversations.

———————

Now, two weeks later, Sam went to the AA meeting that night, and saw that Tony had been invited back for another round. Paul really did not want anything to do with the religious shit, but Tony T. clearly had something he wanted. "You...it sounded like you were telling my story."

Tony smiled at Sam with a beatific grin. "Drunks like us always believe we're terminally unique."

"What?"

"Every alcoholic I've ever met feels that they have kind of a divine right to drink, get sloppy and mean; maybe hit their kids—whatever it is they do, just because they had a weird childhood, or a bad day at work. There's no end to 'good' reasons to feel entitled to get drunk or use. Terminally unique. 'You'd use too if you had my life.'"

"Jesus, man! You are hard!"

"Just doing what I have to, to stay sober one day at a time."

"I may have lost my wife and kids, my job, my pension— maybe even my mind!"

"Good!" chortled Tony, smiling like a ray of sunshine.

"Fuck you, man! It's not funny!"

"I'm laughing at my old me. You sound like I used to!"

"Fuck you, man!" though much weaker this time.

"Congratulations. When you have nothing is the best time to really clean up your life! Get a sponsor! Do 'The Steps!'"

"I don't like the religious part. It turns me off!"

"Have you ever felt like you've experienced a miracle?"

"Maybe."

He told Tony about the two young cops who arrested him, and then actually listened to him, and called his boss.

"That was a gift from your Higher Power. You can call it whatever you want, but there's something working for you."

"We'll see."

He handed him a business card, with several other numbers written on it.

"Give me a call, especially if you have a craving."

Sam wanted so much to cry out, right then and there. He fought to keep it at bay, to pretend it was just allergies. He knew he'd been offered a gift from a complete stranger—and feared that he did not deserve the gift, the grace. He feared his memories, and his awful vulnerability, feared being exposed as less than a man.

Tony shook his hand, and then hugged him. He felt a lifetime of shame wanting to be released. Tony knew Sam had the possibility of a new life opening, untainted by the warped blueprint of the past; that he might yet learn to walk in the sun, head held high; might yet become a new man, no matter how heinous or untoward his earlier deeds; might yet be transformed to the very depths of his DNA; and might one day say aloud to Creator: "I don't know what you want from me, but please, please, allow me to help those who still suffer."

Tony knew, because it had happened for him.

CHAPTER THIRTY-SEVEN
Deeper and Deeper
September 26th, 1988   1624

Sam had been reflecting on his sense of the relative sense of failure he had experienced since coming home from Vietnam. Since a vision of "The World" had been planted as a kind of projected perfect-future-to-be for every man (and woman) who had served, though it was totally different for each and every one of them. In every case, it involved some kind of rebirth, of returning to the States after a year of shit and mud and blood. After being discharged as a civilian, the highest rank of all, and returning to The World where rank was not necessarily bestowed on undereducated, rigid, rule-bound assholes who controlled your life through a series of often illogical and arbitrary rules. Coming home meant a freedom to do and to be that was just the beginning of everyone's fantasy—whether it was to wander the globe with a backpack, make a million dollars, or get a Ph.D.! He had fallen for the illusion as hard as anyone else, carried in his chest, nurtured it, lived every single day with the promise bright and fresh in his heart, built dreams and fantasies around it, constructed whole worlds of how-it-would be on the illusions and delusions it created by its very presence, and then he compounded it exponentially by indulging mightily in every possible psychedelic made by God or man. And then he returned home.

The betrayal was stupendous. Returning home meant curses, strange looks at the mention of his journey, unease even distrust from seemingly "old friends" and family, shitty reception by the VA for medical and dental treatment, even being spat upon and threatened with violence. (Of course, the latter never lasted long once some punk clown caught the wary look of complete readiness in his eyes). Coming home had meant cheating girlfriends, and too much pressure to "talk about it" from his vet father. It manifested on every level. "The World" had not changed a whit, except to have become worse. Nobody gave a healthy shit what he had experienced, the pain he carried, the shame he felt— especially when he saw with his own eyes that he had deluded himself into believing in his bright future (what Neal Sheehan would later call *A Bright and Shining Lie*).

It was that skewed sense of betrayal that drove him to the Police Department initially, the relatively rigid set of rules and regulations; the cooperation and support of other men and women of law enforcement; and the adrenalized possibility of increasingly difficult assignments as an undercover, that in turn, drove him to alcohol—and drugs too, in some situations, just to appear authentic in his role—

though alcohol had become his very best friend, his respite, his shelter.

Now, as he became increasingly sober, the more he realized the tremendous impact his drinking had had on his life since the 'Nam. Despite how sick and nauseated he had felt, he had developed a desire for purity, and a new fire had ignited in his heart with a power and magnificence he had though long lost to him forever.

He was so relieved that he had confided in Paul on the unit. In his dreams, he had begun to experience a wondrous light that permeated him night after night, illuminating his entire world with such intensity, such luminosity, that his eyeballs ached, threatening to burn out of his head. Instead he felt irradiated, uplifted, every cell filled with joy, as if he'd had retrieved a birthright that had been held in abeyance, locked away, hidden, buried, waiting for the arrival of his future self; or, as if his new self were a bank account to which he'd just been given access, that had been gathering interest locked in a vault, anticipating a date determined by the cosmos when he would be deemed worthy. It felt as if the brilliant planning that created the architectural drawings of his life had been finally revealed to him, his own infinitesimally tiny yet powerful role—and he regretted all of the shame and sorrow he had created for himself and others; for the grandiose schemes and oceans of alcohol he'd used to guard against becoming aware of the magnificence and beauty that had been patiently awaiting him. Though the vision burned brightly in him, in the meantime, it was excruciating. He saw himself sitting, perched on a mountaintop, eyes closed, deep in a cosmic dream, connected to all and everything that had ever existed and ever would, waiting, feeling the slow grind of time through millennia, eons, yugas, all unfolding with an internal rhythm of their own, eternal, patient, ever-present, ever-unfolding.

He awoke, crying.

And continued sobbing, body fluids pouring out of every orifice. He could not stanch the flow, toxic waste streaming unabated from mauled and damaged tissues, carrying chemicals of dishonor and dark emotion. He cried as if he had never cried before; cried as if his life depended on it; cried as if it were only in self-expiation that he could live again; cried as if to fail in this holy task were to condemn himself to endless repetitions of the life he had lived before, hidden and ashamed, searching, ever searching to be real; pretending every day at a humanness he did not feel, and being the greatest actor ever born.

He cried as he had not cried in decades, perhaps ever before in his life. At last, he was able at last to mourn for "Little John" Bancroft, shot by a North Vietnamese sniper on a hot, shitty little hill near Quang Tri one April afternoon in 1968. In a kind of tunnel-vision time-warp, he flashed through all of the other shame-filled events of his life as if they were fresh cream through a pastry pipe. At first they seemed solid, implacable, then they shimmered as if gelid, turned transparent, then to smoke. As they dissipated, he cried for all of the joyous times he had missed, dismissed or disowned, all the times he had not been present for Camille and the kids, when he had put his obsessive pursuit of an elusive whole before giving to those who loved him all they needed, wanted, deserved, while he was off somewhere, married to the job, taking care of some kind of nefarious "police business."

Inevitably, his thoughts turned to his father. No matter how much work he had done on the injuries he had caused, no matter how many times he had beaten trees, pillows and waterbeds (often with blown up photographs of his father's face); no matter the many fantasies he had had of torturing and eventually killing him (usually three days later after extensive terror and sometimes dismemberment), Sam remembered with some lingering pride that he had withheld crying in front of him—no matter how terrible the pain, no matter how onerous the shame he inflicted—he had had the perverse satisfaction of denying him seeing his tears from the age of ten—no matter how terrible the recriminations, no matter how horrible the beatings. Never. Not once. It was his redoubt, his bastion against the cruelty, lies, and abominations. Not since then had he shed a single tear in front of his father. It was choice that had become the default position of his life.

Yet now he cried, oceans and rivers of unspent tears, saline streams streaking down his cheeks, letting go, finally letting go of all of the joy and poison he had held for and against his father, all the love he'd carried that he had had to avoid giving in order to not drown in the sea of the hateful vicious napalm that had filled his father's hate-filled heart. And now, now at long, long last, he finally felt capable of loving and forgiving, first himself and now that tyrannical bastard who had so long manipulated him with his unexpressed shame and fear and pain, that he had hidden within him, one of uncountable generations who had followed the rules and mandates into which and with which they had been born without questioning them. He had had to forgive himself in order to forgive his father in order him to be forgiven himself, as Francis of Assisi and all of the great Masters of all time had taught.

After a timeless time, he rolled onto his back, pajamas soaked through and completely uncaring of about it or anything else as his heart surged, solar plexus pulsating, waves of a new vibrant emptiness moving tectonically through his chest wall as a slow ecstasy released him, all of the pores and orifices of his body opening at once as if the flumes of a gigantic dam, to breathe in as deeply as possible this new identity, this new him, freed from captivity. The he shuddered as an orgasmic stream poured through him, his manhood large and turgid as if response to the welling wave, his penis highly aroused for the first time in recent memory.

He collapsed, utterly spent, and when he awoke again it was as if from a dream within a dream, though that to which he awoke no longer evoked the long, sonorous, floating songs of humpbacked whales. Every article of his clothing and bedding was completely soaked. He felt sodden, and smelled as if marinating for two weeks in olive oil, garlic, and balsamic vinegar. All of who he was, all of who he had ever been, and, for all he knew, all he might ever yet be, lay open and fragmented within him like layers of parchment paper fanned and ready for baking brioche.

He knew now he would never be, could never be, the hard man his father had wanted him to be, even the imitation of it he had previously attempted. That part of his life was over, dead. Of course, his father had never been the man he pretended to be either. He had hidden from his own devalued sense of self and his continuing failures to appease his own father (and the multiple images that he had demanded his father assume), the man his father had tried to beat into him, curse and demean him, to shape him, mold him, into the image of the man he himself had never been able to be, so personally crippled by the accumulated weight of accreted emotional energy he had refused or not been allowed to release or integrate. Now Sam knew he could be gentle and strong simultaneously, no longer had to live out of the small, beaten child who had endured the multiple decades of violence and cupidity in stoic silence. He was freeing himself of the manacles he had taken on in order to be loved, and cherished. Now he could, now he would, live and breathe, walk in the sunshine. He was being given a second chance, and he would not blow it, no matter what!

CHAPTER THIRTY-EIGHT
A New Perspective
September 26th, 1988   2149

Paul surrendered to his exhaustion and go to sleep early, hoping to derive more from the wonderful clarity from his dreams. He was a big believer in dreams, especially his own dream work. There had been many times when he awakened from sleep with vivid remembrances, and saved the best of them in his journals.

He fell asleep with the firm intention of manifesting a dream, and had a really good one, vivid and Technicolor. It was one of his "novel dreams." Every six to eight weeks, he would dream the context of an entire book, with characters, plots, narrative and dialogue. They were often quite detailed. He'd had one once that stretched across three consecutive nights, each successive one picking up where the last one had ended seamlessly. Even when he had a nightmare, he brought some colorful remnant back from the "Land of Somnos." Of course, the dream angels visited far more often when he slept more than four hours—which was a major artifact that had been developed since he'd gotten clean this last time.

He had always been told that outlining a book was the best way to keep it organized and consistent. He had tried to do so half a dozen times with his first book, and repeatedly found out that it just did not work for him. He eventually had to decide that he just had to go with his own flow, a process more like dreaming than tax accounting. Sometimes a small detail sparked into incandescent flames, other times he got dropped into the middle of some great action sequence. Then it just developed on its own, as if it had been preprogrammed, similar to a child who develops enough of an internalized database to begin having experiences of his own, on its own initiative. He had found that when writing a book, the characters eventually took over and told him what they wanted! When people asked him how he wrote books, he always responded that he did not write books, that books wrote him! He was simply the channel for material that wanted to come through. He always wrote the ending for poems first, but with this novel, he actually had two and a half different ones!

In some ways the dream seemed fore-ordained, and he was simply on hand to chronicle the details. Sometimes he had what he called a "cosmic dream," traveling through the Universe and visiting other worlds (much along the lines of

Olaf Stapledon's classic *Star Maker*); or in which he was a speck of light dissolving further and further into seeming nothingness, yet retained enough of the power of thought and individuality to capture and bring back ephemeral lessons that were a sign of great grace and blessings for him.

He awakened having had an "organized crime dream," in which he had been associating with "Mafia types" (being that they looked, acted and spoke with heavily-inflected East Coast Italian accents), though they dressed like Yakuza (blindingly white shirts, black suits, shoes, with sunglasses and no ties). There was an enormous amount of cocaine involved, warehouses full of it. (Even though he was clean, he still dreamed about huge slabs of beautiful mother-of-pearl iridescent shale—often seeing, but never using, many kilos of it). In this one, he was living in Mill Valley, high up off Summit Avenue. The dream took place on Francisco Boulevard in San Rafael, in one of the many industrial spaces that had once existed there before it had been taken over by used car dealerships. It was a warehouse filled with thousands of kilo packages stacked about half way up the walls on three sides, with an empty space on the right as you entered, big enough for a panel van or truck. He and his associates were very business-like in filling orders and collecting money, while younger men, further down the hierarchy actually loaded the cellophane-wrapped packages. Everyone was armed, including those whose only job was to brandish automatic weapons, especially AK-47 Kalashnikovs. Paul stood as if a witness, standing apart from himself in the dream, part of him freaking out at what he was doing, part of him just observing. He was not afraid, just very, very mind-blown—especially since he had never really experienced anything at all like it in real life. It all seemed surreal and vivid: the smell of the *cocaina*, the cut and color of their suits, the comings and goings of the vehicles, the presence of well-armed men secreted around and through the building, the suitcases and trunks full of bills that were weighed rather than counted. (A million dollars in hundreds weighs in at just ten kilograms, or twenty-two pounds). There was no dramatic conclusion to this dream, though he was struck by the blasé attitude all of the men (including himself) had about the vast amount of cocaine, and the enormous amounts of money. It was just "business as usual."

When he awoke and pandiculated, he felt the accumulated tension drain from his entire body as he stretched and yawned simultaneously. He realized he had "napped" five and a half hours! He was fully clothed and funky from the long ordeal of the previous night. He started a pot of coffee while he a shower. It was the perfect opportunity for him to write. So, what if it was 0233? It was his fucking time and he could use it in any way that he wanted! He just so longed for the time when he could spend his entire time reading and writing great literature—and no longer having to deal with the everyday working world with all of its rules and constrictions, especially time schedules!

The dream reminded him of struggling through those first three weeks clean from coke, sleeping sixteen to eighteen hours of every day, and craving like a motherfucker every time he swam into waking consciousness. The first time he had regained his mental and physical equilibrium enough to manage to attempt to dress, his only thought was to score (despite the fact that he no longer had either money or resources). He was now officially a pariah. Everyone he had ever known in the trade had turned their backs on him for real or imagined reasons; and of course, there were those who wanted revenge in terms of his life, or at least a broken knee or two.

As he struggled to dress for the world, he heard the voice of the Divine Mother speak to him from the corner of his bedroom. He'd been living on Sacramento Street across from Lafayette Park. He knew it was SHE because no living woman who could have gotten through to him in such a dramatic fashion.

"If you use again, you're going to die!"

The Voice spoke in a beautiful, peaceful, measured voice that froze him in his tracks, thinking he was hallucinating. His muscular contractions locked up and stilled his blood lust for cocaine for just long enough that he had no energy but to simply fall back into bed, mumbling to himself "I'll think about it some more."

When he next awakened, he had managed to convince himself that SHE had just been a delirium dream, and prepared to go score. When he heard the same message again, he sat down on the edge of the bed to contemplate: Did he even give a damn whether he lived or died? It was some measure of his misery that he did so at length—until he started sobbing, and did not stop for the next twelve hours. Movies of all his successes and failures, the tortures and traumas, of his life flowed through him, were displayed in 256 colors, lived briefly and furiously on the bright white screen of his inner cinema before they disappeared into the eternal cleansing fires—and, at length, opened for him a fresh doorway into yet another life, one that had been unfolding without effort and with tremendous gratitude ever since.

CHAPTER THIRTY-NINE
Mornin' Blues
September 27th, 1988   1003

When Paul woke up, he kept his eyes closed for what seemed the longest time, unwilling for the day to begin. He was stiff, every joint aching, sitting in his favorite leather chair—knees achy, neck cramped, mouth filled with excelsior, teeth filmed and moldy, eyes scratchy, butt sore. Sometimes he felt that there was something...almost sweet about running his energy until he got so completely exhausted that he just dropped off in his chair, as if he were reluctant to let go. The aftermath, especially not having brushed his teeth, was always a drag, and he inevitably woke up irritated and grouchy.

He had never really been a morning person; had always loved and cherished the night far more, always choosing to work only PMs or Nocs, even staying up all night on his days off. He was aware that he might still be reacting to some strain of childhood nostalgia, such as when he was ordered to bed at nine o'clock—and snuck out early in the AM when his father fell asleep in his chair, and he was able to sit right up next to the TV and watch 1950's late night television with the volume turned way down—Tales of Wells Fargo (with

Dale Robertson); Naked City; Boston Blackie; Inner Sanctum; Stories of the Century (with Jim Davis).

His father always pretended to love and honor his youngest brother, Francis, the most pampered of all of the siblings, the one who just happened to be a Jesuit priest with a Ph.D. in Philosophy. He very early recognized Paul's bright mind and ancient soul. Though his father had introduced him to Joseph Altsheler, an early Twentieth Century writer of juvenile historical fiction, it was his Uncle Francis (never Frank) began feeding him philosophers, initially Christian: Merton; Augustin of Hippo; Francis of Assisi, Francis Xavier; and then later, branching out: Kant, Camus, Sartre, J.S. Mill, Schopenhauer, William Blake, de Beauvoir, so many others. His uncle became the anchor to which Paul had clung throughout his tumultuous childhood. And when he graduated from grammar school, Uncle Francis told him: "You're going to high school now, and they're gonna try to fill your head full of bullshit. But you know better. You're an old soul."

It wasn't until many years later that he realized that his uncle had been what Alice Miller called his "sympathetic witness," one who validated his tragedy and trauma in order that he was not dropped totally into psychosis. His dearest uncle kept him from drowning in a sea of mediocrity and self-doubt; had encouraged him to dream big, and achieve all he could; who had very likely kept him from becoming permanently "mentally ill." He realized that his uncle's encouragement and recognition had amplified Paul's appreciation for the words of Emil Zola: "I came here to live out loud!"

Alice Miller had recounted the story of young Pablo Picasso being carried around on his father's shoulder after being separated from his mother following a severe earthquake. As they walked around the island for three days, the young boy kept asking his father about the reality of headless humans and bloated horses. His father consistently affirmed the truth of what he was seeing. Years later, when Picasso painted his famous Guernica, he used images recalled from this early experience to imbue the painting with life-like images recalled from memory. He gave credit to his father's honesty for his never having buried the images or blurred the traumatic memories.

The phone rang while he was sipping his first cup of thick, dark special blend (two-thirds French Roast, one-third Mocha Java, drip grind from Graffeo's). His first instinct was not to answer. And he was right not to do so. Tom Sutton was calling to ask him to come in and work some overtime, even though it was his day off. The police presence on the units had been causing a marked increase in anxiety, especially amongst the paranoid patients, creating the need for more staff presence. He only returned the call out of a sense of personal loyalty to Tom, but only after he finished his second cup. He had a standing rule to never speak to anyone before his second cup. Even so, he told Tom he would come in to work in approximately an hour. He wanted to give his brain some time to get into a better groove, write another page or two, hoping to get down some of his reflections and remembrances from the night before.

CHAPTER FORTY
More Questions
September 27th, 1988   1003

"We've been able to track down all of the Number One keys issued to the doctors," said Brian, "except one."

Gloria looked up from the latest crime scene information report. Several of them had come in during the last few hours. Given the massive amount of forensic material (the lab called it "mostly junk," but it still needed to be checked out). Gloria had really been shining in this investigation, so this information really piqued her interest.

"And who might that be?"

"Noah Biederhoff."

"Who's that?"

"A doc in private practice with admitting privileges."

"What? Seriously?"

"Yeah."

"What does he have to say about that?"

"His service says he's sick today."

"And he knew we were checking #1 keys of the doctors?"

"He was cc'd on the memo. And everyone on the list got called!"

"And he didn't come in?"

"It could be coincidental."

"Hah! And my Aunt Harriet has two heads!'

"OK, so it looks bad. What do you want to do?"

"I think you and I should pay the good doctor a visit."

"Where's he live?"

"He lives at The Summit, 999 Green."

"Sweet!"

"And he's not answering his phone? Anybody try his wife's number?"

"Same number."

"Let's get over there."

CHAPTER FORTY-ONE
On the Move
September 27th, 1988   1123

Sophia was having an ancient dream, one that had visited her since childhood. It always seemed that she always dreamed freely when she was in the hospital, one of the few safe places she had ever known

She was a blonde, beautiful princess who was pampered and protected, surrounded by luxury. She was loved by all who saw her, a favorite at court, and considered to be a great blessing. She was applauded everywhere, adored even. Her entire life, she was surrounded by golds, turquoises, lavenders and pastels, frosted with confectioner's sugar.

She dreamed of exotic foreign lands, flying through the air without wings, on magic carpets and magical swans who took her everywhere she might find exciting and filling her with joy.

As she grew older, she remained the favorite of everyone, lauded and praised When she was fourteen, suitors started arriving from all over the kingdom, pledging troth and being willing to wait until she was of age. Her suitors were always tall, exciting, and handsome, impeccably dressed young men from the best families all bearing incredible gifts. Her father, though a bit gruff and distant, provided her with the very best wealth could provide. Her mother had always deferred to her father in matters of state, but as to the marriage of her only daughter, she had strong opinions and her will usually prevailed.

Sophia now lived in her own private wing. Her closets were filled with dresses and gauzy gowns of satin and silk; scores of pairs of shoes made of rare and delicate leathers; rings and jewelry woven of magic gems and crystals, as if the designers had brought down the very stars themselves to adorn her.

Yet, in the midst of all of this finery, she carried a deep darkness within herself that could not escape. It haunted her, followed her everywhere. She was seemingly unable to shake a sense of doom and a peculiar darkness that seemed to seep into her body from the very air itself. She felt as if she were Persephone, continually preoccupied with having to spend half of her year in the Underworld, as if she had been abducted by the Lord of the Underworld and had to spend a third of her life there every year (returning after the winter season).

As she became more and more preoccupied with her inner awareness, she became more and more morose and depressed, befriending the slow mists of an autumn afternoon, the scarlet and gold leaves of soon-to-be-barren trees; of small shadows that flitted behind doors as she approached; the shushing hiss of the curtains' creases that seemed somehow to mock her. Even the oldest trees in the ancient forest seemed to be reprimanding her with their long, slender branches and hollow whispers of laughter.

She chided herself frequently, trying to dismiss what might have been a fatuous inclination, but even in the company of her best girlfriends from other noble families, she could not simply dismiss what she had used to believe were simply fleeting notions. She started becoming more and more withdrawn. The people of the town rarely saw her anymore transported through the streets in her lacquered carriage, smiling and waving as she passed. She even became querulous with her maids and accused them of silent laughter in her wake. They and other courtiers expressed nothing but love for her and amazement at her perceptions. Dark quasi-human shapes formed out of the shadows that visited her dreams and distracted her, allowing her no peace or privacy, beings who mysteriously knew her most sacred, secret thoughts and fantasies—and taunted her with their knowledge.

The further she withdrew, the less able she was to feel safe with herself, or to tell anyone. She continued to wither slowly, gradually losing her grace and spontaneity as these drastic changes progressed. Her father brought the most talented performers, jugglers, and acrobats, presented amazing extravaganzas to lift her spirits—and nothing worked as she slipped deeper and deeper into her own parade. The most esteemed healers and doctors from throughout the realm brought exotic herbs and potions, all, sadly, to no avail. Mages and magicians wove spell and incantations, worked their finest feats of legerdemain. They all ruefully walked away.

For her, the most frightening of all was the spectral figure who invaded her boudoir with increasing frequency. He always came for her wrapped in malevolent ice, spreading a lugubrious mantle of despair around her that gave rise to her choking off the very oxygen from her cells as he took more and more possession of her body.

And then she awoke screaming.

Sophia shuddered, crying, throat and lungs filled with choking phlegm, a deluge of perspiration from her every pore, heart plangently reverberating with the echoes of her despair. She stifled a scream, took a deep breath, then shook herself like a wet dog after she turned. She wanted to run, but there was nowhere to run to.

The dream had been so, so real, so urgent! She had been having therapy since she was a small child, every and all imaginable kind. It intensified after her court appearances when she testifies against her father, told her truth for the very first time; no matter how she much worked, no matter the oceans of tears she shed, the dream kept showing up like her own personal Haley's comet. And now her only refuge was her drawing pad, the sanctuary to which she could retreat, the only world in which she had any real control. She drank the bitter truth of this realization like a draught of hemlock, and wished mightily that she could wreak the violent revenge upon her father that her inner protectors and assassins thought she ought. Her only comfort was that her father was safely locked away in Folsom Prison for the rest of his life.

She had met so many of the ones who lived within her: protectors, defenders, Mary Jane who negotiated with the outer world, Shell Woman whose face she could wear when she had to deal with anyone in authority; Butchie, her little five-year old boy, who kept alive the hope in her for another, better day. Then there were the lamenters, the depressives, those in constant mourning for sins she had committed throughout time, back to and before the beginning of the Universe. There were others she could not yet see or hear, only sense intuitively, waiting to emerge.

In less ferocious moments, she rode the flooding Technicolor rushes of power and prayed for clarity, prayed to be relieved of the breast-ripping urge to scream, and the awful gripping continuing sense of shame. She sobbed as she embraced the desire to be able to be grateful for her life.

She had a momentary flash about the drawing she had made. She knew she had captured the essence of her feelings, though now, in a moment of greater clarity, she realized that it did seem to resemble her father. Some of her self-doubts slipped in to becloud her belief in the validity of her own perceptions. She dismissed this line of thought almost as soon as it arose.

Alice was her rock, her anchor, her lighthouse in the turbulent storms of her inner life. Alice had always been willing to listen, always been there for her to interpret her dreams, to encourage her to journal, to use her talent and desire to write, to use them as clues to unwinding her memories and discovering her true self.

"The more you remember, the better you'll feel!"

"I feel worse now since I started seeing you!"

"You've made tremendous progress."

"But I don't feel better!"

"Feeling worse is the beginning of feeling better."

She had faithfully attended week after painful week. She had remembered, sometimes aided by hypnosis. Alice had told her she could hear the tape recordings when she was strongly, more able to handle the material, to integrate the hidden reservoir she carried, the treasures of her memory banks.

CHAPTER FORTY-TWO
Now What?
September 27th, 1988   1239

Kube put a police placard on the dashboard and they parked in a "No Parking Zone" directly in front of the building on Jones Street. It was a thirty-two-story modern glass-and-steel high rise, designed by Claude Oakland, and built in 1964. It had unobstructed panoramic views north from the Golden Gate Bridge to the Bay Bridge—punctuated by Coit Tower; Alcatraz Island (first named "La Isla de los Alcatraces," or "The Island of the Pelicans); the Richmond Bridge, and the entire length of the Embarcadero. It was one of the most scintillating views as one might have in this city of extraordinary views, for which gift one might easily pay an extra $1000 or $2000 a month. As a native San Franciscan, Ryan had visited most of the vista locations in his city, yet felt that here he had been transported to the Himalayas, and its breathtaking rare air.

"What apartment?"

"Strictly speaking, they're condominiums?"

"People own their own apartments, but not the building? What kind of advantage is there to that?"

"It's still equity."

"It's just a marketing scheme by real estate people," grumbled Kubicek in his best basso profundo.

Ryan took in the quizzical look that passed Gloria's face, then laughed.

"You can take the man out of the socialist country, but you can't take the socialist out of the man."

The doorman was wearing a frock coat with gold braid, and had the hooded eyes and wary look of a former policeman. He also bore the shattered capillaries of a chronic drinker as he watched the disparate trio with some apprehension as they approached. A sharply dressed Latino woman accompanied by an equally sharply dressed Caucasian man, both in the company of a sloppily dressed man who looked like a Slavic King Kong. The incongruity was striking. Nonetheless he did his duty, and asked if he could be of assistance.

"The Hulk," as he had immediately named him, produced SFPD identification out of the inner pocket of his voluminous jacket, showing just the handle of his concealed weapon in the process. The festooned doorman invited them into the marble-floored lobby.

"Jack McKillian. I knew you were on the job. I did twenty-five years with the San Jose PD."

They shook hands all the way around, and then the retired policeman asked again, in a far friendlier tone, "So what do you need?"

"Dr. Biederhoff?"

"2905."

"You know the tenants' apartment numbers?"

"George Schultz used to live here, other prominent people."

"Anything especially significant about Dr. Biederhoff?"

"He entertains quite a lot here. He has a lot of young friends."

"Men or women?"

"Well. Mostly men. Young, well-dressed men!"

The doorman did a visual scan around him, including the approach to the front door. He glanced at each of them in turn, then lowered his eyes and spoke softly.

"This is a very good job. My pension...it's good, but I need this job."

Ryan swept the eyes of his companions, and then said, "We're just trying to catch a killer, Jack. We need a little help here."

The doorman peered up from under the rim of his military-style cap, and caught Brian's eyes.

"What sort of help?"

Taking a deep breath, Gloria stepped forward and, keeping her voice soft, told him they had been unable to locate Dr. Biederhoff, and wanted to access his condominium.

Just then a very well kempt woman of indistinguishable age, somewhere near eighty, wearing very chic and fashionable clothes and walking her miniature poodle, approached the door. Jack moved quickly to open the door for her and her canine companion who appeared to be wearing a genuine diamond collar. He tipped his hat to her, as she reached out a hand to him with what might have been a ten-dollar bill that he smoothly palmed with one hand while tipping his hat with the other.

"I can't let you in without a warrant," he said, "but let me try the house phone."

He went to an elaborate chrome panel set into a marble column, and shook his head after failing to successfully connect.

"We can get a warrant here in half an hour, but we'd really rather not call a lot of attention to your building. You know how it works. If we get the warrant, then the ADA shows up, the press gets involved..."

Kube zeroed in to the heart of the matter when he said, "And then the tenants get word of it, and they get upset. Maybe some of them don't really want the publicity...Your Christmas bonus takes a nosedive."

"I guess, since you're on the job, and me being a public-minded citizen, the least I could do is knock on his door, see if maybe he's in there...sick or injured."

Kube frowned at him. None of them made as if to move.

"I guess, I could quietly give you my master key. But it has to stay between us."

To cover the man's embarrassment, Ryan stepped forward with his hand out.

"Of course. And if we find anything, we will handle it discretely."

"You're not going to toss the place, are you?" asked the doorman, as if he were the wrangler after the horses were out of the corral.

"No. Just a look-see. Dr. Biederhoff seems to be unavailable, and no one has heard from him since yesterday. Have you seen his wife?"

"Ah, Mrs. Biederhoff...she's not...here a lot. She...she's the one with the family money. She's quite a bit older too. She usually stays at their home in Marin, in Mill Valley."

The three investigators looked at each other, completely nonplussed. None of them had ever heard of another residence.

"Do you have an address? Another phone number?"

"No, but I could probably get it."

"Please do. We'll be back shortly."

CHAPTER FORTY-THREE
A Small Rewind
September 27th, 1988   1130

While Gloria, Tim and Kube were busily tracking down the case of the missing key in the relatively bucolic defines of Mill Valley, Dom Sanchez talked to Eddie Chacon in Spanish. He was neatly in a flannel shirt and pressed blue jeans, but he seemed edgy and as if he were possibly withholding something.

Domingo Sanchez was short and stocky with a thick dark Zapata-style moustache. Members of the Detective Bureau called him "The Wooly Mammoth." He was the resident expert in gang-related activities and made the hottest salsa any of them had ever eaten. He called it "Volcanic Meltdown."

"Mr. Chacon, I'm Detective Sanchez. I wanted to talk to you a little bit more. Thank you for coming in."

Eddie grinned and spread his hands in a magnanimous gesture.

"No problem!"

"It seems that you have a pretty solid alibi for when the murder took place."

"That's right. Paul Marzeky saw me, so did Tom Sutton."

Dom continued as if he had not been interrupted.

"What we here have questions about," he said and paused, "'Fast Eddie,' is your juvenile record."

Eddie broke into an immediate sweat, looked around the room as if he might need to go to the lavatory really badly right now.

"Can you tell us anything about that?"

Eddie got his breath, and replied. "Those files are sealed. I've got a new life now. I don't want to talk about it."

"That may be, but we can get a court order to open them, if need be."

"Look, I don't want any trouble. I've got a girlfriend and a baby. I've just started working here. I can't afford to lose my job."

"Then maybe you can tell us a little bit about your childhood."

Eddie wasn't sure what they were looking for, but he was semi-relieved. They seemed to only want to know about the past. He was concerned that they might have gotten onto his latest money-making activity with Maria.

———————

Maria Conchita was ecstatic. She had replayed her own clips from the 11 o'clock news over and over, exulting in new possibilities. She had been an absolute star tonight, getting a scoop on all the other media sources! She had luxuriated in a long hot bath, and allowed herself several glasses of her favorite red wine, Lacrima Christi, the tears of Christ. Legend had it that it was Mount Vesuvius was where Lucifer was cast out of heaven, causing Christ to weep.

Immersed in her fantasies of fame and glory, she decided to push her new source and called him at work.

"This is Eduardo Chacon. How may I help you?"

"Eddie. It's me, Maria Conchita."

"This is not a good idea, you calling me at work. What's up?"

"Do you want to make some more money?" she asked, dangling the bait, even though this time it would be coming out of her personal funds.

"Of course. What do you want?"

"Anything pertaining to this story. Exclusivo, comprende?"

"I heard a rumor about a drawing. I'll see what I can do."

CHAPTER FORTY-FOUR
The Fountain of Memory
September 28th, 1988   0421

Sophia was dreaming. It felt like a dream within a dream. She felt as if she were actually remembering a real event from her distant past while at the same time as if she were observing herself dreaming in the dream. She remembered, sometimes so much, sometimes too well. Sometimes hidden memories arose unbidden like a harvest moon, bringing with it its cornucopia of awareness, thoughts, visions, feelings, sensations, insights, prescience, journeys, hopes, wishes, needs, desires and most especially the dark fruit of her long-lost and suppressed memories.

April 12, 1973 1456

She was three. She was having a party with her dolls, stuffed animals, and all the little friends no one else could see.

Then he came in.

She felt confused. She loved him so much! But he smelled bad!

As he approached, she saw that he was walking funny. Then he wanted to kiss her! Ugh!

She liked his hairy arms, but his prickly face hurt! And he smelled bad!

He reached down and picked her up—ugh!

She wriggled and squirmed. She could not escape!

"Leave me alone!" she screeched directly into his ear.

He roared at her like a wounded lion.

"Whassa' the matter with you? Daddy loves you!"

"You smell bad!"

She smacked him with her tiny fists, hitting him on the arms, neck, face with no effect.

"Give Daddy a kiss!"

"No! You stink!"

He grabbed her soft, pink, spindly little arms and held her fast.

It hurt! It hurt! "Mommy! I want my Mommy!"

Then she started to cry.

"God damn you! Don't fucking cry!"

His face twisted in the ugly way it did, and she cried even harder.

He slapped her across the cheek, and she started shaking, as if she were having a seizure; then started hiccupping uncontrollably as she gasped for breath between tiny squeaks of tear-filled terror.

"Stop goddamned crying!" he said, and then again tried to embrace her as yet another sour wave of stale alcohol breath surrounded her.

She hit out with her little fists, and he dropped her on the floor. The small frightened animals in her brain fled as if before a forest fire. Totally panicked, she ran to her hidey-hole in the closet. Clutching her favorite cinnamon bear, she started breathing harder and faster until her flood gates opened, sending torrents of tears unchecked down her sweet pink cheeks.

He jerked the door open, and screamed again, spittle splattering her like a hydrophobic dog.

"I'll give you something to cry about!"

Her shoulder dislocated as he yanked her brutally out of the corner, and she shrieked in immense pain and wildly smacked him directly in the eye.

Then he alternatively slapped her and backhanded her, again and again.

"Cry, you little shit! I warned you!"

He lifted her and wetly kissed her pretty little face several times. He felt shamed desire rising in his trousers. As lust and hunger welled up in him, he forced his tongue into her mouth, probing her delicate teeth, kissing her repeatedly, while breathing hot, fetid fumes into her little pink face.

Still holding her with one rough hand, he yanked at his belt and dropped his trousers around his ankles. Her continuing screams seemed to inflame him, and his tumescent penis throbbed as he maneuvered her tiny body so as to better penetrate her. She screamed and kicked wildly, indescribable fear streaking through her. She peed her pants and hot urine flooding down his shirt front, but it did not deter him. He tore her ruffled pants off and smashed her face down onto a stack of flat cardboard boxes.

He pulled off his underwear, and attempted to insert his swollen penis into her thrashing backside, missing her anus, and then pushing against her vagina still wet with urine. She screamed and screamed, completely terrified by the unearthly pressure she felt building as he repeatedly attempted to stab her with his organ like a Pear of Anguish.

She was so confused! Why was Daddy hurting her?

Then a searing white-hot poker of pain slashed up through her, tearing her tender little body wide open. He shoved into her as she repeatedly shrieked and screamed before, at length, her threw her to the floor bleeding and crying.

She twisted and screamed at the top of her lungs as she watched him approach. She swiped her face with the back of a tiny hand and then started swinging wildly. She hit him twice in the face before he grabbed her.

"I hate you! I hate you! I hate you!"

"You little bitch!" he said, and picked her up—one hand on her little butt, the other on the nape of her neck—and hurled her across the garage where she crashed face first into a pegboard rack of garden implements, and a trowel gashed her jugular vein. Dark blobs of venous blood gushed from her neck as she lay there, rapidly losing consciousness, limpid, sprawled like a broken angel.

He had swiftly stanched the blood flow, and whisked her unconscious to the ER. No one questioned his being covered in her blood, and the doctors praised him for his quick thinking that saved her life. He spun them a tale about her repeated visits to the expressly forbidden garage, despite his many admonitions.

When she regained consciousness, and seemed able to pass the simple neurological exam (the X-rays being negative), he quickly assured them that he would "watch over her all night long," and refused to have her admitted overnight. She closed her eyes tightly when they got in the car, and were driving swiftly away when he glared at her.

From his mouth issued deep sulphurous molten fumes of hatred spewing her with revulsion and distaste as she dove deeper, ever deeper into the hidden place no one else could go, safe from him and any who might try to intrude.

"If you tell <u>anybody</u>, I will kill Mommy!"

CHAPTER FORTY-FIVE
Champion
September 29th, 1988   0539

She shuddered as tears still dampened her cheeks, and started when she opened them to see Alice sitting by her side holding her hand. She uttered a little gasp, and threw her arms around her and cried again, now in deep relief to find herself in the presence of Alice. She noticed that she had a twisted handkerchief in her hands.

"Oh Alice! I am so glad to see you!"

"The night staff called. You were screaming and thrashing around. They thought you were having a nightmare. You woke up for just a moment and called out my name. I came as soon as I could."

"Oh Alice! You are the best!"

"I promised you I would help you walk through your memories."

"But it hurts so much to remember!"

"It's part of the healing process, to remember your real memories."

"But my mother still doesn't believe me! She tells me none of it is true"

"She believes what she wants to believe! She's just using that to protect herself from admitting her denial of the harm that was caused to you!"

"Maybe I don't really want to know!"

Alice asked her to related what she remembered of the latest dream/flashback. Even though many of the elements were familiar, were, in fact, a rehash of some of their earlier recovery/discovery work, there were new aspects to this latest production of Sophia's unconscious.

"So, you remember hitting him?"

"Yes! Several times. I realize now that I didn't just lay there like I used to think. I fought back!"

"That's excellent! How does that feel to you?"

"More real. More like me!"

"Good. What are your feelings now about your father?"

Sophia closed her eyes and felt deeply within herself.

It was in this rare and precious moment that she allowed herself to be acutely aware of a very powerful desire to kill her father. In this new moment, she was both embraced and repulsed, filled with power and simultaneously frightened to her toenails, by the might and ferocity of her rage, a wrath so total that she could have destroyed him instantly with one laser beam look.

Alice did not immediately caution her against such intensity as had so many of her other therapists. Instead she looked into her now open eyes and simply said, "I understand the impulse, Sophia. It's totally natural."

"It's just exactly how I feel. He raped me!"

"He raped your little child self. You are no longer weak and helpless. If he were to try it today, how would you react?"

"I'd kill the bastard!"

"Exactly! This is another aspect of something we have talked about in my office. There is a small child, that battered, abused little girl who lives still, now, inside of you. She is a part of you, the adult Sophia, that she needs and wants to act for her, to act in her favor, to acknowledge and protect her."

"But how? I can't go back and change what happened!"

"No, but you can open yourself up to her, let her feel your presence and act as her protector. Her champion."

"But how, Alice, how?" Now Sophia was feeling anger breaking through her longstanding sadness.

"Good. You sound angry. That's a good place to start."

"How?"

"If you want to proceed right now, we can. Otherwise we do not have to process any more right now."

Sophia felt a doorway opening in her, built of faith and hope and dreams of a new freedom beckoning to her, welcoming her from beyond the edges of the madness and sadness out of which she had habitually lived—never telling the truth, always being afraid of being hurt, hiding, hiding deep within herself, always going to that place where no one could find her. This new light, this numinous possibility momentarily infused her with a power and a strength to go further to recover all of the obscured sights and sounds and smells so long suppressed, the her that was her real and true self.

"No, Alice, I have waited long enough. I want to know what it is to really feel alive and whole and good. Will you help me"

"Of course. I will help you find your champion."

CHAPTER FORTY-SIX
Intervention
September 28th, 1988   1834

Sam called Tony, the speaker from an AA meeting he had attended. He had questions of a nature that we more in line with his recovery from alcohol than of a psychiatric flavor. Besides which, he wanted to retain his anonymity relative to his real occupation and disposition. After greeting him, Sam mentioned that he had been having some serious doubts about his future, especially about his desire to return to work – perhaps ever. It was difficult enough to think about the simple task of taking a walk, especially without two guns and a blackjack strapped to various parts of his body.

"That's a question all of us drunks have. It always comes up, and is probably one of the most difficult, if not dangerous questions of early recovery."

"Why's that?"

"Because you realize you have survived your detox—and you're going to live. And as amazing as your survival might be, the question becomes: Now what?"

"Exactly."

"I know you're hoping I might have some kind of magic answer for you, but I don't. It's probably the biggest difference between being a drunk and being sober—you have to answer a lot of questions for yourself in a new way."

"I don't want you to 'fix' me. I'm not fucking broken. But you've been sober a lot longer than me. I need some help."

"I'm not trying to 'fix' you. I can't. Only you can do that for you."

"I'm working on it. Jesus Christ, I've only been sober what? 16 days now!"

"All the more reason not to push the river too much."

"But I gotta do something!"

"You still have to do one day at a time."

"I have a family I have to think about."

"You have you too think about first. It's not 'selfish,' in the way that most people use the word. You look around in wonder that you could have quit drinking; that such a thing could have come to pass. And then you realize that your drinking has always been a part of your life; that you have lived for twenty or thirty years. And suddenly it hits you— WOW! I have to go back to some kind of life without drinking! And that's scary."

Tony's thoughts were so in accord with what he was feeling that Sam could barely speak. He felt so goddamn fragile, and so goddamn pissed off. The urge to kill someone was extremely seductive in that moment. To just watch the life slowly extinguish from their face as he closed his hands inexorably around their throat.

Then he reminded himself that that was his old life. He wanted something new and better. That had to include making an effort at reformation—of himself, his life, down to the foundation.

But he was scared shitless at the thought of going out into the world without two pistols and a blackjack concealed on his person. He could not conceive of life without a badge, the symbol of his authority that had opened so many doors otherwise closed; broken up arguments, and stopped fights. And what about his pension? Six more years and he could skate away. Of course, he could claim that his alcoholism was stress induced, and maybe get a medical discharge.

"I've been there too, Sam," Tony sighed. "The only thing I can tell you is one of the universal truths—'One day at a time.' It's all you have, no matter how ambitious you are. You only get one day at a time. The same with the booze. You only have to stop drinking one day at a time. Not for a year, not forever. Just one day at a time."

He knew he was being granted a grace; had been granted a reprieve from a life that would surely have taken him over the edge. How easily he could have killed Camille sometimes, especially when he felt jealous and threatened by her. She seemingly had such ease with the world, such a sense of really belonging. It was one of the things that had always attracted him to her. Yet her ability to make money scared the shit out of him because he really believed that it was just a matter of time before she took the kids and disappeared on him. Probably with her goddamn boss at work, that smiley-faced fuck! He knew he was being paranoid, but sometimes he couldn't control his feelings. Sometimes Camille showered him with the sweet, warm rain of her love and tenderness. Other times he wanted to torture her when she withheld what he felt he needed, deserved to get up and go for just another day; what he required to provide for her and the kids – except that she was doing that far better than he.

"But what you don't understand...Nobody here knows who I really am. And I can't really talk about it either."

"Like we always say: 'You're only as sick as your secrets.'"

"I...really can't talk about part of this, but...there's more at work here than my recovery."

"Nothing should be more important than your recovery."

"I understand that," said Sam angrily, "but I'll have a life again one of these days. And I have to look toward that, even if right now I'm not sure of what that might be."

"That's confusing, Sam."

"I know it is. I...just can't tell you everything right now."

"What does that mean?"

"Just that there might be more to things than it seems."

"When you're ready to talk, please call me. But right now, I gotta go."

"This isn't a fucking soap opera, Tony. I just can't talk about some things right now. Thanks for listening."

Sam decided he had to talk to Ryan. Sam had always believed that cops were different, immune from normal human failings and weaknesses. As a brother officer, he would understand better. But Ryan wasn't a brother drunk.

CHAPTER FORTY-SEVEN
Another New Direction
September 29th, 1988   2232

Paul spotted Sam Jones sitting by himself watching the late-night news. Ordinarily the television was supposed to be off by the time the night staff got there, but sometimes the PM crew made exceptions. Given all of the upset of recent days, it was understandable that they might not want this fellow stay to stay up. Sam had reported a huge breakthrough in an AA meeting and felt "for the first time in years" that he would be able to maybe live without drinking. Paul was intrigued and wanted to talk with him about it. Even though he'd been clean over five years, he always loved to talk to the newly sober. It always gave him a perspective on how far he had come. And he was sometimes able to share some of the changes he had been through, passing along strategies for sane living. It was an amazing fellowship. He never knew when he might meet another who was walking the same path, having experienced a spiritual awakening that led him to a new life.

"I read in your case notes that you had a breakthrough at the AA meeting."

Sam looked up into the earnest eyes of a man near his own age. Sometimes the staff just wanted to get information to put into their case notes, but Paul had the look of someone who was actually interested. All of his cop instincts were telling him that this fellow might be someone he could trust, though he didn't know why. He decided to be civil and answer him civilly.

"I've been drinking most of my adult life. Then I heard an incredible speaker, Tony D., the other night. It was like he was telling my story, only he's been sober a long time. He really got to me, you know?" asked Sam, eyes tearing as he turned his head away and broke eye contact.

Paul was impressed in spite of himself. There'd been some speculation in the case notes about whether or not this guy might be harboring a mood disorder, or maybe even be borderline psychotic, but what he was hearing here gave him chills up and down his spine. Paul's truth sense was tingling, much like Spiderman's "Spidey sense." This guy really <u>did</u> seem righteous.

Looking at his watch, Paul said, "Look, I've got to go to report. But if you're up when I come out, we can talk about it for a few minutes if you like."

Sam looked up and decided to take a small step and discuss a little of his reaction to Tony the other night. He wasn't sure he would be believed if he did. They might think he was crazy too!

"Sure. That sounds good. I'm gonna go lay down and read for a while. I'll be in my room."

"Cool. See you in a little bit. If you're asleep, no big deal. We'll do it another time, Mr. Jones."

Sam held out his hand and said "At least call me Sam."

"OK, Sam. Paul. Paul Marzeky," and shook hands with the man.

Twenty minutes later David peeked in to Sam's room. He was reading "The Big Book" of Alcoholics Anonymous. Sam immediately put his finger in as a bookmark and closed the book around it.

"Come in. Have a seat. Can you talk for a few minutes?"

"Sure. There's usually a lot of work at the beginning and at the end of the shift, so I can't stay long," he said, then shifting gears, he asked "What brings you here anyway?"

Sam looked at the man for a long moment, holding eye contact. He felt that it was not just an idle question, or a standard staff member's opening gambit to elicit information. The guy seemed genuine enough. He put a bookmark in place and set the book on his nightstand.

"I feel like I've been given this amazing opportunity. It's a little confusing though. I feel like I have so much I need to do once I feel better," said Sam, then saw the cautionary look in Paul's eyes. "I know I'm rambling and a little disconnected, it's just that so much has happened in the past few days, my head is still spinning. Give me a minute to collect myself."

They sat in silence for a few minutes and Sam tried again.

"I had a big row with my wife over some trivial bullshit. I had been working really hard to control my drinking, but after that, I just...blew out, I guess. All I could think of was to get a fresh bottle, Bushmills, that's what I drink...or used to drink. I still can't get used to the idea of never drinking again. I went to the liquor store and forgot my wallet. I got a little rowdy at the liquor store. I was gonna come back and pay the guy! I live right in the neighborhood, for Christ's sake. He panicked and pushed a silent alarm. When the cops came, I guess I must have looked kinda crazy!"

"Wow! Quite a story!"

"It's been intense. I'm a lot clearer about what I want. I just wish I didn't hurt so damn much. Fucking Tylenols don't do shit."

"I know. But you been at it," said Paul, and made a motion as if tipping a bottle into his mouth, "for years. You can't expect all that hard drinking not to have an effect on your body."

"I know. But thanks. Sounds like you've got some experience with the process."

Paul examined his motivation, and decided he would do a personal share, but not to bask in his own glory.

"I don't usually tell people about this, certainly never a patient, but I trust you because you're a vet." Paul sighed, then went on. "I've been clean for almost six years."

Sam focused on Paul's face, then sat back and pondered for a minute.

"Thank you, brother. That means a lot to me. I've been remembering so much shit I'm gonna have to make amends for...well, anyway, thanks for trusting me. It feels good."

Paul smiled and held out his hand. "Not a problem. And thank you. For your good work. I gotta go. I'm doing another double tonight."

Sam lay in bed, ruminating about his life, especially about being a cop and whether he could ever be a cop again. Then he remembered that in the morning he was getting a pass to attend an outside AA meeting with Tony, the proviso being that Tony accompany him to and from the meeting and stay with him the whole time. He was scared shitless about going out into the world without two pistols and a blackjack concealed on his person; the many times just flashing his badge had saved him hassles, broken up arguments and stopped fights. It was too much for him to contemplate. He had fifteen years in! What about his pension? Of course, he could claim that his alcoholism was stress induced, maybe get a medical discharge.

Several of the staff stopped by making their hourly rounds. He greeted them in a friendly manner, and sloughed off their questions with polite denials of a need to talk or medications. At three o'clock, Paul stuck his head in the door.

"Are you sure you don't want a sleeper? Or a Valium for anxiety? Dr. Schapiro has ordered both of them for you, if you ask.'"

"No thanks. But, if you've got a minute, I'd like to talk a little."

"I've got to let somebody know where I am. Be back in a minute."

By the time he returned, Sam had donned a robe and was sitting up in a chair by the window.

"I want to tell you something, but I'm afraid you're gonna think I'm nuts."

Paul went into what he called "mental health mode," where nothing a patient told him seemed to affect him, no matter how bizarre or shocking. It allowed him to maximize the patient's attention and willingness to give information that might—if reacted to with shock or revulsion or disbelief—otherwise not be forthcoming. It was like being in neutral gear. Outwardly he manifested with a calm, open face, lips relaxed, eyes alert but compassionate, body posture relaxed, hands open palms out, prepared for whatever might come.

"I saw the perpetrator. I saw him go into the seclusion room. He had a key."

Paul's mind went into high gear as he analyzed many possibilities in a nanosecond and then asked, "Why didn't you tell the police?" He figured he would go with straight logic first and see where it led. Sometimes having a conversation with a patient was a little like walking a maze. You just had to put one foot in front of the other.

"Because I'm a cop."

Sam's response really unsettled him, sending him down multiple pathways of possibility. One was that the man was delusional.

Paul retained his outward poise, and only moments passed before his response.

"If you're a cop, it really makes no sense that you wouldn't report what you saw. You're the perfect witness."

"Unwittingly so. I'm here under an assumed name because my medical insurance will no longer cover me for detox and treatment. Only my Captain knows where I really am. Officially, I'm on vacation."

"Why?"

"Because I've got fifteen years in and they don't want me to lose my pension."

Paul had been so caught up in the flow of the conversation that he had almost forgotten he was talking to a patient, albeit one who seemed perfectly rational, not delusional at all. Still...

"Does anyone else know you're a cop?"

"Here you mean? No. Oh wait a minute, are you asking if anybody else knows I'm a cop? Or maybe you think I'm crazy too? No, man, I'm not crazy. This is not a delusion. I really did see the perp enter and leave the room. The perp saw what's her name, Sophia, but I don't think he saw me. That's why I'm bringing this up. She could be in real danger. And I can't come forward right now. You're gonna have to help me protect her."

CHAPTER FORTY-EIGHT
The Empty House
September 27th, 1988   1439

The doorbell chimed like a carillon. Kube waited briefly, then rang again. They had all drawn-on hospital gloves before unsnapping the safety straps of their firearms, but no one drew. Kube used the master key they had finagled out of the former San Jose cop.

The trio entered, and loudly announced their presence as police. Alternatively, they called out to Dr. Biederhoff show himself, if he were present. As they roamed through the upscale confines of Apartment 2905, only silence greeted them. The condominium had originally been two separate units, but had been combined into one by an ambitious previous owner, creating a very rare three-bedroom domicile. The rooms were graced by twelve-foot high ceilings, and the entranceway led directly into the living room floor that was covered with deep-pile carpeting with floor-to-ceiling windows all around. The space was dominated by stone and bronze sculptures that complimented the elegant furnishings that were as classic and expensive as the building itself.

There were two different conversational groupings built around leather couches and chairs, one arrangement set up around a working fireplace with an ancient, highly-polished mahogany surround topped with a pristine slab of marble. The other was set up a comfortable distance from a set of windows that looked north and east, sweeping across Pacific Heights and the Marina District before capturing the Golden Gate Bridge and Sausalito in the one direction; and reaching out to embrace first Coit Tower, North Beach, Fisherman's Wharf, and Alcatraz—and then encompassing Oakland and Berkeley before perfectly framing Mount Diablo in the far distance.

"Oh my God!" said Gloria Flores, as Kube stood mute and speechless. Even Tim Ryan—a native San Franciscan who had grown up in some of The City's most affluent surroundings—was nonetheless so impressed with the beauty he was seeing that, for a moment, he forgot his role. His eyes filled with tears of joy at this rare display of beauty and magnificence, a gift from the city of his birth.

Gloria unnecessarily reminded them that they had no search warrant, and were merely seeking the good doctor as a potential material witness, not a suspect.

Recovering quickly, Ryan nodded his head toward the interior of the elegant hideaway. With hand signals, he motioned each of the pair in different directions after calling out again for either the good doctor or his wife. After checking all the closets and cupboards, and inspecting closely for any hidden rooms or spaces, they called out to each other.

"Clear!" came Kube's voice.

"Clear!" called Gloria.

"I'm clear here too!" called out Ryan.

Quiet echoed through the otherwise spacious aerie, as if silence itself had a voice that spoke through the emptiness and desolation. Although extremely beautiful, there was a certain lack of softness to the space.

"Very male kind of space," Gloria commented when the trio returned from a quick search of the premises that had yielded nothing more than their original reconnaissance. They let themselves out without leaving a trace and locked the door behind themselves. Jack was anxiously awaiting, fear etching his bloated alcoholic face. He was visibly relieved when he saw them reappear. He hurriedly handed Ryan an address and phone number in Mill Valley. Mrs. Biederhoff did not answer, and Kube left a message with his number to call him back.

Ryan turned to Kube and barked.

"Number Two Walden Lane. Mill Valley. Call dispatch and have them get in touch with the Marin County Sheriff's

ASAP. Have them do a safety check and get back to us forthwith!"

Chapter Forty-Nine
Home again
September 28, 1988 2231

Paul had been shaken by the revelations of Samuel Q. Jones (or whatever his name actually was). He still questioned whether what he had been told was delusional. The night passed quickly, and his thoughts continued to percolate. He had made mention that he was going home to write and one of the day staff sneered: "Anybody can write a novel!"

It was the kind of comment that only someone completely unacquainted with the amount of artistry, discipline, rigor, and just plain work that was required to write a book. It seemed to be a chic kind of thing these days to be a 'writer." There was rarely a week went by when someone didn't come to him and say that he or she was "a writer too." When asked what they were writing, invariably it was a dozen hand-written pages in a notebook, or worse: "I haven't written it down yet! It's all in my head though!"

Whatever the case, Paul went home, and set the water boiling to make a fresh pot of coffee. If he was lucky, he could get his MDR in (a thousand words a day, rain or shine, sickness or health) before he slept, and not have to worry about it between the time he got up and had to leave for work again.

He reflected that Freud used to say that people make jokes about things about which they are most serious. And he realized that he had been "making jokes" about his working to support his writing habit" his whole life. He had always framed working for a living around his real desire to write and communicate. It was part of why he favored the afternoon and night shifts—and partly to avoid all of the political bullshit that inevitably fell upon the early workers. Of course, such choices revolved around identity—who and what one thought oneself to be. He identified with being a writer, and denigrated his role as a vastly underpaid, though highly intelligent worker in the trenches of human misery.

CHAPTER FIFTY
The Story Continues to Unfold
September 29th, 1988   1211

Sophia looked less distressed today, less anxious, more relaxed and mature—though if asked, Alice would not have been able to define exactly what was different. It was more a feeling than anything else. Nonetheless, Sophia was actually smiling.

"What's going on with you today?"

"Sometimes I get so tired of being the way I've always been, of being me."

"Don't have much choice really. Like Oscar Wilde said, 'Every other job is taken!'"

"I know. But still…"

"If you look at what you are going through as temporary or transitory, as a cleansing rather than as an identity, it might help soften the impact a little."

Sophia's face shifted, toughened, hardened, and the words that issued from her mouth were harsh and cutting.

"What identity, bitch?" roared Esmerelda, the Portuguese lesbian woman who was Sophia's protector. "I work hard to keep her from having to experience any more bullshit from men—especially that rapist asshole of a father!"

"He's safely in prison for a long time!"

"But the damage is already done! She's had to suffer for what he did!"

"And you do an excellent job, Esmerelda!"

The alter-personality growled and then purred somewhat like a happy cat. Then Sophia's face softened and her young client spoke again through the same lips.

"I'm sorry, Alice...I did not know she was there...sort of waiting."

"It's OK. I'm glad we have mapped your alters, and to speak directly with them when they arise. I know you have had very little choice most of your life."

"I always get so caught up in other people's needs!"

"It's very easy to do—especially for women. Sometimes guys have it so easy."

Sophia laughed, then her face turned sad and serious.

"But why do they always want to touch me? Why can't they see me as more than these?" she asked, cupping her breasts in both hands, tears flooding her cheeks.

Alice looked compassionately at her client, inundated with memories of her own, of asking herself those same questions—and all the strategies she had had to develop her true selfhood.

"Your earliest experiences with men are related to your father. Men are generally only interested in sexl with women. Their cultural orientation revolves around it—until they learn better. We've talked about this before."

"But it keeps coming up, over and over! I just hate it!" she said, now feeling more angry than hurt. She slammed her right fist onto her right thigh, and continued. "This is what happens when I cut myself. I get so frustrated. I'm just so tired!"

"And you are getting better! You've learned some new ways to avoid self-harming."

"But they don't always work! I get so...," and here her voice shifted again to that of a plaintive, little girl's voice that contrasted sharply with the expletive she used, "fucking tired of it sometimes."

Sophia reached out and took Alice's hand.

"You've had no support most of your life. You just have to keep working at it."

"But you don't have to! You talk to men all the time. I've seen you!"

"I make it look easy. I have bad days too."

"Not like mine!"

"That's why I'm here. To help you sort it all out, and make better decisions."

"I'm so glad, Alice," she said, now grasping her therapist's hand in both of hers. "Sometimes I'm afraid you're gonna get tired of me."

Alice squeezed back for a moment, and then let go.

"I'm won't reject you as long as you're working on yourself. That's my job."

"I...am I just a patient? To you?"

Alice considered what Sophia was really asking, and then formulated an answer to the unspoken question.

"I'm trained to help you learn how to deal with your life issues. And I care about you as a person, and as a client."

"So, you don't think of me as weird? Or diseased? Or damaged?"

"I think you are a very courageous young woman who's experienced some horrible things. And I'm someone who is helping you work through them."

"What about after therapy? Can we still be friends?"

"Like I've told you before, I am both legally and ethically unable to be 'friends' with you after our therapeutic work. That doesn't mean I don't genuinely like you as a person, but there are constraints built into the system to protect both of us."

"It's not fair. I don't know anybody like you."

"You will. That's part of our work. Ultimately what you are doing is learning to create new belief systems to replace your old ones. As you retrieve your memories, as you let go of old emotions, you'll make room for new feelings, to have new relationships."

"But it takes so long!" Again, she looked like a small child.

"Sophia, it's only been a year that we have been working together."

"Nobody ever saw me before you did! They all wanted to give me those...pills!"

"But we're on the right track now. And I will not abandon you!"

"But Alice, I really like you!" she said, again grabbing her therapist's hand.

This time Alice gently disengaged her hand, and looked directly into her client's face.

"I understand what you're feeling. I seem like someone who is everything you want to be. You can learn to love yourself like you think you love me."

"I want it to be you, though."

"Sophia, we've talked about this before. You have feelings for me. That's totally natural. But my position gives me a certain amount of power that makes me attractive—especially because I seem to be everything you've ever wanted to be, the image of me that you see."

"You mean you're not being real with me?"

"Of course, I'm 'being real' with you. But that doesn't mean that we can have a personal relationship!"

"You just said you care about me as a person!"

"I do. That does not mean I can get involved with you personally."

"I...have these feelings, Alice."

"There's nothing wrong with your feelings. And it's natural that you direct some of them towards me. It's called transference. I hold a space for you to feel your own feelings. You project them onto me until you are strong enough to have them for yourself. You see me as someone who has 'saved you.' It's natural for you would feel gratitude."

"I...love you, Alice."

Alice was thrown head first into the whirlpool of her own thoughts and decisions. I'm going to have to refer her to someone else. If she weren't so fragile, especially if she weren't hospitalized again, it would be so much easier. I will definitely have to make an entry about this, and my decision, in the progress notes; and I'm going to request an immediate meeting with my old friend and supervisor Florence.

It's always so harrowing to mediate between a client's fragility and the ethics of my calling. God knows she herself had had a transference with her training therapist, and it had become an issue to be worked on. But she and her training therapist were both on the same page in terms of academic information and intention for the sessions. Sophia was obviously not. Alice paused for a moment, to give Sophia the impression that she was thinking about the measure of her reply.

"I understand, Sophia. I really do. But it's my image that you love. You only see me in therapy, and so I am this amazing person who never seems to make mistakes; who always understands you. But that's my job. It's not who I am all the time."

"Yes, it is."

"I'm not going to argue with you about this. You'll just have to take my word for it. And you really need to think about what I am telling you. I am your therapist. We can never have that kind of personal relationship!" she said, far more sharply than she had intended.

CHAPTER FIFTY-ONE
A Further Unfolding
September 27th, 1988   1849

Sam lay awake, scrolling through his memory banks as if they contained holy artifacts instead of just the bad memories that were gradually being flushed and integrated; replaced, and re-formatted like digital code. The longer he was sober, the more he felt a sense of separateness from his old self, as if who he had been were actually another person. It had been described to him in group that this sort of "depersonalization" was not all that rare, especially when someone was recovering from severe experiences. He believed sometimes that he was be being transmuted by his having survived excessive violence and alcohol. At other times, he felt far more humble, and decided that his moral compass had gone awry for decades, and was slowly returning now to true north. He'd made so many errors in judgment, for years attempting to play whatever role he felt was expected of him, rather than just being who he really was, how he really felt. He had always been so driven by intense shame.

He was examining his very ground of being very closely. He was realizing how unstable he had always been, from the time of his earliest memories; and was just beginning to "see" a grander design of patterns, events, and people unfolding, refolding, and merging into a perfect puzzle that mysteriously managed to be whole and organic; that somehow was always of benefit to all and everything, no matter how scattered or malformed it might otherwise seem from one's very personal viewpoint; how he was receiving rewards from all that he gave without thought or compunction—all of which seemed to be the very best reward he could have had, despite the tremendous pain of letting it all go. At the very least, his present work on himself was pre-cursing a future puzzle piece he would eventually need and use. In a bright, brief flash of illumination, he saw the he might be that person he had always needed most.

It felt like he was in a flow, or a process, of daily developing ever greater awareness. It felt as if he were seeing so much more now, much of which he used to believe was utter bullshit, even though he weirdly treasured many aspects of it. It felt was as if shades had been removed from his eyes and sunlight was entering directly into his brain, as if he were personally known, and valued by this omnipresent presence. He felt the glimmerings of a "Grand Plan," like a giant chess board stretching throughout the Universe in which every creature—protozoan, dinosaur, sycamore, human—played a perfect part, and was loved, needed, and praised for it, whether or not that creature had reached the point at which it was able to be aware of the vast and cosmic love of this massive being whose body was the Universe.

Smiling, filled with these deep thoughts and love, he drifted off into a profound sleep filled with uplifting dreams, though he could not remember their contents.

When he awoke refreshed, still floating in the tendrils of his dreams. It was a relatively rare experience for him, and he reflected that it might be due to his unburdening himself to Paul. He had felt filled with relief then, and still felt altered now.

Then, moments later, a worried-looking Paul entered his room.

"We gotta talk, brother. The shit might be hitting the fan!"

"What do you mean?"

"Somebody told me that the cops had been 'quietly inquiring' about me. They've already talked to me three times! Somebody told me they were talking to the Head Nurse about whether they had ever witnessed me using 'excessive force' toward patients!"

"Holy shit!"

"Yeah. No shit!"

"But why? Why are they zeroing in on you?"

"I don't know. I suspect they might have uncovered some old information about me. Don't you cops call it 'deep background?'"

"So, there might be some truth to it?"

"It's all bullshit from a long time ago! Not one of the people who filed complaints against me were even there when these 'alleged incidents' occurred!"

"You speak pretty good 'leagalese,' man!"

"I been around this fucking system a long time!"

"So? What?" Sam asked, spreading his hands wide in front of him.

"I don't fucking know! Turkey butt!"

"Have they talked to you directly again?"

"Not recently," Paul said and related the "incident" that had happened at the station house."

"Shit! Sounds bad! But if they were really after you, they would have kept you!"

"I'm fucking innocent!"

"And?"

"Fuck, I don't know!"

"Are we still solid? On our deal, I mean?"

"Do you mean, am I going to turn you in to save my skin? Fuck you!"

"Not a very therapeutic way to talk to a patient!"

"Fuck you again! You're the one got me into this with your lies and bullshit!"

"I didn't lie to you!"

"It was your fucking drinking and your fucking lies got you here!"

"OK, that's true. But I never lied to you!"

"OK! OK!" said Paul. Then he took a deep breath and sighed. "Sorry. You're right. I just don't know what to do."

"It might blow over."

"You know better than that!"

"Those Homicide dicks get a scent, and they don't stop sniffing!"

"So, what do you think? What should I do?"

"Don't run away. Or do anything out of the ordinary. They'll be looking for that."

"I know that. What do I tell them when they take me in for another 'little friendly chat'?"

Sam looked at Paul for a very long moment, as if assessing his soul.

"Did you kill the guy? That asshole?"

Paul sputtered for a moment before he could answer.

"Fuck no! And fuck you for asking!"

"Hey! I'm still a cop! I had to ask!"

"Well fuck you very much!"

"I didn't think so, but I had to know. Understand?"

Paul glowered at the other man, and then nodded his head.

"OK. If you're innocent," he extended his hands with palms open toward Paul, "and I believe you are, then the best approach is to tell the truth. Tell them about these 'past incidents;' that you were innocent then, and you're innocent now."

"What if they want more than that?

"Like what?"

"I don't know! You're the fucking cop! What do you think they might ask me?"

"Do you know anything more about this murder than you have told them?"

"That would lead me to talking about you! And if I don't, they might try some shit like 'obstruction of justice.'"

"Too true. But, if you don't tell them about me, they won't have any idea about what you're holding back. Just tell them as much truth as you can!"

CHAPTER FIFTY-TWO
Alice Changes Her Tack
September 29th, 1988   1321

Alice was sitting in the inner sanctum of her former supervisor's office. Dr. Florence DuBois was an older woman who was no longer in active practice. She had become one of Alice's closest friends and advisors, and still acted as her sounding board, confidante and consultant. Alice had summarized the situation with Sophia and asked about alternatives to simply referring the young woman to another therapist.

"These are complicated issues. It sounds like this client's made significant progress. And now, she's breaking through to all her old memories," said the older woman, carefully avoiding the psychoanalytic term "repression," referring to a totally unaware failure to remember traumatic events or memories.

She personally did not believe in repression, though some experiences might be dissociated to preserve one's mental status. Repression always carried an implication of complete victimization, as if an individual had experienced something sent by God that was beyond the possibility of human experience to endure, forgive or retrieve. A victim stance was very dangerous in that it could easily lead one to feel entitled to behave in any way one chose and expect that one should be excused because one was unaware of the source of the behavior—and was, therefore, "innocent" of all responsibility.

Her personal belief was in taking full personal responsibility, even for the nature and conditions of one's birth—though she drew the line at owning any blame or shame for perpetration at any age, but especially in childhood. In that case, the perpetrator was always responsible! Always! The survivor was, of course, responsible for cleaning up the aftereffects of such egregious behaviors, especially the loss of autonomy and sovereignty.

Florence's own sexual abuse as a teenager had led her to becoming the pre-eminent child psychiatrist in the Bay Area, maybe even the United States. Her latest book, entitled *You Can Still Have a Happy Childhood*, embodied her personal philosophy.

She believed in and practiced her own form of Charles Whitfield's Inner Child Work. She had come to gauge spiritual development by the level and extent of an individual's ability to redeem his or her self ("buying back" one's lost vitality and personal qualities lost to shame and trauma). The whole of the process hinged on integrating these lost energies. As a result of her own work on herself, she had come to model her personal motto: "Being an inspiration to others is the highest achievement."

"And so, she is suddenly aware that she has real emotions. And believes she's in love with you. Is that correct?"

Alice wanted to defend her feelings, to more completely define the nature of her relationship with Sophia. But realizing that Florence always had a teaching point behind such questions, she simply nodded her head.

"So, she expressed her 'love' for you, after asking if she were more than just a 'client' to you. Yes?"

Alice again affirmed.

"And you assumed, perhaps correctly, that she might want to create a very personal, even sexual, relationship with you, correct?"

"Yes, but why 'perhaps'?"

"Because you may have jumped to some unwarranted conclusions. She may be trying to express the fact that she feels very vulnerable right now, and needs you more than ever. You didn't explore the subtext of her statements. I would say that she might, just might, have been telling you that she loves you; and simultaneously is having sexual feelings with which she cannot deal, about which she is afraid."

Alice considered this as Florence continued.

"On the other hand, you may be completely correct. She may be wanting an inappropriate relationship with you. My point is, we don't really know because you got defensive. You shut her out of a deeper therapeutic conversation because of your own fear."

Alice felt stung by the clarity of her mentor's analysis, even momentarily resented the fact that she was paying a hundred dollars an hour for it! Then she recovered her equilibrium, and smiled.

"You're right—as always."

"It's not about being 'right,' Alice. It's about not allowing your feelings to interfere. Let's look at the countertransference, shall we?"

While it is expected that the client in a therapeutic situation will project his or her needs onto the therapist (as a kind of place holder) for discussion and integration, Florence was referring to the process by which the therapist may, consciously or unconsciously, seek to get his or her own needs met through the therapeutic alliance, the bond, with the client.

Alice blushed at the implications, but still managed to ask.

"What do you mean?"

"You called her 'beautiful' one time; and 'attractive' another. Perhaps you're attracted to her as well. The countertransference may be interfering with further effective treatment at this point."

Alice felt flustered. She had thought that Flo would tell her had seemed to be telling her that she should transfer Sophia—what she thought she wanted originally. Now she felt she wanted to keep Sophia, maybe even conversely as a way of proving that she was not attracted to her! Sometimes being a therapist was very confusing!

"I'm not sure...I don't think I'm attracted to her in that way. I have always liked her spirit; how hard she works. I admire that. But I don't think I'm sexually attracted to her."

"You have mentioned several times too that you have held her hand, or she has held yours."

"Oh God! I hadn't even thought of that! She has always seemed so vulnerable, so innocent! Oh God!"

"Don't beat up on yourself. It happens. And it seemed to have had so unintended consequences."

"I see. Oh God! I may have contributed to her misunderstanding!"

"You may have."

Florence smiled at Alice, and took a sip of the herb tea that she blended herself.

"But I think it's far deeper than that. Especially with her long trauma history, but it's important that we discuss this—especially since I believe that you really want to keep this client, not refer her."

"That's true."

"And given the high level of trust she has with you, you might be the perfect person to help her transition her feelings; to help her find an appropriate outlet. She's likely going to go through the heartbreak of teen age romance, all of that angst, that she's really never experienced. Your job now is to keep it from breaking her."

"I really thought she was saying that she has sexual feelings for me."

"That may be true! But it's important that you be clear with yourself, with where you stand, with who you are. Then you can deal honestly with her feelings and her revelations."

Alice flushed again, this time with relief.

"I see what you mean. I hadn't really examined my own sexual feelings. I've never been particularly attracted to women though."

"It may be because of the intimacy of her revelations to you within the therapeutic relationship. And her sexual energy might be really powerful now, if she's really just allowing herself to have it untainted, unrestrained, for the first time!"

"You could be right."

"Are you sexually active? Now?"

"No, not really."

Flo raised an eyebrow archly.

"I must admit that I have been feeling...hungry lately. Maybe I just need to get laid!"

CHAPTER FIFTY-THREE
A New World
September 29th, 1988   1357

Sophia covered her eyes, attempting to block the internal pictures that were assaulting her in mute accusation for all of her years of silent covert acquiescence in her own denigration, for not fighting, screaming, yelling, even killing her perpetrator father. She clawed to keep the intrusive images away, but the power of the unleashed truth quickly stripped her bare like a small animal trapped in a pool of piranhas. The torrent of images raced through her like a stream of gammas rays, and slowly her initial shock turned to awe.

As her shame drained, a blinding lust seize her like a grand mal convulsion. She realized in that illuminating moment of awareness that she'd blinded herself with lies and intimidation; been manipulated into believing her sexual pleasure was bad, shameful, even contemptible; that it was her pervert father who had blamed her for feeling alive; who had slathered her with his own shame when he had raped her repeatedly through the years; who had used her while condemning her!

Ancient proscriptions felt lifted from her heart and mind, as if by a supernal source; as if a physical weight, as if discarding an old set of clothes—but of a totally different magnitude, a completely different dimension. She felt lighter, more relatively free to see, to be she, fully feeling and embracing her essential self, feeling bold and audacious as all apprehension slid away like ice from a heated windshield. She touched herself tentatively through her jeans, a light brush with a fingertip growing in strength and sensitivity, to a more firm and bold embrace of her fingers, growing increasingly with a sense of rightness and confidence, as the power of her embodiment, her innate abilities to have the pleasure she had never allowed herself flooded her. She felt fully embodied, in her body, the sweet fullness and joy of it for one of the rare times in her entire life. Where shame and frustration had previously ruled her, her previous vacuity and numbness were replaced by a sense of enormous flowering of titillating rippling waves of pleasure from her vagina, her clitoris.

She could not help but think of Alice, dear sweet Alice who had helped her so much, who so inspired her so much, more than any other human being. She felt ready, longing to really, really live, to be in her own body, to relish in it, to love it, to enjoy it!

Her head was whirling, filled, even saturated with so much...hunger, desire, she wasn't sure what, just that it was demanding. She...wanted to be touched, really touched. In her last session with Alice, she had wanted Alice to touch her, to caress her like no one ever had. And she wanted...to touch Alice! She was so shocked by that revelation that she could only say "I love you!"

Her vagina was raging. She was burning! Her entire body was on fire!

Without any thought, she closed the door and stuck a chair under the door knob. She lay across her bed, opened her jeans, and slipped her hand underneath the edge of her silk panties, her favorite yellow ones with the little ruffle. She touched her clitoris tentatively, then as her Bartholin glands started copiously releasing, and the erectile tissue of her clitoris grew thicker and stronger, her fingers slipped with ever greater facility and dexterity—rubbing, twisting, squeezing, as lightning bolts of pleasure shot through her body, and she abandoned herself to herself in a way that she never thought possible! So much stronger! So...a-maz-ing!

Her vagina was absolutely sopping with sweet-honey as she inserted two fingers, and they danced in and out, in and out, then went back to her clit, massaging moisture around and around her hard, little red bud. She felt a wave growing, a tsunami racing toward the very shores of her beingness. Her toes began to curl, and her calf muscles cramped as she opened her thighs wide, hips pushed into the air as her fingers continued their unceasing exploration. Then she simply let go completely, utterly beyond choice as the divine, extraordinary, amazing wonder of orgasm swept through her—and she lost all thought, all desire, all conflict and conversation, released herself into a timeless ocean of pure, silent bliss that left her weightless, emptied, floating loose and free, totally unconcerned about absolutely nothing at all!

CHAPTER FIFTY-FOUR
On the Griddle
September 29th, 1988   1912

The police had called, and very politely, asked him to come in for "further questioning." To Paul, it seemed like a twisted deus ex machina mechanism in a dystopic fantasy novel.

Paul didn't yell or scream. He did not, in fact, even ask "Why?" Retrospectively, he believed that his lack of reaction might have seemed misleading, given his former brutal interactions with the investigating officers. The only thing he requested (naively perhaps) was that they not put him in a small interrogation room. Although his intuition told him he already knew what they wanted, he did two things before going to the police station (this time it was Central Station on Vallejo Street in North Beach). He called Shirley Stephenson to make sure she was available just in case. (They had spoken after his last interrogation, and she had agreed to represent him should he need her). Then, he took the time to do some deep breathing so as to center himself before he appeared.

For a couple of minutes, Ryan and Kubicek chatted with him in a friendly manner about the unusually wet weather; the Giants; the rather slow progress of development of the Bay

Area Rapid Transit (BART) system, and the fact that some part of Market Street always seemed to be torn up. Then, as if a gigantic gear had turned somewhere in the Universe, Kubicek asked the question about which they all knew Paul had been summoned to answer.

"Mr. Marzeky, why didn't you tell us before, about all these complaints filed against you? The ones for 'excessive use of force?'"

The rage rose unbidden, though Paul stifled it, and actually managed to put a facsimile of a smile on his face, though to a spectator it must have looked more like a rictus than a moue.

"Don't you mean the three 'allegations of excessive force' filed by people who were not even there when the alleged events happened?" and then more forcefully, "Do you mean the unproven allegations made against me?"

"The witnesses seem pretty credible to me!" Kubicek continued in a raspy, carping voice.

"Oh really? What do you know about psych units? About 'reasonable force'? About the politics of a psych unit?"

"None of that is relevant!"

That was it! Paul jumped up, and shouted.

"'All of it is fucking relevant!"

Kube made as if to move toward him, but Ryan signaled with his hand to desist.

Sitting down again, Paul went on in a less agitated tone.

"First of all, none of the women who filed the 'complaints'" he said, and made air quotes with his fingers, "was even in the room when the alleged incidents occurred! Secondly, under State of California law, I am allowed to use 'reasonable force' to protect myself and/or a patient. That's exactly what I did in every case. Thirdly," Paul said, pushing down a third finger of his right hand, "all three of those complaints were made by lazy-ass bitches who didn't come to my aid when I called for help during a take-down! They bloody ass waited until it was done, and then filed complaints against me! I know for a fact that one complaint was filed by a nurse who was sitting in the fucking Nurse's Station eating doughnuts when I called for help!"

"You've been in a lot of take downs?"

"It's part of the job!"

"You wouldn't say an excessive number?"

"No, but then I've never been afraid to take somebody down who needs to go into seclusion either!"

"And who determines that?"

"Depends. Somebody attacks a patient or staff member; or if we use a show of force and it's not working, it's sort of a group decision. Generally, it's the most senior person present."

"Has that been you a lot?"

"Sometimes. Why?"

"We're trying to determine if there is any significance to your history of 'excessive force' complaints."

Paul jumped up again.

"I fucking knew it! You are trying to pin this shit on me!"

"Calm down!" From Ryan.

"Siddown!" From Kubicek.

"Naw, man! I want my attorney! I want Shirley Stephenson! Now!"

As if on cue, there was a knock on the door, and a uniformed officer stuck his head in.

"Marin County Sheriff's on the horn."

"Kube, you take it."

The uniform said, "Sir, I think you might both want to hear this!"

Ryan and Kubicek exchanged a look and headed out the door.

"Make yourself comfortable, Mr. Marzeky. You may be here a while" said Kube as he exited.

"Lieutenant Swanson, Marin County Sheriff's here."

"This is Lieutenant Ryan, SFPD. Glad you could get back to us so fast!"

"I'm not quite sure what you're talking about. I'm calling to notify you of a murder-suicide here in Mill Valley!"

"My department called you earlier for a safety check on one Thelma Biederhoff, Caucasian, 52, 5'6", 140#, Blonde and Blue. 2 Walden Lane, Mill Valley."

"This is very confusing, Lieutenant. That's who I was calling you about! She's the vic!"

"What do you mean?"

"Preliminary findings indicate that she was injected with an overdose of insulin, just before her husband did what looks like a suicide. Noah, he's a doctor, right? Caucasian, 37, 6', 180#, Blonde and Brown, same address. It's the most bizarre thing I've ever seen."

"What's that?"

"He dissected the veins and arteries of his left arm, and clamped them off. Then he took a scalpel and cut through all of them!"

"Oh Jesus God!"

"Sorry about that. I guess that wasn't what you were expecting!"

"Oh, hell no! We've been trying to find her husband. You sure he's the doer?"

"Very little question. She was laid out all neat and tidy, hands folded over her chest. Wearing a white silk nightgown, I guess you'd call it."

"Oh Jesus!"

"And he left a note!"

"Really? Can you read it to me? Please?"

There was a clunk as he set the phone down on a countertop, footsteps echoed across a hardwood floor, and then returned.

"OK. Here goes. Seems to have been addressed to his wife—at least at first." Then he started reading: 'Dear Thelma: I'm sorry for any upset I might have caused you all these years. I deeply appreciate your love and patience. You always knew I was attracted to young men.'"

"Then there's a kind of blank space before he continues, same handwriting. 'It's all my responsibility. She stole my key, and wouldn't give it back! Then she started blackmailing me! I couldn't take it anymore! I knew the shame would kill you! Especially after the last incident. You deserved so much better! I'm really sorry!' "And it's signed 'Noah.'"

"Jesus fuck! I don't know what to say! Can you fax me a copy?"

"Absolutely!"

"Oh hey! Did he have a ring of keys on him?"

"Yeah. We found a key ring in his pocket."

"Can you see if there is a key marked 'Do Not Duplicate' with a large #1 stamped on it?"

"Hold on. I'll talk to the evidence techs."

Moments later, he came back on line and reported a key with a "#1," but it was not inscribed "Do Not Duplicate."

"I guess we don't need a safety check now!"

Stunned, Ryan hung up the phone. Ryan and Kubicek just looked at each other.

"Now what the fuck?"

"I don't know, Boss! This is getting crazier!" He paused for a moment, then commented. "I have a bad feeling about this guy, Boss. I just don't see the doctor as the perp! This Marzeky guy knows more than he's telling us. I just know it!""

"Let's put him on the griddle some more, and see if he cooks."

Paul was pacing in the interrogation room when they entered. Paul scowled when he saw them, spreads his hands wide, and said "Shirley Stephenson!"

"There seems to be some question about your story."

"Shirley Stephenson!"

"Just one question and you can go!"

"Shirley Stephenson!"

"Are you holding out on us? Do you know something, anything, that might further our investigation—anything at all?"

Paul looked first at Ryan, and then at Kubicek. He sighed before replying.

"Shirley Stephenson!"

The two detectives exchanged a glance, and then looked at Paul before Kube spoke.

"Maybe a few days in a holding cell in San Bruno (San Francisco County Jail) will loosen him up!"

"Shirley Stephenson!"

"We're gonna talk again. Real soon. Keep yourself available."

CHAPTER FIFTY-FIVE
The Next Stage
September 30th, 1988   1102

Sophia had been released from the hospital the evening before. Alice was essentially opposed to psych meds, but she considered an occasional dose of benzodiazepines for acute anxiety to be acceptable. She had seen too many so called "side effects" (far too numerous, far too horrible to witness) of the "major tranquilizers," that were, in her opinion, about as tranquilizing as a sledgehammer to the forebrain.

It started in 1952 when Thorazine, which had been developed for use in surgery to "calm agitated patients," became the "chemical straight jacket" of choice for psych patients. The "new major tranquilizers" or neuroleptics, had only shown to be refinements in delivering more force with less dosage size—creating more profit for Big Pharma!

Even though she was offered a spot in a three-quarter way house, Sophia had very reluctantly decided to move back into her mother's house on Greystone Terrace, off Corbett, on Twin Peaks. She loved the incredible views of The City, her city, and in the near distance, the magnificent Pacific. She elected to go there and do a lot of reading and some writing. She had decided to transfer to San Francisco State and major in psychology. It had taken her three years to get an AA degree from City College because she had missed exams and had had to take time off for hospitalization. But her strong warrior spirit drove her incessantly, and she pushed forward while integrating her various fragmented personalities.

Both Alice and her young client were aware of the immanent dangers incipient in her moving back into her mother's house, but there hadn't been a lot of choices. The trust fund resulting from her father's conviction had made her mother executrix, and she was unwilling to relinquish control. Her mother really did not want Sophia living anywhere else, or having any greater autonomy. Sophia's shining dream was of living totally independently without meds. To this end, she had talked to Alice at some length about a law suit against her mother so that she could gain control of her money. In the meantime, Sophia committed herself to intensive outpatient follow up care (twice a week for at least two weeks). The first appointment had been scheduled for today, her first day out of the hospital. They were in Alice's office on Clement just off of Arguello. She had decided to walk as the day had been a beautiful one, with the fog having burned off just an hour before.

"Have they caught him yet? The man at the hospital?"

"Not yet. The investigation is 'ongoing,' they say."

"What's that mean?"

Alice laughed, Twillin trilling, Sophia thought to herself!

"Basically, they don't really have a clue!"

Sophia's face clouded, and she asked in a tremulous voice.

"Do you think he'll come after me?"

Alice started, then smiled her most beneficent smile.

"I think you're safe. As far as I know, no one except the police know you were a witness!"

Sophia started crying, sputtering through her tears.

"He just looked so much like my father! Do they believe me?"

"Oh absolutely! I've had several conversations with the detectives. They don't doubt you at all."

"I'm so glad! I just hate it when people don't believe me because I'm...different."

"I don't want you to worry about that right now. Just focus on getting better."

"Do...how do you feel...about what we talked about last time?'

"I had a long session with my consultant."

"Oh?"

"I told you in the beginning that I had her. You signed a Release of Information so that she and I could talk."

"I remember now. I had forgotten."

"I'm glad. She really helped me get a lot better understanding about our dynamic."

"Oh?' said Sophia, looking a little perplexed and shading into manifest anxiety.

"Don't look so worried. It's a really good thing."

"Really? I hope so."

"What is your greatest fear?"

"'Greatest fear?' About what?"

"About yourself right now."

"I... I am afraid you'll drop me. You won't be my therapist any longer."

"Thank you for trusting me enough to say that. And for trusting yourself too."

"What does that mean?"

"I know how difficult that was for you."

"Does that mean we're OK?"

"Absolutely. And there's some things we need to talk about too."

"Wait. Wait. Tell me again. You're not dumping me."

"I'm not dropping you."

Sophia smiled brightly, and said "Thank you, Alice."

"And we need to talk about last week some more, in another context."

"What does that mean?"

"I want to own that I have been very concerned about you, and that sometimes I have treated you more like a friend than a client."

"How's that?"

"Florence pointed out to me that I have held your hand at different times, and I have allowed you to hold mine."

"Yes."

"I want to acknowledge that I might have contributed to your confusion. Generally, therapist do not touch their clients, unless that is within the description of the therapeutic contract. Even then, such therapists usually have a Massage License. It makes it legal to touch their clients."

"But you have helped me so much, Alice!"

"And I will continue to do so. But from this point forward, I have to be a little more professional."

"No more holding hands, huh?"

"That's correct."

"What about how I feel?"

"That's all legitimate material to talk about and work through."

"Talk about?'"

"Of course. That's what we have been doing all along. Now we have a new arena to work through."

"But...I don't want to just talk about it."

"Sophia, we've already talked about this. We really cannot have the type of personal relationship you were talking about earlier."

"But we can talk about it?"

"Of course. There's a reason for everything, and I will help you to get to the roots of all of what has been troubling you. We will work on this as we have worked on all of the other issues that have come up in your life for the last two years."

"But I'm awake now, Alice! I want to feel more, experience more...with my body!"

"As you free up your mind, you will."

"But I don't want to wait!"

"You don't have to. You are free to experiment. Just be careful."

"I don't know how to...what to do."

"We can talk about this more, but I think it's important that you be very clear with yourself about what you want. You're a very attractive young woman and very vulnerable. You have to be really sure what it is you want."

You're right. I'm not actually sure what I want. But I want to be alive! I want to feel more! I want to move out of my mother's place as soon as possible."

"How will you manage that? Do you have any money other than what your mother controls?"

"Goddamn her" growled Esmerelda in a very deep voice. "The fucking bitch!"

"I mean no harm here. We all need to be practical."

"But what do I do now?" answered Cecilia, the victim alter, and started weeping.

Alice checked her impulsive desire to comfort Sophia, and recycled the energy, and reminding herself that it was countertherapeutic.

"I want to address Sophia."

"I'm sorry, Alice. They just show up sometimes."

"All for good reasons, Sophia. That's why I asked to address you. The more you stay conscious and make decisions, the stronger you will become."

"I understand. But how much longer will this last?"

"You know I can't really tell you that, but you are making really good progress."

"I just want to live a real life!"

"Does that include having a relationship?"

I... think so.

"Here's the real question: man or woman?"

CHAPTER FIFTY-SIX
Turmoil
September 30th, 1988   2041

Surviving Viet Nam had been a matter of paying attention and watching your brothers' backs as they watched yours, the men with whom he lived and died a thousand deaths daily. Sam had proven himself to be brave, loyal, and trustworthy. He had carried the vision of a new life with him home. Home, that special protected location always held in memory: one lived for, hoped for, dreamed about. He had never forgotten his friends and brothers, never would—and how powerful it was to be a part of something larger than himself, something special even if it was driven by a delusional sense of patriotism and promoted by liars and propaganda artists.

There was never any question of morality. It was always a matter of survival above all else—and doing whatever it took to make that happen. They had had a special bond, one the fucking brass hats could never destroy, no matter how much the fucking politicians had tried to keep them from winning.

He had to believe that they had made a difference. Without that sense of propriety, he would just simply kill himself. He had fiercely loved and been loved by these comrades-in-arms, his band of brothers.

They who had suffered so much fear and despair, so much shame and degradation, so much pain and frustration; who had endured the manic-depressive fluctuations of pleasure and pain that had so defined this war of attrition; who shared the bonds of muscle and thew, of vision and honor; who knew the dignity of another man's tears and the blessing in a comrade's blood; who had walked in the shadow of the valley of death, and walked out again; who were stoned to the bone and fierce of heart; whose trust in each other was a living prayer that eradicated all boundaries; who were a prophecy's fulfillment so subtle as to be overlooked like a diamond in a box full of cut glass—they knew. They would always know. They had paid with their hearts and minds, their eyes and ears and noses, buying the thousands of exotic, quixotic sights and sounds, tastes and smells, demanded of warriors throughout the ages, imprinted in their cells, an eternal, indelible bond, joining them mind-to-mind.

THEY WERE BROTHERS.

He had returned to a world that just did not give a shit! A fucking world in which everything was commodified; that had neither then nor now gave any honor or respect to anything or anyone, other than money. He returned angry, lost and dissociated—unable to connect with the so called "core values" of the insane addictive treacherous society, or yet have found an identity amongst the rising tide of the disaffected and revolutionary youth of his generation. No matter how accomplished he became at playing the game; no matter how much money he made; no matter how much love and closeness he developed with Camille and the kids—it was never enough. He always felt like a hamster on a merry-go-round, always wanting more, and with no idea how to ever catch up! He missed it, the wild, crazy, chaotic insanity of the war! He'd knew it sounded crazy. It was something only another vet would understand, but he fucking missed it sometimes—the intensity, the bonding, the immediacy, the connection of battle and bonding, of gristle and thew, of being armed and dangerous 24/7.

Of course, there was so much shit he did not miss at all, especially the politics and the bureaucratic bullshit; and all of the fucking fear, the leeches, snakes, mud, crotch rot, C-rats—but most of all, he did not miss the incoming, or having little yellow men trying to kill him—and having to killing them to survive, always to survive, to push away the foul panting breath of death stentoriously breathing down his neck, and scorching his eyebrows.

He remembered the immortal words of Country Joe Mc Donald:

> And now my friend we meet again, and
>
> we shall see which one will bend
>
> under the strain of death's golden eyes,
>
> which one of us shall win the prize
>
> to live, and which one will die.
>
> 'Tis I, my friend, yes 'tis I
>
> Shall kill to live, again and again,
>
> To clutch the throat of sweet revenge.
>
> For life is here only for the taking.

CHAPTER FIFTY-SEVEN
The Work Goes On
September 30th, 1988   2154

When Paul had come on shift that night, Sam immediately told him they needed to talk.

"Yeah, we do! Probably be a while."

Sam felt as if he were on the edge if a precipice. He was willing to either jump or not. He had not felt the kind of edgy courage he was feeling now since he first came home. Not even working undercover vice was as intense. He had been very moved by Tony's story. Sam longed for that kind of new life, craved it, like a phoenix leaping into the consuming flames only to be born anew.

It had been a loud, busy night, so it was well after 2100 meds when Paul came to Sam's room. Sam was lying in bed contemplating the diverging paths that seemed to be opening in front of him. He felt as if time had multiple possibilities, all determined to some extent by his choices NOW and splintered into even more subsidiary roads and directions depending on those choices, and that those in turn determined as-yet-more uncreated futures. At the heart of it, though, he felt an emerging glimmering of peace, something he had rarely experienced, as if he had never before deserved it, as if it were a gift he'd had to earn. It felt counterintuitive to his twisted belief system, one in which grace had no address.

Paul staggered in, exhausted, and fell more than sat into the chair at his bedside, and sighed deeply.

"You look like shit, brother!"

"Thanks a fuck of a lot! Your buddies from Homicide had me in for another session today. It fucked with my sleep!"

"They're not my 'buddies,' though they are fellow officers!"

"None the fucking less! They threatened to send me to jail for three days unless I tell them why I am withholding! That fucking Slavic guy is like a fucking terrier after a rat! He just won't let go! And he knows, somehow he knows that I know more than I am letting on!"

"You haven't told him anything, have you?"

"Oh, hell no! I gave my word!"

"Thank you for that!"

"I fucking told you I wouldn't, and I won't!"

Still immersed in himself, and the sensations of peace flooding through him, Sam spoke in what might have otherwise seemed like a *non sequitur*.

"Honor! It's an amazing thing!"

"What? What the fuck you talking about?"

"You keeping your word with me! We are brothers with different mothers!"

Paul laughed.

"Wow! I thought for a moment you were going schizzy on me!"

"Not a chance, man! Not now when I'm saner than I've ever been!"

Paul laughed, and said, "That may not be saying too much about your state of mind!" He leaned over and they dapped.

"No, listen. I went to an AA meeting here on the unit. The speaker fucking lost everything just like me! And he came here to 'inspire strength and courage'" said Sam, making air quotes with his fingers.

Paul sat up abruptly.

"Jesus, you're really serious!"

"Well of fucking course! You fucking think I'm just some kind of fucking drunk?!"

"Whoa! Whoa, man! I didn't mean that at all!"

Sam hrumpphed, and then smiled.

"I think I may be able to help both of us!"

Paul raised his eyebrows, and said, "Really?"

"Really!"

"How's that?"

"I'm seriously thinking of talking to them, tell 'em what I saw!"

"What? Are you fucking crazy?"

"No, I really am not! Saner than I've ever been, in fact."

"But what about your job? Your benefits?"

"This is more important!"

"I don't understand!"

"Part of this is them threatening you."

"Don't mean nothing!"

"It's my shit that got us here!"

"And how is telling the truth now going to help?"

"It'll get you off the hook!"

"So?"

"So, it's important to me! I won't have you to sacrifice yourself for me!"

"Your safety is important to me!"

Sam blushed then, and a small sob escaped him.

"Thank you. That means a lot to me!"

"It's true!"

"I know. I know. It's fucking beautiful."

"You're welcome."

"But I need to stand in the fire and own my own shit!"

"What do you mean?"

"I'm here on this unit because I'm a fucking drunk! But I'm also a cop! And I'm a witness to a murder. Ergo, I have to stand up, no matter what!"

"Holy shit! You really mean it!"

"Of course, I do!"

"Jesus!"

"I do need to call my Captain and talk to him about it. I don't want him getting in the shitter over this!"

"When? I mean when are you going to do this?"

"I don't know. Right now?"

"It's late! You want to go waking up your Captain at this time to unload on him?"

"He's a friend. We worked patrol together a long time ago. He'll understand."

"Then what?"

"I guess I'll talk to the detectives."

"Tonight? Er, this morning?"

"I don't know. Maybe. Yes!"

"Jesus! When you go all-in, you really go all in!"

CHAPTER FIFTY-EIGHT
The Way Opens
October 1st, 1988   0011

Ryan and Kubicek had picked up Chinese from the Eagle Café on Grant Avenue. After they ate, they gave in to the bone-deep fatigue they were both experiencing as a result of less than three hours sleep a night since the case had begun. Ryan was sleeping in his favorite office chair when the Duty Sergeant roused him. Kube was racked out on the couch across from him, snoring. Sam Smith was on the line, calling from the in-patient unit and had a strange tale to tell. Although he had been questioned repeatedly by both uniforms and plain-clothes detectives, they all had seemed to have run up against the same wall. The man had essentially refused to divulge any personal information—which deficit had been attributed variously to early recovery, brain damage, or an undiagnosed psychosis.

The initial police report stated that the man had had a gun on his person when he was apprehended by the SFPD, shirtless and half-shaven. A note in his chart requested that SFPD be notified before his release, not an uncommon request when somebody in custody was about to be released, but this note made a special request that a Captain Quillan be contacted personally.

As Sam waited, he felt as if he had taken a magic potion that uplifted him. He felt his new life emerging as if the carapace of his old like were falling away from him, paid for by his truth, the same truth that would just keep getting stronger. He was undaunted by what lay ahead, even if he had to face it completely alone.

Ryan and Kubicek were not quite sure what to expect when they entered the unit, though they were nonetheless hypervigilantly alert. The man they knew as Sam Smith greeted them with clear eyes and a slightly mocking smile.

"Mr. Smith, I'm Lieutenant Ryan, SFPD."

"May I see your credentials, please?"

"Of course," he said, and produced them. Sam scrutinized them carefully, and nodded his head. Then he handed them back.

"If you have any information that would assist our investigation, I want you to tell me immediately. Failure to do so may be considered as obstruction of justice, and is a felony."

Sam smiled wanly, and then leaned forward with his elbows on his thighs.

"If you're going to take such a hard line, I may need to have my PBA attorney present!"

"What 'PBA attorney'? What are you talking about?"

"The Policeman's Benevolent Association. I'm SFPD. Samuel Jones, actually. Detective Sargent Samuel Q. Jones. Auto Theft, though I'm kind of on 'administrative leave' undergoing 'the cure' here because I've used up my medical benefits."

"Can you prove any of this?"

"My Captain is aware that I'm going to talk to you. I just told him half an hour ago that I was a potential witness to the murder. He'll confirm it."

"This is crazy. I never heard of such a thing."

"It's a little complicated."

When Ryan called Captain Quillan, he asked the essential question.

"Does the Chief know about this 'arrangement' you authorized?"

"That's my fuckup. Sam's my man, and I wanted him to get the best possible treatment under the circumstances. I mean, when Betty Ford Center fails..."

"There may be hell to pay for this! He has obstructed my investigation!"

"I made the best call I could in the moment, and I'll stand by it. I'll take the hit. Technically, Sam was drunk and off duty, and carrying his gun like he's supposed to. He just got a little 'carried away,' you might say, when he realized he didn't have any money."

"What about the store owner?"

"He's not gonna' file any charges. He's 'new money' from Hong Kong. He got scared when he saw 'the crazy man with a gun.' He's very happy that we took care of the problem."

They exchanged direct phone numbers, and Tim told him he would be in touch. Then he decided to question Sam.

"You saw the perpetrator?!"

"Yeah I did. And if you get me with a police artist, I can get you a pretty good picture of her."

"Her?'"

"Yeah. She had tits!"

CHAPTER FIFTY-NINE
Yet another Dimension
October 1st, 1988   0821

"Jesus, what kind of fucked up bullshit is this?" asked the Kube, still thinking of the contradictory evidence they had gathered from the two witnesses who claimed to have seen the perpetrator—only one claimed it was a man, while the other said it was a woman! "And now this crazy stuff from Marin! Fucking Jesus!"

Ryan and Kubicek were standing by the fax machine, reading over the purported suicide note of Dr. Noah Biederhoff. They were assured by the Marin County Sheriff's Office that there was only one set of fingerprints on the note. They told him further that, pending all the lab tests and such, their Medical Examiner was tentatively calling it a murder/suicide.

Ryan kept looking at the note and shaking his head. His handsome face bore all of the marks of consternation.

"'She stole my key, and wouldn't give it back! And then she started blackmailing me!'"

"What the hell is that all about? And we've got two conflicting witness statements—one says it was a man, the other that it was a woman! Jesus!"

Kube was actually rather conciliatory for once, and replied, "We'll get to the bottom of this. Don't worry!"

"I'd just like to clear this case before I retire!"

Then Ryan started laughing.

"What? What? What the fuck?"

An ardent fan of Raymond Burr, Ryan commented: "Perry Mason would have called this 'The Case of the Unwitting Witnesses!'"

CHAPTER SIXTY
Just Another Night
September 30th, 1988   2252

At staff report, Charge Nurse Lisa Tremaine was adamant about keeping Iverson heavily medicated.

"I do not want anyone injured. I know the doctor has refused to write a standing PRN for Haldol." There was a collective groan that rose off the gathered staff like fog above the ocean, voicing their collective displeasure with new doctors who wanted to pretend to be godlike by under prescribing psychotropic drugs that were most effective at knocking down the more severe manifestations of psychosis. Iverson had so far been cooperative with taking the Ativan whenever it was offered, which was as frequently as they could give it within the dosing guidelines. It never really seemed to affect him. He probably liked it!

She waited a moment for it to subside, then continued. "He doesn't believe that Mr. Iverson is psychotic." Another groan like a Greek chorus. She looked over both shoulders before continuing, and then said in a mock-stage-whisper: "I personally do not give a damn what he thinks. We're gonna snow that bastard! Any time he acts out; any time he is inappropriate; any time he even looks like he's gonna get out of hand—PRN him. And if he refuses, immediately call for back up, and give him his meds IM!"

Most of the staff members were quite pleased with her attitude. Some of the younger staff looked puzzled, some even as if they disagreed with her stance. But none of them voiced any objections. They had all heard the stories.

"If these young doctors worked here eight hours a day, even for one day, they'd change their tune about being 'patient advocates!'"

The PM shift had dosed him with 2 milligrams by mouth (PO) of Ativan at 2014 for "agitation." He was not legally due again until 0014 on the noc shift.They were preparing the night shift for his usual early morning rambles around the unit. The only legal and allowable option for giving him more meds was if they could document his becoming "agitated." The nursing staff had decided to use the PRNs liberally, giving it every four hours, especially since Iverson was well known for his agitation and violence. Two years previously, he had seriously injured a staff member during an admission, but the administration had refused to follow up with criminal assault charges because some shyster ambulance chaser attorney threatened to file a lawsuit against the hospital during the period when they were being inspected by the Joint Commission on Accreditation of Healthcare Organizations (JCAHO). It would have been terribly bad press and added extreme extra stress to an already overworked staff.

The most common opinion of those who did not work nocturnal (noc) shift was that it was "easy duty." The usual line was "You get paid a shift differential just to sleep all night." Another prime time, and erroneous, assumption about "The Mole Patrol" was that most of the patients slept all night—though statistically more encounters that led to seclusion and restraint occurred on noc shift than any other time.

Conversely, it was often quiet enough at night to allow for staff to take a nap in lieu of the contract-guaranteed breaks and lunch. College students reading and studying on the night shift were legendary

The greatest advantage, though, was the almost total lack of administrative brass and political bullshit. Most admissions were scheduled during the day, though they could, and did, occur at any time. While better staffed, the day shift was under the omnipresent scrutiny of legions of administrators who, for the most part, made patient care secondary to managing, and massaging, an efficient bureaucracy.

Even for all of this, noc staff was often considered to be the best clinically. Those who had been in the field a long time often gravitated to noc shift so as to best maximize their personal or creative time, while still maintaining a presence in the psych world. A Licensed Psychiatric Technician (LPT) was usually the designated medication person, while the Registered Nurse took care of all of the Doctors' Orders and administrative duties. The LPT carried the keys to the Narcotics' Cabinet, and was responsible for all meds dispensed. He or she was accountable for change-of-shift medication count. RNs were always in charge, and paid twice what the Techs were—although starting catheters and IVs were the only actual tasks that legally set them apart. Noc shift also seemed to be the time when some delusional or otherwise "crazed" individual decided he (usually he) wanted to go mano-a-mano with the night staff in the modern equivalent of a quick draw.

CHAPTER SIXTY-ONE
Preparation for Battle
October 1st, 1988   0253

Paul was already experiencing another busy shift (he asked himself, what did he expect? It was an acute psychiatry unit!).

Janak Iverson was another manic, intrusive male patient who just triggered him terribly. They had had to seclude and restrain him for obnoxious and threatening behaviors. Paul ran through the list of negative adjectives attributed to Janak Iverson: volatile, hostile, intrusive, dramatic, paranoid, loud, belligerent, intense, manipulative, obtrusive, hyper-sexual, arrogant, florid, demanding, and just plain rude. They all really applied. As did the many diagnoses: "Manic-Depressive, Manic," and "Schizoaffective" were the two primary Axis Ones applied, while "Borderline Personality Disorder," "Oppositional-Defiant" (which should have been changed to "Conduct Disorder" since he was over eighteen), even "Narcissistic Personality Disorder." No matter what was the truth of the matter, he was a scurrilous, nasty, slimy, manipulative bully who preyed on young, or disabled women for money and sex.

And not for the first time, he wished that the goddamn doctors had to deal with the constant irritation patients like him created! They never wanted to listen to line staff, being convinced of their own PR and the belief in themselves as godlike, omniscient and simply awesome clinicians who knew better than everyone else. If they would just put people like Iverson on Prolixin enanthate or Haldol decanoate! If these patients got a once-a-month injection, they would no longer have the option of not taking their pills when discharged, only to be re-admitted (sooner than later) for the same symptoms for which they had been the first time. It was one of the primary tenets of biological psychiatry, that controlling the symptoms was controlling the illness itself. So, if that were the case, why not use the best option available?

Of course, this line of thinking ran totally counter to his fears of the Therapeutic State (TS) that seemed more and more evident every day. It was becoming increasingly evident in many aspects of daily life, especially with increasing police intrusion, more draconian laws, and bureaucratic nonsense foisted upon the population "for their own good," the State acting *in loco parentis*. Forcing meds on people was something he had to do, but not something he necessarily liked. One of the tenets of the TS was maintenance of the façade of placidity, the bland ostensibly neutral stance that was required of one in the face of brutality and insult from patients.

The official party line was that it was "counter-therapeutic" for staff members to exhibit their personal feelings about the behavioral aberrance of patients—as if disgust and anger were simply to be controlled in favor of the mandated bland seeming indifference. Since the medical model postulated that all patients be considered "sick people," and therefore not responsible for their often-inappropriate behaviors (including spitting, insulting, hitting, punching, biting, even urinating, on staff!) It was simply expected that the staff should absorb such insults and injuries without having feelings or opinions about it! This gave rise to a collective assortment of under-medicated assholes with long psych histories like Iverson who had been led to believe that they were relatively untouchable and non-responsible for exhibiting any kind of outrageous behaviors they might want. It tended to lend them an air of quasi-invincibility, especially when they could so easily call Patients' Rights Advocates with complaints (seeking retribution actually), no matter how hurtful or harmful the behaviors had been. It was especially bad with manic patients because such relative immunity fed their grandiosity. Hah! According to the medical model, everything was pathological! Only the dead were without symptoms!

For Paul to constantly suppress his anger and frustration had inevitably had the effect of triggering his depression, not that being depressed was brand-new for him. He had experienced episodic bouts all of his life. It had always been part of the draw of cocaine and other stimulants for him. They ameliorated eliminated the immense sadness and sorrow he had always carried (albeit temporarily and delusionally) by manipulating his dopamine reward pathway. Now he could feel it building again, like the leading edge of a cold front into a clear, bright sky bringing huge thunderheads that might suddenly darken his inner landscape with turbulence, violence, and chaos. It was especially galling for him to have to keep a close cap on his inner weather and not allow his true feelings to show. This was in contradistinction to the most healing approach he had ever taken, driven by completely expressing his feelings without regard to social conventions or prohibitions.

Of course, this had led to him being written up for being excessively honest (though they called it "inappropriate" and the "use of excessive force"). He had been written up at various facilities even though what he had done was within the confines of his job description. But honestly, the only therapeutic impulse he felt toward Iverson was to beat the shit out of him! Maybe he needed to go back into therapy himself!

He reflected that guys like Iverson represented everything he hated about other men. Perhaps it was another flashback to his father. Perhaps it was just one of the seemingly unending series of his critical self-judgments. Iverson, just like that fucking Hawkins, seemed to amplify all of the worst character traits of men—the brutality, the violence, the lack of feeling and compassion, the unwillingness to listen and the general lack of gentility.

He had even briefly considered the idea that maybe the guy really was just a sick puppy, and that for him to push everybody's buttons was a symptom of his pathology. It sucked having to put up with it, but he had to admit that Iverson embodied many of those same traits that he despised. Not for the first time, he wished he were someone else! In his own weird way, guys like Hawkins and Iverson were really honest, even though totally offensive. Jesus! What if what he believed to be his spiritual awakening was actually just a gigantic pile of delusions? Maybe he and Iverson were actually brothers under the skin! Jesus Fuck!

His ruminations were interrupted by the appearance of the Nursing Supervisor.

"Is there fresh coffee?" asked Tom Sutton.

"Yeah, I made some, so you can't complain that it's weak. The shit they make here would gag the Pope!"

Paul was feeling from managing the tension of dealing with the obtrusive, intrusive Mr. Iverson. But then, there was always somebody! Paul was always calm in the face of threats or actual violence; but as soon as the deal went down and the patient was locked in the seclusion room, his hands would shake and he'd break into a cold sweat. Maybe that was part of being a professional!

By the time he had resumed his favorite resting position behind the counter of the Nurses' Station, he was sipping his second cup of the new brew. He pulled the oversize loose-leaf binder containing the Unit Procedures into his lap, fully intending to pursue the agonizing task of reading them as required by Nursing Regulations. Instead, his insatiable mind turned, yet again ruminating on the economy and Ronald "Ray Gun's" ruinous fiscal policies. It was so ironic that only thing he and his father had ever agreed upon was that they both hated the insipid, B-grade actor, who once had the temerity to comment that "homelessness is a lifestyle choice!"

He reflected too, on how fortunate he had been, choosing to move to San Francisco after coming home from the 'Nam. The City was really such a small town, even though it had three-quarters of a million population. The psych world was far smaller and even tighter. He had rarely had to interview for a job. Every position he had ever had was offered predicated on word-of-mouth recommendations, and the fact that he was a licensed, male Tech with lots of experience.

Despite the fact that he liked the power and authority the job invested in him, it was still only intended to provide him with enough money to free up his time to write. Writing had been the only available outlet for him as a child to relieve the unbearable oppression of his father's tyrannically controlling presence. He learned how to commit to paper the winged thoughts and searing torments he was experiencing. Although he did not realize it at the time, documenting his life experience (even at that point) was part of the process of developing a sympathetic witness (a la Alice Miller) through and onto the pages, something he did not have anywhere else in his life, the kind of nurturing presence he despaired of ever finding. Through the years it had become increasing more true as he had matured, and was now one of the mainstays of his life. Art saves lives! It had saved his.

CHAPTER SIXTY-TWO
Into the Lion's Den
October 1st, 1988   0325

Janak Iverson rolled his neck, eliciting two distinct cracks. He extended his highly tattooed arms, and then stretched the tension out of his thin, wiry frame before finally shaking his body like a dog emerging from water. He donned a fresh pair of hospital pajama pants and decided to discover what kind of shit he could get into. He'd slept two good hours and was feeling frisky, ready to cause havoc, fuck up other people's routines. Inserting two sticks of spearmint gum into his mouth, he began chewing vigorously. The time on the unit clock—flush-mounted above the Nurse's Station with bolts directly into the studs—registered 0325, but he didn't care! Just did not give a healthy fuck! He really liked messing with square people—so rigid and uptight, especially at night when he was at his personal best.

Maybe I'll call Patient's Rights Advocates again! That'll mess with the motherfuckers! Although, on consideration, he remembered that his most recent attempt had been fobbed to a supervisor who told him quite bluntly that they were no longer going to investigate all of his complaints.

"Fuck 'em! Let them earn their money."

He'd been repeatedly told that his judgment was "severely impaired." But that was based on what he knew to be erroneous information. There was absolutely nothing wrong with him! They were all conspiring against him—all of them: the police, the government, art galleries, psych agencies, the fucking lot of them! Every goddamn psych unit on which he had ever been incarcerated treated him shitty, acting like the fucking thought police, criticizing his behavior and his life plan, always messing with his divine mission!

Iverson took a rare moment to reflect on his recent good fortune. Despite being locked up here (again!), he had escaped New York City with his skin intact. His very pregnant girlfriend's father had threatened to remove his epidermis one inch at a time for what he had done. Fortunately, the young woman had never really known his real name—and he had managed to skate out at the very last moment before his commitment hearing for Bellevue (in a stolen car, but so what?)

He laughed mightily reflecting on it, another of the utter ironies of his life, as he approached the Nurse's Station, then cursed. Fuck! It was that goddamn Marzeky! Instant bummer! Motherfucker must never take a night off! Never gives me any play! Motherfucker always wants to lock me down! Maybe if I complain to Patient's Rights about him, maybe that'll get his ass suspended...or fired!

He quickly put a smile on his face as he approached one of his legion of enemies working around the clock to keep him from his holy tasks.

CHAPTER SIXTY-THREE
Deeper into the Morass
October 1st, 1988   0337

Retrieving his journal from his backpack, he pursued his thoughts about money and creativity, what he always called "the artist's schizophrenia"—plenty of time and not enough money (like when he was temporarily disabled); or plenty of money and not enough time (like when he was dealing drugs). The latter had turned out to be a cruel joke on him. He had originally proposed working ten hours a day (at an average of $50 an hour). It had morphed into a tumultuous driving obsession working twenty hours a day and getting strung out for three years filled five-day binges!

Therapy had allowed a loosening of the bonds of deprivation that had haunted him since his Kafkaesque childhood, the depth of his inner penury, feeling and believing that he had to monitor his every penny, his every action, just to survive. The entire process of being stable and supporting himself seemed so at odds with what he had always espoused for himself in his vision as a quasi-hippie and a seeker after occult truths. He had often loudly denounced any and all who had "sold out" to make money. He so resonated with an old Steve Miller line from *Space Cowboy*: "All you back room schemers, star-trip dreamers better find something new to say, cause it's the same old story, it's the same old crime—and you got some heavy dues to pay!"

Therapy had helped him see his motivations as survival skills, not aberrations. One of the nurses with whom he worked reminded him of the old saying "Neurotics build sand castles in the sky; and psychotics live in them." Her entire façade was built around a haughty arrogance toward both patients and staff. She expected others to buy into her pretensions of who she was.

He often pondered this conundrum. He had, for the very longest time, sincerely believed in the appearance of things, that other people took him at face value, as who he projected himself to be with his wry humor and raucous stories, and his carefully constructed façade of strength and power. In a blinding flash of self-discovery, he was severely disconcerted when he realized he had been deluding himself. It reminded him of the Jefferson Airplane lyric: "When the truth is found to be lies, you know the joy within you dies." That is exactly what had happened to him. It irked him to admit that he was, after all, only human.

CHAPTER SIXTY-FOUR
Into the Lion's Den
October 1st, 1988   0341

As he approached the desk, Iverson's thoughts tumbled and rolled, smashing into each other as if agitated by a cyclotron. What had started for him as a snow flurry of dislike and distaste for Paul Marzeky, very quickly grew into an avalanche of major proportions, awakened by the full range of his inner tormenters. The primary voice that lived within him—the one he called "The Controller," the one who directed and protected him—started screaming, sending white-hot tendrils up from the bottoms of his feet, through the nether regions of his brain and out into infinite space. His eyes were boiling by the time Paul stepped into focus, center stage for all of the burdens and obstructions plaguing him.

"Mr. Iverson, I'd like you to take some more Ativan," said Paul. The patient's glazed eyeballs looked like ball bearings rolling around the empty tumblers of their sockets. Iverson seemed like the poster boy for an article in an obscure journal that addressed manic crisis precipitated by benzodiazepines in manic-depressives. When he looked at the man, nobody was home.

"I need some help! RIGHT NOW!"

Loretta scurried up the corridor, and Warren came running up from near the seclusion rooms.

"The Controller" had completely overshadowed him. Iverson believed he was 7 feet 10 inches tall, and carried 520 pounds of rippling muscle. Pure and distilled malignance was emanating out of every pore.

KILL HIM! NOW!

Iverson lunged at Paul, who pushed the grasping arms beyond him, and attempted to wrap his arms around a body that suddenly seemed to be made out of steel ropes.

"I REALLY need some help here!"

GET OUT! NOW!

Janak ripped out of Paul's grip as easily as if Paul were made of feathers. Skinny little Warren grabbed for Iverson's upraised arm in order to twist it behind him, but the crazed man roared and just pushed him away.

Janek roared, cursing and screaming, as he became even more immersed in his psychotic process.

"Fucking Earthlings!"

Loretta arrived, having first pushed the alarm button summoning extra help. Warren had grabbed the man's left arm, and wrapped it tightly in both of his hands. Loretta grabbed the right and pulled it to her chest, though it quickly slithered out as if coated in motor oil. Paul was hanging on mightily to both of the man's legs, and voiced it aloud for all to hear.

"I can't hold him!"

Three more staff arrived, and grabbed various appendages, mostly to little or no avail. The man seemed to be feeding off the struggle he'd created, as he struggled toward the front door, dragging all of them with him.

FREE YOURSELF!

Iverson drew a deep breath, and used his inhuman strength to fling his arms heavenward. He again dislodged Warren and simultaneously backhanded Loretta. She caught his arm on the return when he seemed to be aiming a punch at her, and chomped down on his wrist with her strong and excellent teeth.

"Oh no you don't you son of a bitch!" she screamed. Then she re-secured his arm, and he shrieked in pain.

Even with all six staff hanging off of him, Iverson was making steady progress toward the door as the alarm bell continued to shriek. A loose circle of other patients had gathered around them, like iron filings to a magnet.

ESCAPE! ESCAPE!

Paul looked peripherally out of the corner of his left eye. He thought he must be hallucinating, as there seemed to be a human figure flying through the air toward them!

In less than a second Sam crashed head first into their staggering tableau. The extra weight and the velocity of his leaping dive proved to be the crucial, as the psychotic man crashed slowly to the floor. First his left knee, then the right gave way as Iverson lost his battle with gravity—and fell to the floor like an elephant inundated by a band of hyenas.

"MASTER! HELP ME!" he implored as he collapsed completely.

A cloying reek seemed to emanate from him as he again attempted to rise. Shaking like a cypress tree in a Force Five hurricane, he managed to get one foot flat under him, as all of his bodily systems worked overtime—furious breathing quickening; adrenals pumping; cortisol surging, limbic commands battering his neurons, urgent and intrusive.

KILL THEM ALL!

In this melee, some staff had grabbed other staff members' body parts. One such misadventure resulted in Iverson momentarily getting a hand free. As he reached with the temporarily freed appendage to grab Jane's unsuspecting face, a black clad arm wrapped itself around his exposed neck.

A montage of Technicolor images flashed through Paul's brain, as he attempted to sort out who was who and what body part belonged to whom. There was a profusion of hands and arms in the encircling cordon securing the condign man. He looked up and saw Dominica, kited out in full drag—lipstick smeared, eyes wide and fierce, mascara running down both cheeks—securing the head of the raging man, applying a perfect choke hold, right wrist held tightly with her left hand, simultaneously applying pressure to both carotid arteries as she grunted and ground her teeth, with drool foaming the corners of her mouth.

Sam seemed to synch with Paul as he locked eyes with Dominica. In a moment of shock and recognition, he started shouting.

"It's her! It's her!"

Dominica released her choke hold immediately. Iverson remained unconscious on the floor as she jumped to her feet, and ran toward the sally port door. A heartbeat later, Paul and Sam pursued her. She ripped frantically at the edge of her skirt as she ran. Arriving at the door, she produced the key sewn into the hem of her skirt, and inserted it into the lock. As Sam approached, she balled a fist, intending to "clock" him. He neatly ducked under, grabbed her arm in mid-air, and pulled it behind her back.

Paul shouted for additional help, as Sam addressed him.

"This is who I saw coming out of the seclusion room!"

CHAPTER SIXTY-FIVE
Another Turn Around the Floor
October 1st, 1988   1127

"Ms. Twillin?"

"Yes."

"Lieutenant Ryan here."

"Yes, Lieutenant."

"We've had a breakthrough on the case. We'd like to have a little chat with your client."

"Does she need an attorney?"

"No, ma'am, nothing like that. We just need to tighten up some of the details. We have a suspect in custody."

"I see."

"I'm calling out of courtesy. We need to speak with Sophia."

"And where shall we meet?"

"I'd prefer not to have her come into the station..."

"Me too. Shall we meet at my office?"

When he agreed, she gave him the address and called Sophia to explain the nature of the meeting to her.

"It's the same two detectives you met before."

"Am I in trouble, Alice?"

"Not at all. Can you come to my office around 1345?"

"It's a beautiful day. I might walk."

"Whatever you like."

Sophia was shy, but smiled with true delight when she found out that the two detectives simply wanted to go over the facts of the case with her, most especially the drawing she had produced. The entire tone was far more pleasant than she would have thought possible, but then they were "Just tying up loose ends," and wanted to "Put a bow on their package for the DA."

That apparently included speaking with Sophia "on the record" concerning who she had seen going into the seclusion room, and the drawing she had made of a "tall, white man."

Sophia admitted to being quite anxious, but determined not to "fall apart," and had refused Alice's well-meant advice to taking an Ativan before coming to her office. Nonetheless, she was initially tearful and frightened, though she seemed to gain strength the more she was questioned, and found, somewhat to her amazement, that she had an easy strength and courage within herself that allowed he to answer without compunction or fear. It was something they had been working on in therapy, and both of them had benefitted from exploring Sophia's greater independence.

"Sophia, you said you saw 'a man' going into the seclusion room on that day."

"Yes."

"And you gave us a drawing of what you thought he looked like."

"That's true."

"Well it turns out that your drawing was pretty accurate, except you could not have seen his eyes, could you?"

"I told you! I told you! I made the eyes like I thought they should look!" she said, her voice rising as she got teary-eyed.

"No one is saying you did anything wrong, Sophia. We just have to make sure we're all on the same page when we go to trial. OK?"

Somewhat reluctantly Sophia nodded.

"You saw him from the side and back, is that correct?"

"Yes."

"And he was going in to the room, correct?"

"Yes."

"But you didn't see him coming out?

"No!"

Kubicek turned off the tape recorder at a nod from Ryan.

"Now, just between you and me—the eyes you drew were your father's?"

Sophia looked up tearfully at Alice, who simply smiled and nodded.

"Remember? We talked about this. It's OK. Tell the truth."

Sophia turned to Ryan, and said, "When I get really scared, I remember...my father...hurting me."

"And?"

"Oh! Oh yes! I must have drawn my father's eyes because that...person looked so evil!"

"Thanks, Sophia. We'll be in touch."

CHAPTER SIXTY-SIX
Shifting Demographics
October 2nd, 1988   1132

It had been an enormous, even astounding, few days. The Mayor was pleased. The Board of Supervisors was pleased. All the top police brass was pleased. The Regents of the University of California San Francisco were pleased. Paul had been issued an official apology by the SFPD, and the personal thanks from both Ryan and Kubicek (though less graciously from the latter). He had had a Letter of Commendation put in his file signed by the Hospital Administrator, citing his bravery, courage and leadership. The sense of relief was palpable on both the Acute Adult and the Detox Units. The tension had been lifted, as if fresh air in the aftermath of a hurricane.

The census had shifted, as it always did, peaking generally around the end of the month just before disability payments were made on the third day of the following month. The Psych ER was still flooded with the migrant hordes of homeless and dispossessed—most with a strong Axis II diagnosis of Borderline, Narcissistic, or Histrionic Personality Disorders, saying what had become the "magic words" to get admitted—" I'm feeling suicidal," and being willing to demonstrate some level of self-harm. There were, of course, those who argued that such pathology was indicative of deeper issues, even though the superficial behaviors were clearly manipulative. It was, as always, a difficult line to walk.

The arrest of Dominica Lawrence (aka Daniel Lawrence Shipley) led to her being held in segregation, and placed on suicide watch, in San Francisco County Jail in San Bruno. There was talk of transferring her to Unit 7-B at San Francisco General Hospital, the forensics unit for criminals who were also mentally ill, but the potential backlash to that solution—political figures wanting desperately to avoid too much media coverage, especially making a heroic figure out of the woman who called herself "The Avenging Angel," overruled the whatever clinical issues might have been involved.

Maria Conchita Alonzo had tried numerous times to get an "exclusive" with Ms. Lawrence and failed, resulting in her being arrested for Criminal Trespass and Interfering with the Police in the Application of their Duty. She barely escaped Obstruction of Justice charges. Eduardo "Fast Eddie" Chacon did not fare as well. When Maria testified that he had approached her asking for money in return for inside information; and her producer testifies to the same, "Eddie" was charged with extortion, Abetting Criminal Trespass (the key), Obstruction of Justice, Impeding a Police Investigation, and Lying to a Police Officer. His Pre-Licensed status has been revoked and he was sitting in San Bruno awaiting trial.

Samuel Q. Jones (aka Sam Smith) was released quietly the day after the big fracas. He unobtrusively left by a service door, accompanied by Ryan and Kubicek who slipped him into an unmarked car, and drove swiftly away. The Police Chief had requested an immediate meeting with him, even before he went home—though no one other than Sam knew that he was not going home to his wife and children. She had asked him to find "somewhere else" to stay for the immediate future. But he had made arrangements to stay at least briefly with his superior officer and friend, Captain George Quillan, an old-school, multi-generational San Francisco cop, who'd been asked/tasked to attend the same meeting at the Chief's office.

Though no one seemed to know what the meeting was about, Ryan and Kubicek had been "invited" too. Sam had initially been concerned that he might be getting anything from a reprimand to a suspension, but felt hopeful nonetheless. He was clean and sober, and had a "new lease on life," as they say. He had made connections with several AA people, and found a regular meeting that Tony had recommended, one he'd been attending every day at noon.

He had talked to Camille and the kids, and they were going to have dinner at Camille's favorite restaurant on Sunday (she loved the Trianon). He was hopeful about that, though he wasn't harboring any designs about returning to St. Francis Wood any time soon.

CHAPTER SIXTY-SEVEN
The Story Unfolds
October 2nd, 1988   0834

Alice had been privately assured by Ryan that it was "highly unlikely" that Sophia would ever be called to testify—especially since Dominica Lawrence had signed a full confession. She was being kept under very close supervision with fifteen-minute checks and other precautions—most especially because of her extremely rapid moodshifts, accompanied by everything from tears to hysterics to stone cold rage and demands for her release. She kept blaming it on her "high testosterone level," and how it could have all been averted if "that bastard" (Biederhoff) has simply agreed to her blackmail, and paid her off!

"It wasn't like I was asking for that much! Just enough to get my reassignment! Not even my Adam's apple or vocal cords!" she insisted as she smoked cigarette after cigarette during a further interview. (She had refused to talk otherwise).

Sometimes her voice would change, reflecting her moods—the more tender and vulnerable ones (she called her "feminine" ones) came out when she was sad or distressed, while the harder emotions were expressed in rougher tones (the "masculine ones"). Dr. Noah Biederhoff had been her erstwhile sponsor for the primary replacement surgery, but had refused to steal the money from his wife's estate to provide for Dominica's surgeries.

She had gotten involved with the good doctor when, near the middle of one of her required pre-surgical therapy sessions, she had seduced him into having sex with her in his office. In the heat oi the moment, they failed to lock the door. He had pulled up her skirt and torn off her silk panties before inserting himself rock-hard into her anus. Noah was in the process of giving her a reach-around when the door burst open, and the coke fiend Unit Clerk, Raz Something or other, burst in unannounced. Though he backed out quickly, he had gotten a full view of the felonious and highly unethical activities, though not of her. The clerk had started blackmailing Dr. Biederhoff into supplying him with boxes of 26-gauge insulin syringes. When Raz Whozits (nobody ever seemed to remember his real name) was caught sleeping at his desk on a Monday morning—bags under his purple smudged eyes, completely toxic from a weekend of shooting coke in the bathtub—he threatened to "mutilate" the Assistant Medical Director who had awakened him. First repeatedly invoking the strictest confidentiality, Noah leaked the word that he suspected the man of using drugs on the job as well, and hinted that he might have a psychiatric history. The hospital arranged for the man to be transported to Seton Medical Center (just across the San Mateo county line in Daly City) on a seventy-two hour hold as "Danger to Others." He apparently escalated tremendously there. His outraged outbursts were dismissed as "delusional," especially his stories about the esteemed Noah Biederhoff. The last Paul had heard was that he had been swallowed whole by the State system like Jonah by the whale. He was never seen again. There was some speculation that he might have been eliminated by Dominica, but there was no proof of that.

During one of their subsequent encounters, Dominica managed to secure Noah's Master Key. Since she had been hospitalized on the Adult Acute Unit numerous times for suicidal ideation (usually accompanied by the most superficial slashes to one or both wrists), she figured she could always benefit from having such a treasure. On her most recent "incarceration" as she called it (following yet another argument with Noah about money), she became severely depressed. Then, Zack Hawkins had threatened to cut off her dick. When the huge ruckus broke out on the unit, she thought she had been unobserved using the key, and simply dispatched the condign man with a choke hold, and slipped out again. She thought she was safe. Janek Iverson had flirted with her, and rejected her when he found out she still had a penis. He had threatened to "fuck her up completely" if she didn't leave him alone. When she saw him struggling and relatively immobilized during a takedown, her fragile restraint shattered, and in the heat of the moment, she had applied the choke hold that led to her discovery.

She was sobbing as she spoke, voice filled with rage and righteousness.

"If I could only have my surgery! I just know everything would be all right! I just know it!"

"But why did you kill Zack Hawkins?"

"He threatened to cut off my...you know, genitals!" she responded in a voice heavy with sadness and shame.

"And for that, he had to die?" Kubicek asked, intrigued and incredulous.

She answered in a gruff, strangled baritone as she pulled against the handcuff that secured her to the metal table, and lunged at The Kube.

"A girl has a right to protect herself, doesn't she?"

CHAPTER SIXTY-EIGHT
Authority Speaks
October 2nd, 1988   1156

Sam felt extremely anxious, almost overwhelmed as he entered 850 Bryant, The Hall of Justice building, accompanied by the two working detectives. This was going to be his second meeting with The Chief that day. The earlier meeting had been bitter and thankfully brief. Sam had been immediately suspended without pay "until further notice." He'd been asked to return for this meeting with Ryan and Kubicek, who were, however temporarily, assigned as his "minders."

Accompanied again by them, he entered the Chief's anteroom. They were greeted by his long-time secretary and gatekeeper, a shrewd middle-aged woman nicknamed "Dragon Lady." Only today the dragon was smiling, and pointed them directly to the mahogany door that led to the inner sanctum. Sam was both gratified and concerned that they were being given top echelon treatment.

The Chief was sitting behind his large, highly polished desk, talking to a dark-haired man in a plush chair who had his back to them. He was smoking a large cigar and tapping the ash into a cut crystal bowl on the edge of the Chief's desk.

Sam immediately noticed a Deputy Chief standing to his left of the desk, conversing with a nervous-looking Captain Quillan, who smiled briefly at him, and then returned to his conversation.

The Chief looked up and stood behind his desk while gesturing with his hands to chairs arranged in front of it. As they started to seat themselves, The Mayor turned in his chair, and smiled at them. Sam figured this was a very good sign, since His Honor had been under such intense political pressure since the murder. There had been organized protests at City hall, even talk of a recall attempt. They immediately stood to attention, including Sam, who was in mufti, and was not actually required to do so.

His Honor spoke in the mellow, mellifluous voice for which he was so renowned, while gesturing expansively with the hand holding the cigar.

"Gentlemen, please sit down. This is the Chief's meeting. I am only here at his invitation, to observe!"

Now they all looked a bit confused, especially Kube, who ordinarily did not attend any ceremony, even those in his honor.

The Chief, a thirty-five-year veteran who had worked his way up through the ranks, and therefore held the respect of most of his officers, also gestured them down as he unwrapped and prepared a Havana for himself—apparently a gift from the Mayor.

"We're here for a number of reasons today. First, I want to welcome Sergeant Samuel Q. Jones back to active duty, as soon as he is cleared medically—which they tell me shouldn't be more than another couple of weeks. I understand that you've had quite a time of it, recovering. How are you feeling?"

"Fine, sir. Thank you," said Sam, even more stunned.

"Good, good. I'm sure you're quite anxious to get back to work."

"Uh, sir, yes sir! Thank you!"

"I also understand that you were quite instrumental in apprehending the perpetrator of our recent murder case, while you were...'undercover.'"

"Uh, yes sir. That is, I..."

"That's OK, Sergeant. I know all about it," he said, glancing over at George Quillan.

"In recognition of your service under extreme circumstances, I am taking this opportunity to present you with the SFPD Silver Medal of Valor. This is a special award, and as such you will not be invited to the Medal of Valor ceremonial dinner and presentation. Nonetheless, the award and my appreciation are real. Please stand up."

All gathered as the Chief came around his desk, and pinned the Silver Star with the red, white, and blue ribbon on the left side of his chest. They all saluted as the Chief did. The Mayor smiled and shook his hand.

"I also want to announce that a Letter of Commendation, signed by both The Mayor and myself is being inserted into the Personnel Files of both of you detectives," he said, nodding at Ryan and Kubick, who responded in kind.

"Thank you, sir."

"Or rather, I should say Captain Ryan and Lieutenant Kubicek! Congratulations!"

The Chief returned to his desk, and produced a number of crystal cut glasses, and a bottle of 21-year old Bushmills. He handed them around to everyone but Sam, at whom he smiled somewhat ruefully and handed a glass of sparkling water. When everyone had been served, he turned to Captain Quillan, and raised his glass.

"And to the well-deserved retirement of Captain George Quillan!"

A wave of utter surprise swept through the non-brass present, as glasses were raised

"Here, here!" rang out.

George told Sam later that he had struck a deal with The Chief, so that Sam could be reinstated with no loss of grade or back pay; and that he himself would take an early retirement (he had twenty-three years in, after all!). He was sworn to confidentiality about the arrangement, especially in terms of the media finding out, and making the entire situation public.

As they left the office, Sam shook hands with Ryan and Kubicek.

"Thank you both. I really am glad to be part of a police force that has guys like you!"

They shook hands all around, and Ryan commented wryly, "Thanks for your assistance with the case!" and they all laughed.

"Any time, gentlemen, any time. If you ever get an opening in Homicide, let me know!"

CHAPTER SIXTY-NINE
I am You, and You are Me
December 21st, 1988 1312

As she improved, and came into better community with her various selves, Sophia's attraction to psychology, and especially therapy, began to assert a stronger pull on her attention than her attraction to Alice Twillin—who was, after all, her role model of healthy femininity. She decided to take an Introduction to Psychology course at San Francisco State during the spring session. She had already had several serious confrontations with her mother about gaining control of her own money. She had consulted with an attorney, and filed the necessary paperwork to have her mother removed as financial agent for her disability payments, her father's Social Security survivor's pension, and the trust fund he had set up for her in accordance with the plea agreement he had reached at his own trial. She decided that it was time she be her own woman.

CHAPTER SEVENTY
Peace, or at least, Relative Calm
January 13, 1989   1456

Paul had taken a ¾ time noc shift position at UCSF Langley-Porter Neuropsychiatric Institute. It gave him time to think and to write. And, if he went back to school, time to study. In the meantime, it allowed him time to let his thoughts roam unimpeded, especially about his past and his future. They almost inevitably led him to considering the history of this his favorite city, and how it too had evolved—and the deep ties San Francisco had to his own work.

He had even come to forgive Ryan and especially Kubicek. He reflected on the history of the SFPD and realized they had come a long way too.

The SFPD was officially organized in August of 1849. Due to a less-than-diligent attendance to escaping prisoners from the Brigantine Euphemia (then serving as a floating jail), coupled with the replacement of the entire police department after the elections of 1851 and 1856 (in accord with the laws of the day), the Vigilance Committee wrested control of the justice system from the regularly established authorities and administered justice on their own account. Its anonymous members dispensed quick and deadly justice along the roaring Barbary Coast (now North Beach) and in China Basin where the term "Shanghai" had grown to infamy, referring to knocking unwary drinkers unconscious with a chloral hydrate ("Mickey Finn"), who would awaken in the middle of the Pacific Ocean on the way to an uncertain future in the China trade.

Even though he hadn't arrived until 1969, he had loved being a hippie! And the Beats! He had so deeply empathized with the uncertainty that had inspired their characters and their lives, their spiritual search in the existential and sometimes nihilistic void—especially the pervasive sense of alienation that had spawned so much creativity, and the despair that had materialized as a loose association of souls united by common purpose and dedication who became known as The Beat Generation. (He had heard various definitions: beaten down; beatific; even just dead tired beat of the world and its rising corporatism).

Paul wanted to be slotted into such an idiosyncratic niche. He had finally had to decide that he would never be another Bob Dylan or Henry Miller. He had decided too that not living up to the standards they had set was something for which he could forgive himself. They had always been heroes to him, and he realized that it had finally become time for him to be his own hero, forged in the crucible of his own destiny, his own choices, his own real lived life experience. He did not have to write his magnum opus on a roll of wrapping paper to be hip!

Paul had come to realize that he was very, very proud of who he had become, even if there were no other standard against which to compare himself. He was his own model, his own hero, his own archetype—something he had never really considered possible previously. He was proud of the long way he had come, and in the words of Kris Kristofferson (a brother vet), "All alone all the way, who's to say, that you've thrown it away for a song? Boy, you've sure come a long way from home!"

He opened the latest of his journals (number 7 in an infinite series), anxious to get a few vagrant thoughts down before they were whisked away by the Cosmic Vacuum Cleaner. He'd had another brief brush with what he called his "cornerstone memory" or "keystone memory" upon which all the other memories were based, the template that supported the façade of his life. He'd come away feeling the need to write about it, and increasingly, to mourn the loss of the deep past even more thoroughly.

What came instead was an addition to the narrative flow of a new book, whose working title was *Spirals of Time.* It was an almost transparently autobiographical novel about a Viet Nam vet too depressed to work. The book had only two characters, the protagonist and his psychiatrist. The alternating chapters portray his reflections on his life, and conversations with his shrink. Although he had been accused of being narcissistic on this account, a far more literate friend had told him that it reminded him of Samuel Beckett, the minimalist Irish playwright and novelist. He felt complimented, and at the same time, hoped to create a context, even a genre, that would one day bear his own name! As James Baldwin had commented: "It is this power of revelation which is the business of the novelist, this journey toward a more vast reality, which must take precedence over all other claims."

Paul was marveling at the skill and adroitness with which he maneuvered his characters (admittedly only two) through life situations and the crispness of his dialogue. Although he sometimes thought that the only true artists were those who were recognized and lauded by critics and an adoring public, he realized that true creativity was something far more than living the relatively unfettered artist's life devoted to great literature, or paintings, or music. As Henry Miller said in *Big Sur and the Oranges of Hieronymus Bosch*: "Whoever uses the spirit that is in him creatively is an artist. To make living itself an art, that is the goal."

It was this very sentiment that drove Paul, and gave him comfort in his darkest hours, knowing that there had forever been those who had struggled mightily to express their deepest visions, who had walked the long and lonely roads, and left signs for him to follow.

He was extraordinarily grateful.

www.ingramcontent.com/pod-product-compliance
Lightning Source LLC
Chambersburg PA
CBHW072018020726
47501CB00006B/1863